Praise for Catching Jordan

"I stayed up all night reading *Catching Jordan*—I couldn't put it down! Jordan Woods is my heroine!"

—*Simone Elkeles*, New York Times *Bestselling author of the* Perfect Chemistry *series*

"Sweetly satisfying."

—*VOYA*

"*Catching Jordan* has it all: heart, humor, and a serious set of balls. With a clever, authentic voice, Kenneally proves once and for all that when it comes to making life's toughest calls—on and off the field—girls rule!"

—*Sarah Ockler, bestselling author of* Fixing Delilah *and* Twenty Boy Summer

"I fell in love with the hero on page 1, and *Catching Jordan* just gets better from there. This feel-good romantic comedy about high school football is the novel I've been waiting for. I loved it!"

—*Jennifer Echols, author of* Love Story

"Kenneally makes football accessible—and even enjoyable—for those who might not ordinarily follow the sport. Her protagonist is a strong-willed female quarterback who's determined to continue playing during college. Jordan (or "Woods," as her teammates call her) is a fearless captain and the teamwork and camaraderie that's so implicit in the story are great takeaways for readers of any age."

—*RT Book Review*, 4 Stars

"Debut author Kenneally does a solid job of depicting Jordan's conflicted emotions, the pressure she is under, and her testy relationship with her father."

—*Publishers Weekly*

"A beautiful novel with a competitive spirit both on and off the field. With a real and captivating depiction of high school relationships, *Catching Jordan* shows the same reverence for the human heart that it does for the game of football."

—*Karsten Knight, author of* Wildfire

Praise for Stealing Parker

"A realistic portrait of a teen who… searches for love in forbidden places. Another engrossing romance from Miranda Kenneally with a hero who will melt your heart.

—*Jennifer Echols, National Award-Winning author of*
Such a Rush

"Readers of this teen novel will appreciate its realistic and witty dialogue as they navigate its tightly packed plot."

—*Kirkus*

"*Stealing Parker* is fresh, fearless, and totally romantic. Kenneally hits another grand slam!"

—*Sarah Ockler, bestselling author of*
Twenty Boy Summer *and* Bittersweet

Things I Can't Forget

MIRANDA KENNEALLY

sourcebooks
fire

Published by Sourcebooks Fire, an imprint of Sourcebooks, Inc.

P.O. Box 4410, Naperville, Illinois 60567-4410

(630) 961-3900

Fax: (630) 961-2168

teenfire.sourcebooks.com

Library of Congress Cataloging-in-Publication data is on file with the publisher.

Printed and bound in the United States of America.

VP 10 9 8 7 6 5 4 3 2 1

This story is for all of my readers.
I hope you find your truth.
And to my biggest fan, Don: thanks for
encouraging me to always go my own way.

sketch #323
what happened on april 6

Girls like me do not buy pregnancy tests.

I drag my pencil down the paper, drawing tears rolling from her eyes.

Girls like me sing in the church choir. Every spring break, I go on mission trips to Honduras, where we renovate houses for the underprivileged. I do all my homework every night, and before I go to bed, I kiss Daddy's cheek and tell him I wish he'd go to the doctor about his blood pressure and start getting more exercise than walking Fritz and scooping his poop.

I've only kissed one boy my entire life.

Emily called that day, crying. "Kate," she said between sobs. "You can't tell anyone. Not even your mom."

I drove to Walmart two towns away, over in Green Hills, so no one would see me buying the test. I trembled as I carried the box to the self-checkout lane. I scanned, bagged, and paid, and bit back tears, because my best friend of fifteen years—since we were three years old—might have accidentally gotten pregnant by her long-time boyfriend.

I didn't even know they had had sex. It's not something they would tell. If anyone found out that Jacob, son of Brother Michael—our preacher at church—got a girl pregnant out of wedlock? Chaos.

It wouldn't look good for Emily either. She's like me. Always wears clean T-shirts and none of her jeans have holes or loose strings. She would never even think about smoking a cigarette. She doesn't go over the speed limit. She plays the violin and has a scholarship lined up to attend Belmont University in Nashville.

But Emily made a mistake.

I use my black coloring pencil to shade her hair. My red pencil fills in her lips, turned upside down in a frown.

And then I made an even bigger mistake: I helped her.

you were my first kiss

I haven't been to Cumberland Creek Camp since I was eleven, since I was a camper. Now I'm eighteen, a high school graduate. I'm someone who has no business being a camp counselor, that's for sure. I can't start fires. I can't tell poison ivy and poison oak apart. And since I tipped over in the Cumberland River sophomore year, canoes and I have had a serious love-hate relationship.

But my friendship bracelet making skills are first-rate, so my church—Forrest Sanctuary—nominated me to be the camp arts and crafts instructor. I never would've agreed if Emily hadn't been nominated to be a counselor as well.

"It'll be a great summer!" she'd said. "We'll meet new people and get to hang out by the lake and make s'mores and go creek stomping together. Like when we were eight!"

But now I'm here alone.

I need the money for college, and it's too late to find a job anywhere else in this economy, and I figure if I do this for the church, maybe God will think about forgiving me for what I've done.

Back in the day, the Chickasaw Indian tribe believed that this land—these mountains in Tennessee—were where heaven meets the earth, and lots of locals say God often communicates to people here. Through signs. Through visions. Through just feeling closer to Him. When I was little, it was always the talk of camp. *Would God speak to anyone this year?* I remember hearing a rumor about how a counselor had this deep feeling she needed to go see her boyfriend. So she drove away from camp and made it to his house just in time to find he'd slipped and fallen down the stairs and was bleeding heavily from his head. He lived, thanks to the sign.

Everyone wants a sign at some point, and this summer I need one more than ever.

I park my car along the tree line beside the basketball court and make my way up the trail, past the cedar and oak trees, keeping a watch out for copperheads and black widow spiders. Last time I was here, a deer tick bit me and burrowed into my skin. Two weeks later, I had a rash the shape of a dartboard stretching across my pale stomach. Everybody wanted to see it. And I mean everybody. Even Will Whitfield. But when you're eleven, you don't pull your shirt up for anybody except your mom and the doctor.

Anyway, the whole reason I'm thinking about Will Whitfield is because I see him standing in front of the camp director's cabin, along with the other counselors. The cabin's name is Great Oak because camp is divided into two lands: Birdland and Treeland,

and all the cabins are named accordingly. *Cardinal, Redwood, Wren.* My favorite cabin is White Oak because it's nestled up in the hills overlooking the lake and it's closest to the Woodsong Chapel, my favorite place. Emily and I made a lot of good memories here, memories that I hoped would continue this summer. But this job doesn't pay much—not enough for her to rent an apartment in Nashville.

Her parents kicked her out of the house after they found out about the abortion.

They said they'd pray for her soul.

I hope they're praying for my soul too.

• • •

A guy wearing no shoes is staring at me.

Boys don't usually stare. Except for Bruce Wilson, captain of the high school math team, and he hardly counts because I never wanted to return his stares.

Shoeless Boy is beautiful. His tan face is kind and maybe a bit mischievous. A red bandana keeps his dirty blond hair in check. His khaki shorts reach his knees and sunglasses hang off the collar of his black T-shirt. He's carrying a guitar case in one hand and has a laundry basket full of clothes under the other arm.

He sets the guitar down and waves. I wave back. He grins, and my knees feel kinda wobbly.

He reminds me of someone...

A lady blows a whistle. "If y'all will gather round," she says to

5

the group of ten counselors. She's got a mass of curls and she's... large. I can't think of another way to describe her. My face flushes. I shouldn't think mean things like that.

"Welcome to the sixty-fourth summer of Cumberland Creek Camp!" she yells. Everyone hoots and screams in response. I clap along with them, but my heart's not in it. Not while Emily's living by herself, working two jobs to make enough money to pay her rent. I've already promised myself I'll send her half of every paycheck. I'll make $300 a week here.

"You okay?" Will nudges me.

"Great, thanks," I lie. We went to the same school—Hundred Oaks High in Franklin—and I had a crush on him for just about forever. Now he's finally got a girlfriend...who's also a counselor here this summer. She took Emily's job.

Parker wraps her arm around Will's waist and leans toward me. "Hey, Kate."

"Hey," I reply with a smile. A non-jealous smile, I pray. I always imagined he and I would get together, but I don't think they're the kind of couple who breaks up. Parker goes to my church and we went to school together, but we never talk. Her long brown hair is tangled with messy plaits in it. She's like a beautiful wild child.

The whistle screeches again. "I'm Megan Anderson, the camp's director."

Two girl counselors squeal, "Megan!"

"Let's have a seat on the porch and we'll do introductions,

go over our training schedule, and then take a tour of camp, for those of you who haven't been here before," Megan says.

Everyone rushes for the folding chairs and porch swing, but I make myself comfortable on a tree stump next to the deck. Sunlight filters through the leaves dripping above us.

The boy who had been staring at me got a coveted spot on the porch swing. The two girls who squealed "Megan!" sit on either side of him, and he's laughing and looking back and forth between them. He must be a returning counselor. I can't help but notice how pretty the girls are, with their short shorts and tanks and tan, skinny legs. My body and legs are skinny too, but I desperately need a tan this summer. I also need to gain some muscle back after my soccer injury.

"Okay," Megan says, tooting her whistle. "We're going to play an introduction game. Y'all have to pair your name with an animal and tell us a bit about you."

Everybody groans, but they're smiling. I remember playing this game when I was little.

Megan starts us out. "I'm Monkey Megan and I just finished getting my master's in education from Tennessee Tech."

A buff guy with brown hair announces himself as "Bumblebee Brad. I'm the games director this summer." He says he just graduated high school but doesn't mention where he's going to college. I notice a series of deep purple bruises peeking out from beneath his T-shirt sleeve.

Will says he's Wallaby Will and Parker is Platypus Parker and they are going to college together at Vanderbilt.

My turn. I swallow the lump in my throat. "I'm Kangaroo Kate—"

Shoeless Boy laughs and croons in a deep Southern accent, "Oh, cool. I can ride in your pouch."

"What does that even mean?" his swing mate asks, elbowing him in the gut.

"Filter, dude. Filter," Bumblebee Brad says to Shoeless Boy.

Megan blows her whistle, giving everyone an evil eye. That whistle'll get way old way fast. "Tell us a bit about yourself, Kangaroo Kate."

My face burns. I decide not to tell them this is my first job. Ever. "I'm going to be a freshman at Belmont University in Nashville this fall. I'm the arts and crafts director here this summer."

Shoeless Boy stares at me some more and I stare back. Ride in my pouch? Really?

We move on to other counselors. A girl sitting on the swing says, "I'm Alligator Andrea and I'm a senior at Middle Tennessee State University, where I'm majoring in communications. I'm also the president of Chi Omega Tau."

This guy Iguana Ian howls like a wolf, and everyone cracks up.

"Huh?" I whisper to Parker, who's sitting on the steps.

She plays with a clump of her long messy hair. "Chi-O-T. Coyotes? It's a sorority."

I raise my eyebrows. I didn't know Christian girls joined sororities.

Next up is Shoeless Boy and I hold my breath, waiting to hear his name and interests and what he's doing here this summer.

"I'm Marsupial Matt—"

"That's not an animal," I interrupt, and everyone gives me weird looks.

"Sure it is," he says with a laugh.

"It's a classification, not a specific animal. A kangaroo is a marsupial."

"I know," he replies. His mouth curls into a smile.

"What does that even mean?" Andrea asks, using the same tone as before.

"It means that a kangaroo is a marsupial." He shrugs and glances at me again.

She flicks his thigh, then musses her hair, watching him for a reaction. So Andrea likes Matt.

He looks so familiar.

He clears his throat. "Now, as I was saying, I'm Marsupial Matt—"

I accidentally snort and laugh, and Matt smiles. Will's mouth falls open as he looks at me.

"Fine," Matt says to me. "I'm Matt Brown the Mutt, and I'm from Bell Buckle. I'll be a junior at MTSU this fall. I'm majoring in literature and I'm getting a minor in classical guitar. I'm the camp lifeguard."

I love that he plays classical music and likes reading.

"Oh, and I'm in Delta Tau Kappa," he adds. I've never even considered joining a sorority and it seems like everyone here does that kind of stuff. On weekends they probably throw raging keggers and underwear parties. I've seen stuff like that on TV.

Nearly everyone is older than me and is a returning counselor. Parker, Will, and I are the only new hires. Most people are dressed in shorts and tees, but this one guy is dressed in camo pants and big brown hiking boots. Eric ("I refuse to play the animal introduction game") wears a Braves cap, chews gum, and is twenty-one and a senior at Auburn. He doesn't laugh along with everybody else and he rolls his eyes when anyone mentions a frat. He seems very into the whole Camping Experience because he keeps bringing up fly-fishing and trailblazing.

"It's great to meet everyone," Megan says. "Let me go over our schedule for the next two days. Tonight we're going to focus on ethics and Bible studies we'll do with the campers, but tomorrow and Sunday we'll do a run-through of a week at camp. We'll grill out and we'll go swimming, canoeing, kayaking, and creek stomping. I encourage you all to get to know each other. Each week you'll be paired with a new counselor of the opposite sex. Our groups of campers consist of twenty boys and girls, and your cabins will be side-by-side. You and your co-counselor are responsible for your group all hours of the day, except for during activities, when campers rotate among us."

I wrap my arms around my leg and drop my chin onto my knee. Thinking of children reminds me of Emily's baby and what I did. I shut my eyes.

Megan tells us who our partners are for week one. Parker pouts when she hears she's been paired with über camper Eric while Will's paired with Andrea. Matt's with Catfish Carlie and I'm matched with Bumblebee Brad.

He lifts his chin and winks at me. Not in a creepy way, but in a friendly way. I decide I like Bumblebee Brad.

"One last thing," Megan says, twirling her whistle like she's doing nunchucks. I'm afraid she'll put somebody's eye out. "Everyone gets weekends off. But no one is allowed to be here over the weekend—it's a liability for the regional conference. As some of you know, we had to fire two counselors who broke this rule last year."

We take a break before our camp tour and our first session: "A Practical Introduction to Sharing God's Love with Young People."

I dart away from Great Oak before I have to speak to anyone. I go to my Volvo, to grab my sketchpad and pencils and to check my cell, and surprisingly, I don't have any missed calls. I can't believe my parents haven't called a bazillion times already. And Emily usually calls me once a day, but I haven't been answering.

Not since our fight.

I angle my phone toward the sky. I don't seem to be getting any reception here. Not even one bar. I should be using this time to talk to God about everything anyway. And I'm glad I don't have to feel guilty about not picking up Emily's calls.

I drop the cell into my car's cup holder, stealing a deep breath. I take in the purple and pink sunset. This isn't bad so far—I mean, besides the fact most of these counselors seem obsessed with their fraternities. I noticed Andrea playing with her necklace made of Greek letters, and the Jeep parked next to me has a "Greek for Life" Delta Tau Kappa bumper sticker and no doors (must be Matt's).

He drives a Jeep with no doors?

I lean my head against my steering wheel and pray and hope and think about the sign. The sign I desperately need.

Without Emily, without soccer, and without my relationship with God, who am I anymore? *Can you forgive me?* I pray.

Can I forgive myself?

The memory of the fight floods my mind and won't go away. I clutch my steering wheel.

• • •

Three weeks ago, I let myself into Emily's room to find her sitting at her desk, mascara and tears staining her cheeks. I hugged her and helped her to the bed.

"Mom found the paperwork," she whispered. "She found the paperwork from the women's center in my backpack."

I rubbed my face. Told my heart to stop pounding. "And?"

"She and Dad asked me to move out. They're beyond pissed."

"They want you to move out now?" I exclaimed. "We graduate in three days!"

"After I graduate." She pointed at an ad for a studio apartment on her laptop screen. "I guess I won't work at camp. I'll go to Nashville early so I can make more money. It's only three months until college starts." Even if she didn't have her parents' support anymore, at least she had her scholarship.

I clutched the bedspread, not looking directly at her. Her parents kicking her out didn't surprise me. They're all about appearances. They're the type of people who wear fancy clothes so people will think they're rich, but behind the scenes they're drowning in debt. Having a daughter pregnant out of wedlock would make them gossip fodder for our entire church.

"You can move in with us if you need to," I said.

She nodded and the tears flowed down her cheeks again. I hugged Emily for the longest time. Then I chewed on my thumbnail.

"Stop biting your nail," she said. Since she had come back from her symphony camp in D.C. last summer, she'd been bossy. I took my thumb out of my mouth.

"Can we pray together?" I asked quietly.

"Why?" Her eyebrows furrowed.

"I need to."

Several heartbeats went by before she said quietly, "I can't pray with you anymore."

"Why?"

"I've told you. I don't buy it. Any of it."

I leaned over onto my knees. I didn't understand what she was saying. All I knew was that I needed my friend and I needed to pray.

"For me?" I asked. "Please."

"I don't get why you need to pray. Nothing happened to *you*." She folded her arms across her stomach and hunched over.

It didn't just *happen* to her. It happened because she decided to sleep with Jacob. "That's not true," I said. "I sinned. I sinned to help you—"

She sniffled. "You didn't sin."

Why couldn't she understand that I'd shoved aside everything I believe in, everything at the core of who I am, to help her? By taking her to the women's center, by holding her hand while the doctor spoke to her, I gave up who I am. I gave up the relationship I had with God and openly defied Him to help her. I sat in the exam room while it happened.

I told her all of that.

Her face went red and her eyes glossed over.

"I'm just asking you to pray with me," I said. "Please."

"You're being a judgmental bitch," she replied, wiping a tear off her cheek. Her eyes popped open, as if she couldn't believe what she'd just said.

I couldn't believe it either.

Pain crushed my chest. I stood up from her bed and wiped

my hands on my jeans. "I just…needed to pray." I barely got the words out before I started crying.

She jumped up, knocking a pillow to the rug, reaching out a hand to me. "Kate—I'm sorry—"

Without saying anything, I left her house and haven't picked up a call from her since. Not because I don't miss her, because I do, but because I lost part of myself that day and I don't want to lose even more.

• • •

I pray for the sign; I want Him to tell me that what I did, helping to end a baby's life, is okay. Because everything within me says it's not. If I hadn't taken her to the center, maybe she would've changed her mind about aborting the baby. Maybe her parents wouldn't have freaked out on her.

I have a billion what ifs and no way forward.

I pray to God, telling Him I want *my* Emily back. Because without her, and without knowing what I'm supposed to do next, life kind of feels like french fries without the salt.

Here in the now, something smashes into the driver's side window, rattling it. I jump, hitting my head on the car's ceiling.

"Ow!" I rub the top of my head.

I climb out, carrying my sketchbook and pencils. Matt hustles up to retrieve a basketball bouncing beside my car's front left tire.

He's not wearing a shirt, and seeing his muscles nearly makes my heart stop. Then his blue eyes and tan biceps are right in front of me.

"Sorry about that," he says, smiling down at me. He has a dimple in his chin.

He should be a bicep model. Is there such a thing as a bicep model? Like hand models who model watches and rings? I guess a bicep model would show off tattoos.

"You okay?" he asks.

"I'm fine," I say, touching my head.

He tosses the basketball up and down. "I wanted to ask…do I know you?"

"You look so familiar—"

"Did you go to camp here when you were little?"

"Yeah."

He grins and looks around. "Are you King Crab Kate?"

I cover my mouth with a hand. "Oh my gosh—you're Miniature Poodle Matt!"

He drops the ball, rushes forward, and hugs me. His arms and chest are all sweaty, but I hug him back.

"I totally won our cannonball contest," I say. "I beat you so bad."

"Sure, keep telling yourself that," he says, releasing me. We fought about that contest for days.

"You shared your ice cream with me." I smile.

"I took you to the Thursday Night Dance!"

I touch my mouth, remembering how he pulled me behind

16

the art pavilion and quickly pecked my lips. He looks at my face and I know he remembers.

"You were my first kiss," he says, pointing at me.

And my only, I think.

Now we're both laughing.

"Matt!" Brad calls out. "Can we get the ball back?"

After he hurls the ball back into Brad's hands, Matt picks up his black T-shirt from the asphalt and slips it over his head, then gestures toward the path. We fall into step with each other and stroll down the trail.

"Why aren't you wearing shoes?" I ask.

He looks down at his filthy feet. "Cutting to the chase, eh?"

"Yep."

"A few years ago? I got into marathoning. I've done seven."

"You've run seven marathons?" I exclaim.

"I want to try to run the Chicago marathon barefoot."

"Barefoot."

"Why not?"

"Sounds cool. Maybe after that you could run a marathon dressed up as Miss Piggy or Elvis or something."

He stops walking and a smile spreads across his face. "Or I could run the marathon dressed as Miss Piggy. Barefoot."

"Pigs have hooves, not feet."

"Now you're getting too complicated for me. I can't run a marathon in hooves."

We've paused next to this big fat cedar tree, smiling at each other. He peels bark away from the tree's trunk, catching my eye. I can't believe this is the Matt I knew when I was eleven. He's changed so much. The quiet, skinny boy I knew wore glasses and had a comb-over. Always had a *Hardy Boys* book in his hand. Shy. He rarely smiled. But I remember how he smiled at me.

And now he's a literature major with a mess of dirty blond hair who could be a bicep model.

I say quietly, "I'd love to run again."

"Again?"

"I used to play soccer. I fell and tore my ACL last fall."

Matt winces and checks out my knee. I want to cover the long, thin scar.

"So you didn't play again after that?"

"No. I did a lot of physical therapy this spring. Maybe I'll be able to play intramural in college." *It's a total long shot.*

He asks, "Were you a good runner before?"

"Pretty good. I played center midfield."

He looks impressed. "I'm sorry you got hurt."

I clutch my sketchbook closer to my chest, trying to forget how much my injury had hurt. Physically and in my mind. I haven't gone running since it happened, because I'm scared I might tear something again. I stick to the exercise bike now.

But I miss feeling my long black hair flopping against my back in the wind. My heart pounding and blood rushing through me as I sprint faster than anybody. I miss being part of a team where we spoke a common language: soccer.

Looking down at my scar, I say, "It happens, I guess." But God didn't have it happen to anyone else on my team.

I point at the restroom pavilion, indicating I need to use it. We walk over there to find that Parker and Will have snuck into the darkness behind the bathroom pavilion and he's got her pressed up against the wooden wall. They are kissing fast and furiously and their hands are everywhere. I'm a little curious, because no boy has ever kissed me passionately like that, and I spend way too much time imagining what it would be like. Tingles rush up my spine and my face goes rosy, for spying, for being jealous.

"Geez," I mutter.

Matt and I stare at Parker and Will, then move inside the pavilion filled with picnic tables.

"Guess they couldn't hold out." Matt chuckles softly. He's okay with this? With Parker and Will getting all handsy at church camp? It reminds me of how uncomfortable I was in my high school cafeteria, where the football players made out with girls all the time, slipping their hands under shirts and skirts.

"Sometimes you just can't wait," Matt says.

"Oh?" I say with a tiny voice, wondering what kind of guy he is now.

"Yeah, like, a couple weeks ago? My mom sent me to pick my

little sisters up from ballet, and on the way home, I saw this new restaurant called Just Tacos."

"Just Tacos."

He nods. "But it was weird. They had a lot more than just tacos there. They had fajitas and quesadillas and enchiladas. I told the waitress that a burrito isn't a taco and she said, 'It's a big taco.' I cried bollocks on that one."

All this laughing feels good. "So what does Just Tacos have to do with kissing?"

"Besides the fact I absolutely love both?" he asks.

I nod. How many girls has he kissed since he pecked my lips that time? He was thirteen then, so probably a bunch.

"So I was driving home and I got really hungry for a taco. I took my little sisters inside and we totally pigged out, and when I got home, my mom was pissed because she had cooked a roast."

"Because you just couldn't help getting the taco?"

"Exactly." He puts his hands in his shorts pockets and glances from the ground up to my face. The lantern light filling the pavilion really brings out the green flecks in his blue eyes. "It's good to see you again, King Crab Kate."

"It's good to see you too, Miniature Poodle Matt." We smile at each other some more. "You've changed a lot. You're more confident."

He blushes. "You've changed a lot too."

I raise my eyebrows.

He looks me up and down, at my khaki shorts, tank top, and the cross charm hanging from my neck. His eyes move from my long black ponytail hanging over my shoulder to the freckles dotting my nose. My breath hitches in my throat.

He adds, "You're a lot taller. I bet you can ride the big kid rides at the fair now."

I playfully nudge his shoulder and take in his eyes again. I don't want to look away.

He coughs lightly into a fist and points over his shoulder at the bathroom—*I need to go too.* I push open the screen door to find Andrea and Carlie chatting next to the sink. I decide to listen—subtly, I hope—before walking inside.

Carlie is drying her hands on a paper towel. "Matt seems happier this summer."

Andrea fluffs her short blond hair. "He's still not over it…"

Carlie throws the paper towel away, then uncaps her lip gloss. "I could've sworn he was checking you out when you first got here."

"He told me he's not interested in dating at all right now."

"Ian asked me to share a bed in Dogwood. Thank God, it's been months since I've gotten any."

Andrea laughs, and my heart speeds up. It's nothing new, but it always upsets me when I hear about other Christians doing it. Don't they hear the same lessons as I do in Sunday School?

"I sooo want Matt," Andrea says. "I haven't fooled around in like, a year."

I can't listen anymore. I let the screen door slam behind me and walk into the bathroom. Andrea and Carlie shoot me looks before I push the stall door open and sit down. A beetle is crawling on the floor, so I edge my sneaker away from it.

What hasn't Matt gotten over?

"I can't believe that new girl was eavesdropping," I hear Andrea say as the door slams shut.

When I come out of the bathroom, Andrea's sitting on a picnic table, talking with Matt.

I bite down on both of my lips. I loved our conversation, and now he's off talking to Andrea already. I tell myself he's not the same boy I knew when I was eleven anymore. He's twenty, a grown-up. A bicep model.

He's not interested in dating anybody…?

He looks over at me and waves. I wave back and inch away toward Great Oak, passing by Parker and Will again. Now they are holding hands and talking quietly. If I'd gotten the chance to date Will Whitfield, would he have tried to put his hands all over me? I'm not that kind of girl.

But I didn't think Emily was that kind of girl, either.

sketch #332

what happened on april 17

I sketch an outline of Emily's figure, thin and hunched over.

That day, she had sat on her porch steps and buried her face in her palms.

"I have to do it," she cried.

"You don't," I said. "I'm sure there are options."

"I'm not giving up my scholarship."

She'd gotten an offer to attend Belmont University's prestigious music school in Nashville, where she would study violin. Her grandfather played violin too, and the first time he heard her play, he knew she'd go a lot further in life than he did. His claim to fame was playing the fiddle in front of crowds of three hundred at the Rutherford County Fair. Emily wanted more, and between junior and senior years, she'd played for the National Youth Philharmonic in Washington, D.C.

I fan my colored pencils out on Great Oak's cedar deck. As I draw the scene, I add heavy mascara to Emily's eyes, something she never wore before D.C. I smudge her cheeks, to show her tears and the stress she was under that day in April. I make her lip gloss glisten and make her tight yellow skirt cling to her legs. I draw myself looking confused. Eyebrows tilted down. Hands stuffed in my armpits.

Neither of us admitted it, but that summer had changed her. She had started using words we'd only heard in movies. She showed off more cleavage and went quiet during Sunday school. She didn't participate anymore. With a voice full of wonder, she would say things like, "Do you think God really exists?" I told her, of course there is a God.

But I couldn't understand why she was questioning that, and that made me think about my own beliefs. Church was all I had ever known, and Emily had come back from D.C., telling me most kids there didn't believe or they belonged to some other religion that I knew nothing about, like Judaism and Islam. Why didn't we learn anything about those religions in Sunday School? Why didn't we have more than a few temples and mosques in Tennessee? The only thing I knew about either religion was what I had learned in history class: the Holocaust, 9/11.

I knew what I was supposed to believe: God is great. God loves me. I don't want to go to Hell. I know some people wonder whether Heaven and Hell truly exist, but do those people question whether gravity exists? Or oxygen? You can't see those with your naked eye, either. I can't see cologne on a guy's body, but I can smell it. I may not be able to see Heaven, but deep inside, I can feel it.

Anyway, Emily's boyfriend of three years liked her physical changes a lot, and when the three of us would hang out together, Jacob and Emily disappeared upstairs into her bedroom more frequently. I figured they wanted to kiss in private.

Before she went to D.C., she'd once told me about how Jacob had gone up her shirt and unsnapped her bra.

"Emily, that's wrong," I had said.

"Prude," she'd replied with a laugh.

Maybe I was a prude, but that's how I wanted to be. We had been told to save ourselves for marriage. After that, she tried to talk to me about physical stuff she did with Jacob, but it always made me uncomfortable.

A small part of me was jealous. I wanted a guy to kiss me. To touch me.

But Mom sent me to Sunday School every week and she taught me to follow the Bible's instructions (thou shall not steal, thou shall not lie), to do what our pastors say. And for good reason.

Like, my pastor told us not to drink. That made a lot of sense after James Macanley drove his truck into a backhoe and slashed his forehead open on the windshield. He had to get seventeen stitches. Sex before marriage isn't smart because you can get pregnant or contract some nasty disease. Taking drugs is stupid. Why mess up your brain like that?

God's laws just make sense. And like I said, before Emily went to D.C., I honestly never knew there were other options, other beliefs. It was like a part of my brain opened up to this whole new world. A world I didn't understand.

Using my pink coloring pencil, I shade in Emily's Converse, which she was staring down at.

That day on her porch in April, Emily wiped her eyes and said, "I want to play for the National Symphony. I can't have a baby."

In elementary school, my Barbies married Emily's Ken dolls. In middle school, we shared deodorant after gym class. Freshman year, when Kristen Markum called me a Jesus Freak, Emily got in her face and told her to shut up. I loved Emily more than anything.

"Have you prayed about it?" I asked her.

"I need to do what's best for me. I think God would want that."

"I don't know what He wants," I replied, and bit my lip.

"I want to get an abortion," she said so quietly I could barely hear her.

I dug the heels of my hands into my eyes to stanch my tears. If I were her, I would've married the father and had the baby.

I wanted to tell Emily that at nine weeks, a fetus can wrap his tiny fingers around his nose and toes. At fourteen weeks, which was about how far along Emily was, a fetus learns to suck his thumb.

"Shouldn't we talk to your mom?" I asked.

"No!" she blurted. "No one can know."

"What does Jacob think?"

She glanced up at me, her eyes watering. "He can't know either."

"But it's his baby."

"But it's my body."

I rubbed my chest, squeezing my T-shirt. "What happened? Didn't you use a condom?"

She smiled sadly. "This one time it kind of slipped off and Jacob didn't notice until we were finished."

I paced around in circles until Emily told me to stop. My face felt stretched and stung from tears. I could tell I was getting on her nerves. I could tell she thought I was immature. But this was a living, soon-to-be breathing person we were talking about. A new life.

"Could you put the baby up for adoption?" I asked.

"Jacob wouldn't go for that. That's why he can't know."

"Why did you sleep with him?"

She lifted her hands. "Because I love him and wanted to be with him. Isn't that obvious?"

The thought of saving myself for my future husband—the person who would love me and understand me better than anybody—thrilled me. I can't wait to share myself with a guy someday.

"Don't you think you'll love the baby you made with him?"

She let out a sob. Cried for a minute straight. She loved the baby growing inside her.

She said, "I want my future. I want to compose music and play for the National Symphony. I want that."

I sketch the flowerbeds and grass around Emily's front porch.

That day, I silently prayed to God, asking for help. And right then, Emily picked a few white clovers out of the ground. She started tying them together, like when we were kids. She and I would sit outside for hours, singing songs while making flower bracelets and necklaces and rings.

I watched as she made a bracelet, and smiling a slight smile, she handed it to me. I slipped it over my hand, onto my wrist. I knew Emily was still the same ole Emily, even if she'd changed in D.C. She was my friend who I loved.

I sat beside her on the step and hooked my arm through hers. "Your secret's safe. I'm here."

Megan's calling us back to training now, but before I put my pencils away, I draw the clover bracelet, looping it around my wrist.

never have i ever

After two hours of ethics, and in a very un-camping-like move, Megan announces we're having pizza delivered for dinner.

"Really?" Eric says, throwing his hands in the air before going back to cleaning supplies in his tackle box. He must be pissed we're not out hunting deer with bows and arrows and grilling it up. This isn't *Beowulf*, Eric. It's 2012!

"Everyone give Matt your topping preference," Megan says.

With my hands in my back pockets, I approach the picnic table where he's hovering over a sheet of paper with a laughing Andrea. She touches his elbow and whispers in his ear while I stand there.

He clicks his pen, edging away from her. "What'll you have, King Crab Kate?"

"Pepperoni and mushrooms, Miniature Poodle Matt."

Grinning, he writes my order down in shaky cursive. It's cute.

"Anything else?" Andrea asks me. She moves so close to him she might as well sit on his lap.

"Nope."

"We'll tell you when the food gets here," she replies, and goes back to acting like I don't exist.

"Thanks," Matt says to me, fumbling with his pen. He glances up at my face. "I'm sorry if I embarrassed you with that whole riding in your pouch thing."

"It's fine," I say. "I have no idea what you meant, but it's okay."

"I have no idea what I meant either." He smiles, pushing the pen behind his ear. He places his palms on the picnic table and leans toward me. "So you're going to Belmont this fall—"

"Let's start unpacking supplies," Megan interrupts, so I smile at him before moving away. We all start sorting through big white boxes of camp T-shirts, games, spatulas, frying pans. I dig right into the new paints and crayons, and start surveying the arts and crafts closet in the open-air pavilion. I have to admit, I love being surrounded by fresh air and listening to crickets and other bugs making their noises. It's relaxing and I can let my brain float away into a world of colors.

I love painting and sketching. My Uncle Steve is a cartoonist and has been drawing political comics for *The Tennessean* for the past twenty years, but it doesn't pay much—Uncle Steve has borrowed money from Daddy on occasion. Grandpa Kelly always says that drawings don't get you anywhere in life, really, and while I spend lots of rainy Saturday afternoons doing water-colors and sketching, it's something I do to de-stress. My parents think I have the ability to become a lawyer, like Daddy and Aunt Missy and Grandpa Kelly.

The truth is, I have no idea what I want to major in. Architecture, a career that requires a lot of math, aka something I am truly terrible at? Art, a career where I'd make no money? Interior design, like Mom? Pre-law track, like Daddy? I should decide soon: college starts in three months, after all, and if I could figure out what to do with my life, I wouldn't waste time taking classes that won't count toward my major.

I unload a bag of my own supplies into the closet. I brought a painting I did when I was a camper: a watercolor painting of White Oak cabin. I tack it on the inside of the door, to remind myself of how much I loved Cumberland Creek as a kid.

"That's beautiful," I hear a voice say, and turn around to find Parker standing there with Will.

"Thanks. I did it a long time ago."

Her eyes widen. "I didn't know you're into art."

"My one true love." I give her a smile.

"Really?" Brad says, striding up with hands in his pockets.

"I also love soccer. And coffee."

Brad chuckles. "Do you need caffeine to survive? Because they don't serve Coke at the cafeteria here." He shudders, as Carlie walks over.

"I totally forgot about that," Will whines. "I remember when

I was little, how at the end of a week of camp, I always begged Mom to take me straight to McDonald's for a Coke."

"I did the same thing," I say with a smile. "We'll have to get a secret stash."

"Don't say that too loud," Brad says quietly. "Megan's a real stickler for us following the same rules campers do."

"I'm surprised our lights-out time isn't nine p.m. like the campers," Ian says.

"I'll have to get some of those Five-Hour Energy things," Parker jokes.

"I don't know what I'm gonna do without cigarettes," Carlie groans. "Last summer I died without them. But some nights I was able to sneak away and smoke down by the lake."

The Middle Tennessee regional conference is made up of six churches, and each nominates members to be counselors here every summer. I've never been to any of the other churches, but based on how Carlie and Andrea act, I can't imagine those churches are anything like Forrest Sanctuary.

"People smoke here?" I whisper to Parker. She goes to my church, so she should understand what I'm thinking.

"So what?" she says quietly.

"So I didn't think people would do that sort of thing here."

"I don't care one way or the other," Parker replies, rolling her eyes. "It's not my business."

After hearing that, I edge away from the conversation and

finish unpacking my art supplies. This is church camp. I don't think it's right for counselors to sneak away at night to go smoke. And since I sinned majorly, I need to show God that I'm still a good person.

The pizza comes, and after we say grace, we divvy it up. Andrea grabs a seat right next to Matt. I had been planning on trying to sit with him. He looks over at me and raises his shoulders, as if to say he's sorry.

I sit down beside Brad and sip my water. "Is your arm okay?" I ask, checking out those bruises again.

He shoves his sleeve down, trying to cover them. "It's fine."

"Looks painful."

Brad nods. "It was. A game of pick-up basketball got nasty."

"Did you get into a fight or something?"

"Nah, I fell onto the asphalt," he says, but I don't believe him one bit. The bruises look like finger marks. He pulls down on his T-shirt again. "Do you have any brothers or sisters?" he asks.

"It's just me," I reply. I nibble at a pepperoni, then focus on Matt across the pavilion. He laughs at something Parker just said and scratches his cheek before folding a slice in half and taking a huge bite. He and I keep glancing at each other so much I guess it finally gets to Andrea.

She stands up and says, "We should play another introduction game. To get to know the new hires better."

"Who's up for a game of Never Have I Ever?" Carlie asks.

Ian says, "Yeah! I'll get the pennies."

"Let's move it over here," Matt says, coming to sit beside me on the bench. I'm sandwiched between him and Bumblebee Brad.

Everyone squeezes around my picnic table except for Megan and Eric, who's going on and on about how his girlfriend dumped him.

"I'm sorry," Megan says, not sounding sorry at all.

"Two years gone. That's all," Eric replies. He wipes his mouth with a napkin and taps his big brown combat boot on the concrete floor.

Matt leans over to my ear. "Megan wants Eric bad. And Eric wants Megan's job bad. And Megan is trying to protect her job while trying to win Eric's love."

I cringe.

"Exactly the response I was looking for," Matt says with a laugh. "Last summer I about put my name up for the director position just so I wouldn't have to deal with them anymore."

I shake my head at him, smiling. "Why didn't you?"

"Because that would require me to be responsible. Now, are we ready to play?"

Everyone has a pile of pennies in front of them. The rules are this:

Someone says something they have never done. For instance, I have never gone deep sea fishing. If a player has gone deep sea fishing, he or she has to throw a penny in a bucket in the center of the table. The pennies don't really mean anything except to show who's done what. It's like a game of Truth or Dare with cash but without the dare. I would rather have the dare than deal with truth after truth after truth.

Carlie goes first. She taps a penny on the picnic table. "Never have I ever gone skydiving."

Ian is the only person who throws a penny in the bucket.

"That's hot," Carlie says to him. "You must be fearless."

"Totally fearless," Ian growls, and I get the sense that if no one else was here, they'd totally sweep the bucket of pennies to the floor and start going at it on the picnic table.

Matt whispers in my ear again. "They hook up every summer. She gets away with anything 'cause her mom is vice president of the regional conference."

Ian says, "Never have I ever worn ladies' underwear."

All the girls throw a penny in the bucket, and Will pretends like he's about to, then he changes his mind. Parker smacks his arm playfully.

Will goes next. "Never have I ever scored a B in a class."

Everyone throws a penny in except for me and Parker.

"You're a braniac, eh?" Matt says quietly to me. I like the way his breath feels warm on my ear. Our shoulders touch.

"I'm going to bed, y'all," Megan says, leaving the pavilion. "Don't stay up too late."

Eric then announces he's going to ensure the camp's main gate is locked so that intruders can't get in.

"Now we can play for real," Andrea whispers, twirling her blond hair.

"That guy is such a douche," I hear Ian muttering to Brad, who nods.

"Never have I ever gone skinny dipping," Andrea says.

"No one believes that," Brad says, as Ian and Carlie throw pennies into the bucket. Yay, Matt doesn't toss a penny! Will drops a penny in the bucket, then shrugs sheepishly at a gaping Parker. She rolls her eyes and throws a penny in too.

"Never have I ever been in love," Brad says.

Andrea and Ian throw pennies into the bucket. Parker's face grows pink and Will lowers his chin. They aren't in love yet? Matt raps his penny on the table for a second, then tosses his in.

I clutch my penny, wishing I could say I've been in love. I glance sideways at Matt, to find he's looking out of the pavilion into the woods. Who has he been in love with?

"Your turn, Parker," Carlie says.

Parker gets this really coy look on her face. "Never have I ever kissed a girl."

All of the guys toss a penny into the bucket. And then Carlie and Andrea do too.

My mouth falls open.

Matt leans over to my ear again. "I bet they kissed each other. For practice."

I can't help but laugh. Andrea shoots me a look.

"Who's next?" Brad asks. "You go, Kate."

I chew on my thumb. "Never have I ever eaten coconut ice cream."

Everyone glances around at each other. Andrea snorts. Matt, Carlie, Brad, and Parker throw pennies in.

Matt grins at me sideways. "I'm a vanilla guy, myself."

"I like strawberry," I reply.

"Coconut tastes like ass," Ian announces, tossing a penny in.

"Your turn, Matt!" Andrea says loudly.

He leans his head back, thinking. "Never have I ever driven heavy construction equipment."

Nobody throws a penny in.

"Boring," Carlie says. Her mouth lifts into a smirk, and she glances between me and Matt. "Never have I ever gone streaking across the MTSU campus."

Matt sneaks a glimpse of me, then raps a penny on the table before tossing it in the bucket.

"I still can't believe I missed seeing that!" Andrea exclaims.

"That takes balls," Will says, shaking his head.

"I heard what they made you do with that banana in the dining hall," Ian says to Matt, laughing.

I sit up straight.

"My frat made me do it," Matt whispers to me, avoiding my eyes. "To get in."

He's been in love. He might still be in love. His body has

transformed from that of Bill Nye Science Guy to that of Adonis. Girls talk about him in the bathroom, and it's not to make fun of him. He streaks across campus to impress other guys.

And my pile of pennies is mostly untouched.

• • •

I roll my suitcase over the bumpy, dusty trail toward Birdland. Megan said we should go ahead and get our cabins set up for this week. Brad and I have been assigned to the Cardinal cabins.

Andrea and Carlie pass by me, carrying sleeping bags and pillows, chatting about some shirt they like at Abercrombie.

Ian sprints by me, slaps my arm, and yells, "You're it!"

Brad and Matt chase behind him, whooping.

Their noise echoes in the wind. The wind rustles the fragrant pine trees. I try to find the moon over the tops of the trees, but they're too tall. These woods must be several hundred years old— they're large and in charge.

That's when Parker and Will come walking up. He's carrying two sleeping bags over his shoulders and she's hugging his waist and laughing. They pause to kiss.

I clear my throat to let them know I'm here.

They break apart and she wipes her mouth with two fingers. "Hey, Kate," she says.

"Where's everybody going?" I ask.

She looks at him. He looks at her. Will says, "We're all sleeping over in Dogwood. You can grab a bed in there if you want."

"Girls are sleeping in the same cabin as boys?" I ask. I thought it was just Carlie and Ian.

"It's not a big deal," Parker says with a shrug.

"It's a big deal to me." Emily and Jacob always snuck off together and look what happened. And now a bunch of counselors are basically going to share a bedroom?

I bite down on my lips, trying not to remember how Emily's face looked after the abortion. Splotchy red marks dotted her cheeks and pain filled her glossy eyes. She kept asking me what the doctor was going to do with the baby and I didn't have the heart to tell her. I just kept squeezing her hand.

"Guys and girls shouldn't share a cabin," I say. "It's probably a sin. What if someone gets pregnant? I'm not helping you if that happens."

"What did you say?" Parker's eyes pop open. She grabs Will's elbow. "I told you I'd try to be nice, but if she acts nasty, it's really hard for me to care."

"It's okay, it's okay," Will says in a soothing voice to Parker. "You're right."

"Nasty?" I whisper.

"Maybe 'nasty' was the wrong word," Will says carefully, shifting the sleeping bags in his arms.

"What's the right word?" I ask, almost scared to know.

"Judgmental," Parker says, staring me down. Will squeezes his eyes closed.

Emily said the same thing about me. That's why we got into the fight. That's why I haven't talked to her in three weeks. In the past, people at school would call us Jesus Freaks, and Emily always told me not to worry, that they were raised differently than us. And I believed her—until she called me judgmental and said that church isn't all it's cracked up to be. Why do Emily and Parker, who were both raised in the church right alongside me, think so differently now? What changed?

Was I supposed to have changed?

Is that why I've never had a real boyfriend?

"Judgmental?" I say softly. "Really?" I add, even more softly.

"Really," Parker exclaims. "Like last year."

"What do you mean?"

"When my mom left my dad for another woman last year, you weren't supportive at all."

I take a step back.

She goes on, "You acted like I didn't exist when I needed friends more than anything."

I open my mouth to argue, then close it. She's right. Brother John always said if you associate with people who sin, there's a good chance you'll sin too. So I steered clear of Parker, because after her mom left, she started hooking up with lots of guys at school and supposedly she seduced a teacher. Who does that?

That line of thinking didn't do me much good, though—I

ended up helping Emily do something so, so wrong. I did it because I love her.

"I forgive you," Parker continues. "But that doesn't mean I have to spend time with you." She turns on her heels and marches toward Dogwood.

Will gives me a shrug. "Night, I guess."

Then he follows her and I'm left standing in the middle of the trail, surrounded by drooping branches and darkness.

• • •

That night, I sleep alone in Cardinal, with only the whir of a box fan to keep me company. The fan blows warm air across my shaking body. Tears coat my cheeks and no matter how much I try to empty my mind, all I can think about is what I did to Emily's baby. Emily's baby, and what Emily and Parker said about me being judgmental.

I'm not happy, and I'm making everyone around me miserable. If I don't figure my life out, the loneliness will continue into college. Into forever? What if I never have a best friend again?

What's going on in Dogwood right now? If I were in there, would Matt be sleeping in the bed next to mine? What does he wear to bed? Pajamas? A T-shirt and shorts? Only boxers?

I shake those thoughts out of my mind and clutch my pillow.

I've tried to live a good Christian life. I follow the Bible to a T. I listen to everything Brother John says. I'm trying harder than ever and it just isn't working. This is not the sign I was looking for.

I'm a good, good girl.

A good, good girl who's got no friends.

A good, good girl who helped her ex-friend get an abortion.

I don't deserve any friends.

I focus on the humming box fan, watching one blade spinning over and over in the same circle.

• • •

The next morning when I wake up, I grab my shower caddy and head to the bathhouse. I cut across the dewy grass. Nobody's awake yet. That's a good thing since my face feels puffy and I need a long cool shower to rinse off the sweat and shame from last night. I shriek when I find two massive granddaddy longlegs in the shower stall, then laugh at myself. They can't hurt me.

When I'm done, the clean underwear, T-shirt, and shorts I put on make me feel like I just left a spa. But the guilt is still fresh. I run my things back to Cardinal, where I dry my long black hair and put on sunscreen, as if it could stop the freckles. When I step back out onto the porch, I jump.

"Matt!"

"Morning to you too," he says, yawning.

"You scared me!"

"I thought my morning breath had upset you."

He's lounging on the porch swing. Sunglasses sit on top of his head. I take in his biceps and lazy smile and the blond stubble covering his cheeks and dimpled chin.

"You doing okay?" he asks.

"I'm fine," I lie. "Did you sleep well?"

"Will's snoring sounds like a freight train."

We smile at each other. A long, still moment. He makes me feel calm, like wrapping up in my robe after a hot shower. I can't explain it. But then I remember he's a streaker. How far did he have to run when he went streaking?

Instead of dressing as Miss Piggy, what if he ran a marathon naked?

And then I'm wondering what he looks like naked.

And then I'm shaking my head and rubbing my eyes.

"I thought I'd see if you'll help with breakfast?" He scratches the back of his neck, peering up at me.

"You're cooking?" I ask.

"It's my day to fix breakfast for everybody. Want some expert tips on scrambling eggs and making doughnuts over a campfire?"

"You can make doughnuts over a campfire?" I exclaim.

"Oh sure." He smirks a little. "I can't do anything fancy like Boston cream pie or anything, but I can make killer cinnamon doughnut holes."

"I love those," I say quietly.

"Well, I'd love some company." He stands up, clutching a shaved tree branch.

"What's that for?" I ask.

"My walking stick? It assists me in walking."

I giggle. "Are you injured?"

"Naw. Of course not. I'm the lifeguard! Who would hire an injured lifeguard?"

"My mistake."

"Your mistake indeed."

"You're hilarious," I find myself saying.

He elbows my arm and glances over at me. Using his walking stick, he makes his way to the cafeteria on the hill. The building's green paint is flaking off and the air smells like grease. He unlocks the doors and we raid the fridge for eggs, bacon, juice, and biscuit dough.

"Grab that big can of Crisco off the shelf, please," he says, nodding toward it.

We lug all the supplies back down to the fire pit area next to Great Oak. He says, "Let's get us some firewood." Out in the woods, we pick up logs.

"That one's too wet," he says.

I drop it and pick up another.

"That one's too big," he says.

I drop it and pick up another.

"Get some tiny branches for kindling, please," he says.

Matt arranges the logs in the fire pit, then grabs a wad of paper towels and stuffs them under the sticks. Then he turns the Crisco can upside down and lets the goop drip onto the wood. He lights a match and throws it on the wood pile. A flame bursts up.

I jump back, panting. "Are you a pyromaniac?" I blurt.

"Crisco's amazing," he says, smiling. Squatting, he begins tossing tiny sticks and grass onto the fire until the flame gets hot enough to catch the thicker logs.

"Isn't that cheating?"

He laughs. "I wasn't aware there are rules for starting a campfire when you're starving for breakfast. I mean, sure, if this was a Boy Scout competition I totally would've been disqualified."

"Maybe I'll use your Crisco trick when it's time for me start my own fires," I tell him.

"I just converted you to my Crisco Cult!"

I laugh. "Now what do I do, oh master of the Crisco Cult?"

"Grab that cast-iron kettle and hang it over the fire," he tells me. "And dump the rest of the Crisco in it so it'll melt. Then we'll fry up the doughnuts in it."

"What doughnuts are we gonna fry?" I ask, glancing at our supplies.

"Take the biscuit dough and start rolling it into balls."

The first thing Matt does is get the coffee brewing (he has a secret stash). It's a humid June morning and the fire's roaring, so I'm wiping sweat off my face like crazy. For a second I'm terrified Matt thinks I look hideous, but then I glance over at him and find that his face is covered in dirt and he's all sweaty too.

Once Matt has the eggs cooking in the skillet, he pours us each a cup of coffee. I watch as he briefly shuts his eyes and murmurs a blessing.

He sips his coffee and asks, "Why didn't you share a cabin with us last night? Were you afraid that I snore too loud?"

I bite back a laugh. "Nah. I just don't think my parents would like it if they knew I was sharing a room with boys. And what if the regional conference finds out? They'd be mad."

Matt slaps his palm with the spatula. "Eh. They'd never know. But I know what you mean. My mom would kill me."

"Really?"

"Oh yeah. She's the youth minister at Bell Buckle Chapel and spends most of her time teaching sex ed and trying to keep teenagers out of each other's beds. Especially her own kids. My brother Jeremiah's practically a man whore."

I stop moving. "A man whore?"

He chuckles. "He's got a new girlfriend every day." He points at me with the spatula. "I'm not exaggerating. One time, this girl Laura came to lunch at our house and by dinner she'd been replaced by someone named Mary."

I laugh, rolling biscuit dough into a ball. "And what about you? Are you a man whore?" I stutter, trying not to seem interested in his answer.

"I wish," he says with a sigh. When he sees the look on my face, he quickly says, "Just kidding. I'm a one-girl kind of guy."

"So it's just Andrea?" I ask, baiting him.

He pauses and picks up his coffee cup from the picnic table. He sips. "Naw. I'm single right now. You?"

"I'm single all the time." I blush.

"So…you have a moratorium on dating?"

"No," I say slowly. "I just haven't dated anyone."

"Ever?"

I hesitate. "Ever. Unless you count our date to the Thursday Night Dance that time." He's so easy to talk to, I can't help but tell the truth, no matter how embarrassing it is.

He takes a swig of coffee. "Are you picky?"

I don't know how to answer that. This is probably the longest conversation I've ever had with a boy. Well, besides Jacob, and he belonged to Emily. I still can't believe she broke up with him.

I sip some coffee.

"I'm picky too," he says before I can respond.

I change the subject. "Now what do we do?"

"Throw some bacon in that skillet, woman."

"'Woman'?" I burst out laughing.

He adjusts his bandana, smiling at me, and my stomach leaps into my throat, and I feel this longing deep inside—a longing to have a friend.

sketch #336

what happened on may 5

After making breakfast with Matt, I sharpen my pencil so I can sketch, to keep my mind off my pathetic dating history. But my plan doesn't work.

One day in May, I pulled open the front door and Jacob marched in, brushed past me, and headed for my living room. No hello, no hi, no nothing. I dug my fingernails into my palms and took a deep breath. I trudged into the living room and sat down beside him on the couch. His face was buried in his palms. Emily had broken up with him a week before, right after the abortion.

I had never seen him that upset. Come to think of it, I'd never seen him upset at all. Jacob always had been a carefree kind of guy. I sketch his hair: black curls pulled back into a low ponytail. I draw the sticker-covered skateboard he always carries around, as he smiles and talks to everybody. Like Emily, he's insanely musically talented. Sometimes he wears a kilt and plays silly music on the bagpipes. Once he played "Happy Birthday" for me and

I couldn't stop smiling. Lots of girls wanted him, but he'd been with Emily since they were fourteen years old.

I draw the blank TV screen that Jacob had stared at that day. Draw tears leaking from his eyes.

For a moment I wondered if he knew about the abortion, about what I had helped Emily do to his baby, when he spoke. "What did I do wrong? Why did she break up with me? Please—" His voice broke.

I continued to dig my thumbnail into my palm. "She hasn't told me."

He glanced up, flashing me a look. "That's bullshit."

I sucked in a breath through my nose. "I'll try to get her to talk to you, but I can't promise anything."

"I need to know what's wrong, Kate. Tell me." His eyes dug into mine. "Does she not love me anymore?"

I wanted to tell him that Emily loved him so much, but she wanted her future more than a life with the baby they hadn't planned for. But she couldn't stop thinking about the decision she'd made without Jacob, so she broke up with him. If Emily had had the baby, would she have had Emily's auburn hair? Would he have had Jacob's black curls?

And then I started crying for Jacob and Emily, who wanted to be together so badly. They loved each other, but her guilt was messing that all up.

That's not the only reason I cried.

Deep down, I was jealous of that love and I wanted a boy to show up crying for *me* because he loved me so much.

"She loves you," I told him.

He abruptly stood up. "This is not what love is," he said, and left my house.

I start an outline of my body, sitting alone on the couch after Jacob left.

Then I scribble over it and start a new picture. A picture of Matt teaching me to use Crisco to start a campfire. I smile and reach for my yellow coloring pencil to draw the flames licking at my feet.

snake!

Before going swimming, kayaking, and canoeing this afternoon, Megan's giving us time to plan our individual sessions. Will's in charge of the Monday ice cream night, so he's fiddling with homemade ice cream makers. Brad's been counting hula hoops, unfolding a giant parachute, and inspecting a tug-of-war rope because he's in charge of field games. Andrea's the camp videographer, so she's playing with various cameras and her laptop. Carlie's writing out clues for the treasure hunt.

Matt already cleaned the pool, so he's lounging in a camping chair, lazily strumming his guitar, playing what sounds like a Hawaiian version of "Kumbaya."

I'm inventorying the paintbrushes when Will plops down on the picnic table bench beside my closet.

"You okay?" he whispers, glancing over his shoulder at Parker. She sees him talking to me and her face looks pained. It's like she'd rather him talk to a Playboy Bunny than me.

"I'm fine," I tell him, placing paintbrushes in a plastic box and storing it on the shelf.

"Matt said you seemed upset this morning."

I focus on my watercolor painting of White Oak and remember the time I found a frog in a bush outside the cabin. He was so scared, he peed on my hand. Part of the reason I like art so much is the escape. The escape into a world that I fill with my colors and music.

"I'm sorry Parker yelled at you last night," Will says, lounging against the table.

I organize the boxes of crayons into a straight line. "I'm sorry if I hurt her," I tell him. "I didn't mean to." I just don't want someone else to go through the same pain as Emily and me.

"You should tell her that, not me."

I let out a sigh. "She doesn't want to talk to me."

"How do you know? She's a pretty forgiving person."

I don't say anything.

After a few seconds, he goes, "She forgave me."

"What did you do wrong?"

His eyes meet mine. "Left her when she needed me most."

I want to tell him that I don't have a best friend anymore.

"Listen," Will says, drumming fingers on the picnic table. "This is none of my business and I hope you don't take it the wrong way, but I want to tell you something about your church."

I brace myself. "Yeah?"

"Forrest Sanctuary destroyed Parker after her mom left."

I smooth my hair. Until last night, I had had no idea Parker was so badly affected. I mean, she and I were never all that close growing up—I had Emily, after all. And Parker was always fooling around with random guys in high school. So I ask Will about that.

"Why do you think she was so screwed up?" Will asks slowly. "It must suck to give your whole life to a church, only to watch everyone disappear when you need help."

This reminds me of how Emily's parents kicked her out after the abortion. How I played it differently. I stuck by, only to have her call me a judgmental bitch.

I feel bad for not having noticed what Parker was going through.

"So Parker's mad at me because I go to her church?" I ask quietly. "Because she's mad at our church?"

Will lifts his shoulders. "I think she's just, um, wary of people?"

In high school, people called me a prude and Jesus Freak because I had no problem telling people that I care about church and God. It didn't make people rush to invite me to the movies on Friday night, that's for sure. But I had Emily to hang out with, and I had soccer, so all was okay.

Until it wasn't.

I say, "Parker's lucky to have you."

He grins. "I'm lucky she agreed to give me another shot."

No guy has ever stood up for me this way. I glance over my shoulder at Matt.

"Is Parker feeling better now?" I ask Will. "Since her mom left?"

"I like to think so. But as you saw last night, she's definitely not anywhere close to being fine…She doesn't really have any friends who are girls."

I know how that feels.

"I'm around if you want to talk more," he says, then leaps up and dashes across the trail to Great Oak, where he pulls Parker into his arms and pecks her lips. She grins.

My mouth edges into a smile.

• • •

We're walking down the path toward the lake, where Matt will train us to canoe and kayak. I look for trail markers that I can remember when walking my campers to the lake. Breadcrumbs, like Hansel and Gretel, but all I see are trees, trees, and more trees.

Parker is a little ways behind me, so I slow down.

"Hi," I say, clearing my throat.

She just looks at me and passes on by like I said nothing. I open my mouth to speak again, but nada comes out. The thing is, I wasn't in the wrong last night. This is a job at church camp. Should guy and girl counselors really be sleeping in the same cabin together?

Rules exist for a reason, right?

Maybe I'd been less than tactless, accusing Parker of sinning, but I was just trying to help. And I feel bad for not noticing her pain during high school, but it's not like she paid much attention to me then, either. She never checked on me after my surgery or asked why I didn't play soccer anymore. The first time she confronts me, she bites my head off, leaving me embarrassed and alone.

Or have I made myself that way?

Am I embarrassed and alone because of who I am as a person?

"You lost?"

I look up to find Eric standing in front of me, narrowing his eyes. His camo outfit truly blends in with the trees. The rest of the group is way ahead of us.

"Just thinking, I guess."

"You can't do that when you've got ten girls to watch out for, okay? You can't take your eyes off them even for a second, or you could lose one."

"Okay, I'm sorry," I say, hardly believing how intense this guy is.

He stalks off. I follow everyone down to the algae-spotted lake, where Matt is pushing canoes and kayaks into the water. Shirtless. His tan biceps and smooth chest just about make my heart stop.

"Ogle much?" Andrea asks me.

My face goes hot. Matt looks up as he unties a canoe and pushes it into the water. He gives me a little wave.

Matt makes everybody put on a lifejacket and hands each of us an oar. Will and Parker share a canoe, and so do Andrea and Carlie, but the rest of us get our own kayaks.

Matt takes my hand, helping me step into my kayak, the rough callouses of his skin scraping against mine.

"Okay, everybody," he yells, clapping once. "The rules of canoeing are simple. If you want to go right, then put the paddle in the water on your other right."

I laugh.

Andrea drops her oar in the water and it starts floating off, so Matt leaps into the water and rescues the oar and returns it to her with a smile. I bet she dropped it on purpose, just so she could see him get all wet. I don't blame her.

I paddle around the lake slowly, drifting in various directions. Will's pointing into the water and Parker's peering down, smiling. Is it a turtle? A school of fish?

Eric circles the lake like it's his job to secure the perimeter from bears or something.

My kayak gets stuck on the side of the bank, and when I touch my oar to the bank, to push away from the land, a coiled brown and white snake catches my eye.

I scream.

I scream again. I thrust my paddle into the water and start paddling away as quickly as I can. Can the snake come in the water? I think they can swim.

Was it a copperhead? A rattlesnake? A water moccasin?

I look up from paddling to see Matt dive off the dock and swim my way. I stop thrusting my oar into the water and lean over onto my thighs, swallowing. Everyone is staring at me like I'm a major moron, which I guess I am. But what if the snake had bitten me?

A minute later Matt surfaces next to me and shakes the water out of his hair. "You okay? What happened?"

I chew my lip. "I saw a snake."

His eyes dart around, probably to make sure the snake isn't about to retaliate because I ruined its nap. "Snakes scare the bejesus out of me."

"I'd never seen one before." My body is trembling.

"They're more scared of us than we are of them," he says, treading water, bobbing like a cork. "But they are still scary as hell."

I'm disappointed that he curses, but I keep my mouth closed. I'm not messing up the good start with him.

He says, "Can you get yourself back? Or do you want me to try to squeeze in and paddle for you?"

My heart pounds at the idea of him squeezing into a kayak with me.

"There's not enough room in here," I say, smiling.

"Too bad," he teases. He grabs my hand. I suck in a deep breath. "You sure you can make it?" he asks.

"Totally sure." I paste a smile on.

"Okay—I'm gonna go rescue that runaway over there," he says, jerking his head toward an orphaned canoe nestled up against the banks. "Race you back to the docks."

He takes off swimming in the opposite direction and I start paddling as hard as I can, smiling to myself about our race. He doesn't seem to be going all that fast. I hope he's not the type of guy who lets a girl win.

After a billion years of paddling, I beat him back to the docks. I shakily climb out of the kayak onto dry land and face an inquisition.

"What happened? Are you okay?" Will asks, crossing his arms.

"I had a run-in with a snake."

"A snake?" Megan asks, playing with her whistle.

"I doubt she saw a snake," Eric announces, wiping sweat from his brow with the back of his hand.

"I promise you," I say, catching my breath. "It was a snake."

"I have a book you should read before campers arrive on Monday morning," Eric says, puffing his chest out. "It will tell you everything you need to know about dangerous animals in Tennessee." Eric looks pointedly at Megan.

She blushes. "Yes, you should read it," she tells me. "And please, no more screaming."

"Are you sure you saw a snake?" Eric asks, scanning the banks.

"Yes, I saw one," I say again, wringing my hand. "Maybe you should read the chapter on snakes in your book."

"I don't think there are any snakes around this lake," Eric says. Is he pretending he didn't hear what I said?

"I dunno if that's true," Matt says, leaping onto the docks from the canoe he just rescued. "Last year I killed a copperhead that was swimming near here."

My heart swells as I smile at him.

"I've got a picture of it on my phone!" Andrea says, nodding quickly. "He smashed it with an oar!"

Eric checks his ginormous watch that's the size of a compass. "Whatever."

I suddenly want to start studying everything I can about the outdoors so I can one-up him, like Matt just did.

"Regardless of whether there are snakes in the lake," Megan says, "you can't react like that in front of children, Kate. It's unprofessional and it will scare the kids."

I look around at the other counselors and nod. Parker raises her eyebrows at me.

I turn to gaze across the lake at the deep green woods. When I was younger, I learned about how Henry David Thoreau went out into the wilderness and lived by himself at Walden Pond for a long time and wrote his magnum opus. I'm not saying I want to go write a magnum opus or anything, but I'd love to have a tiny cabin to myself in the mountains, where I could paint landscapes until my hand falls off and not be around people like Monkey Megan and Eric "I refuse to play the animal introduction game" and Alligator Andrea, who probably is an alligator disguised as a sorority girl.

Parker appears beside me and whispers, "I would've screamed if I saw a snake too. And I want to be a vet!"

I slip my thumbs into my belt loops. "I'm, uh...can we talk about last night?"

Megan blows her whistle and beckons for us to follow her back up the trail, and Parker walks off with Will without responding to me.

"I can't believe you killed a poor snake!" Parker snaps at Matt, passing by him.

"It was swimming near a group of eight-year-old campers who were canoeing. What was I supposed to do?" Matt replies, drying his face with a towel. He waits for me to catch up. "You okay?"

"I never want to see a snake again."

"Me neither." He jerks his head toward Parker. "For multiple reasons."

I laugh. "Thanks for swimming out to save me."

He looks over at my face. "You saved me once too."

sketch #340

At twilight, I rock back and forth on Cardinal's porch swing. I use a piece of charcoal to sketch, making sure to keep my hands away from my face and clothes, so black dust doesn't get everywhere.

I draw thirteen-year-old Matt with glasses and a bit of acne on his face.

I hate it when Christians don't act Christian-like. The boys in our group had been teasing him for writing music and lyrics.

"Only girls do shit like that," a boy had said to Matt, making him turn redder than a strawberry. He clutched the neck of his guitar, glancing at me. Most of the other kids looked away, but I held his stare and tried to show him he wasn't alone.

I got the impression this wasn't the only time he'd been bullied. He never smiled and hardly ever spoke.

But now, as a guy about to be a junior in college, he seems sure of himself. He's grown into his skin.

I draw a picture of eleven-year-old me pulling Emily over to Matt.

"Can we hear one of your songs?" I asked him.

He smiled and began to strum his guitar while watching my eyes.

By Wednesday night, he'd written a new one. Something about comparing a girl's beauty to that of a redbird.

"Vibrant, free, elegant, and lovely."

When he sang it for me, I kept my head down and buried my clasped hands between my thighs. The song ended, and he reached out a hand, grabbed my shoulder, and squeezed.

"Thank you," he said.

I never knew what he was thanking me for, but I said you're welcome and the next night he gave me my first kiss.

This afternoon, when I asked how I saved him, he didn't answer.

I touch my lips, probably getting charcoal on them. How did I save him?

I use my red coloring pencil to fill in an outline of a redbird.

his snores are louder than a bulldozer

"This is inhumane."

Parker is upset about creek stomping.

Once a week, we'll take campers down to Cumberland Creek, where we'll wade around and catch crayfish. Some crayfish are the size of a quarter. Some are the size of a brick.

"We should just let the kids walk through the creek and splash around," Parker complains to Megan. "We don't have to remove poor animals from their little homes under rocks. From their families!"

"Is she always this opinionated?" Megan asks Will.

He smiles and gives a little shrug. "It does seem kind of inhumane."

Parker loops her arm around Will's elbow and pecks his cheek. Megan watches them, not disapprovingly but longingly—it's almost as if she's as jealous of their relationship as I am. Then she focuses on Eric. Still wearing his combat boots and camo pants, he's standing on the bank whittling a stick. The rest of us are in water shoes and shorts and bathing suits, in case we slip and fall in the chilly creek.

"Are you coming in, Eric?" Megan asks.

He scrapes the stick with his knife. "I'm good. I've got this activity down pat."

She nods slowly and after staring at him for a moment too long, she turns to face the rest of us. She blows her whistle, and I wince.

"Let's get going," she says. "Pay attention to where the deep spots are, so you can point them out to campers. The most important thing to remember about this activity is that you should always have a first aid kit handy. Be careful not to slip and fall. Try picking up some crayfish."

"Get them right behind the claws," Eric calls out from the banks. "That way they don't pinch you. The big ones could snap your finger off."

"Right," Megan agrees.

Parker harrumphs behind me.

Will and Matt move ahead of the group, stopping to flip over stones in the water, to look under them.

"Eric is still pissed he didn't get the camp director position, huh?" Andrea whispers to Carlie.

"Yeah, and Megan is up for that big Bible education job at the regional conference," Carlie whispers back. "Mom told me that the conference is watching how well she runs camp before giving her the job."

"She's seriously uptight this year."

"She's got a hard-on for Eric, that's why," Carlie says. "She needs to majorly get laid."

I accidentally stick my tongue out at the thought of that, and Parker laughs at the face I'm making. I trudge through shin-high water to wade next to her.

"Is this your first job?" I whisper to her.

"No." She bends down to pick up a shell. "I worked at Chuck E. Cheese last summer. It was baaaad."

I watch as she examines the shell, turning it over in her palm. "This is my first job," I say. "I didn't realize it would be so much like high school. All over again. You know?"

"My dad says gossip never goes away, no matter where you are in life."

"Great," I say in a flat tone, making Parker smile. "My dad has never mentioned if gossip is bad at his work or not." He's a tax attorney, which is like the most boring kind of lawyer there is.

Parker carefully places the shell back down in the creek and wades off with Will, taking his hand in hers. It reminds me of the buddy system.

When I was little, we weren't supposed to go anywhere at camp without our buddy. Emily was always mine. We used to hold hands as we waded in the creek. We did cannonballs off the side of the pool together.

I never imagined that one day I would have no buddy beside me.

That's when Matt slows down to wade next to me.

"Hey, King Crab Kate," he croons, making me beam.

"Hi, Miniature Poodle Matt."

We angle off from the group, and at first the silence is scary and makes me want to chew all my fingernails off, but then I peek over at his face and see the calm smile there. I bend down to turn over a rock. I find three tiny crayfish the size of my thumb but let them scurry away. The bubbling water noises make my heart slow down.

I rise to my full height again, to find Matt waiting for me, and we keep trudging down the creek. The water is chilly but the air is hotter than a sauna.

"So what's this about you and a banana in the dining hall?" I ask, even though part of me doesn't want to know.

He drags a hand through his hair, ruffling it. "I wish you hadn't heard that."

"Why are you in a frat?"

His eyebrows furrow. "They're my friends. The guys were just messing around," he says, flushing.

I wouldn't want friends who make me do questionable things with a banana, but I let it go because I don't want to embarrass him.

Parker told me that after her mom left, she needed friends more than anything. Did she hook up a lot because she was lonely? At the time, all I saw was that she fooled around with too many people, when now I know that she was hurting.

So maybe there are two sides to Matt wanting to be in a fraternity.

"I don't know much about frats," I say. "How many guys are in it?"

"We have ninety-seven members right now. We'll take on more in the fall."

"That's a lot of friends."

He nods and smiles. "I know some of the guys better than others."

"But what's up with the banana?" I laugh softly.

"It's not for a lady's ears."

He bends down and moves a rock. He spots a crayfish and picks him up, looks him in the eye, and then puts him back down beside the rock.

"You're majoring in literature?" I ask Matt.

A smile appears on his face. "Yeah."

"What do you like to read?"

"Anything, really. I love everything from Dickens to John Grisham to John Green to Judy Blume."

Judy Blume? I've smiled more this morning than I have in months. "What's your favorite book?"

"*The Once and Future King*, by T. H. White."

"I haven't heard of it. What's it about?" I ask.

"King Arthur and how he pulled the sword from the stone and became the king of Camelot…What's your favorite book?"

"*Where the Red Fern Grows*. About the dogs and coon hunting?"

"I hate that book," I hear Parker muttering to Will. "All those poor raccoons got killed to make hats."

"I love that book," Matt says, grinning over at me. "I think that's the first book I ever cried at. When the dog got into the fight with the mountain lion."

"You cried?"

"You're not a real man unless you can admit you cry."

"Oh really?" I tease.

"Shush," he says, laughing as he picks up a tree branch from the banks. He snaps a stick from it, then drops the branch in the water. The current carries it away. "What other books do you like?"

"I don't read a lot," I admit. "I'm more into art."

"Is that why you carry around the little portfolio and pencils?"

I peel a strand of hair away from my damp forehead and nod. "Do you want to become a writer or something? Is that why you're majoring in literature?"

He squats and dips his hand down beneath the surface, scooping up water. "Maybe. I mean, I'd like to do that eventually, you know, when I find the right idea for a story, but I think I'll probably become an English teacher in the meantime. Like my dad."

"But don't you have to wear shoes at school?"

He splashes my shin. "What are you going to major in?"

"I have no clue," I say. "Daddy thinks I should do the pre-law track, but I don't think it sounds all that exciting."

"Agreed," he says, laughing. "One time I looked at an LSAT

study guide, just to see what going to law school might be like, and I fell asleep. I drooled all over it."

I laugh, and two steps later, I slip and nearly wipe out. Matt grabs me, stopping me from crashing down into the water. He helps me to my feet.

"Is your knee okay?" He peers down at my scar.

I'm grasping his elbows. "I'm fine."

The creek forks and splits to the right, but we keep walking straight.

Andrea wades past us, peering over at me.

Having never stepped a foot in the creek, Eric is waiting for us at the other end. My water shoes make squishy noises when I step out onto the grass.

"Did you catch any crawdaddies?" Eric asks me.

I shake my head, glancing at Parker. "I wouldn't want to hurt them."

She finds my eyes.

"If you didn't even try, how will you teach campers how to do it?" Megan asks me, clucking her tongue. I'm surprised she hasn't blown her whistle in my face and asked if I can do anything right.

"I don't see why campers have to do it at all," I say.

"Me neither," Matt says, adjusting his bandana. "They could just enjoy nature."

"Creek stomping is a rite of passage at Cumberland Creek Camp!" Megan's face looks like it might explode.

I watch Brad as he mouths "rite of passage" with his jaw draped open.

To fill the silence (I guess), Eric announces to the group, "Some campers might want to save their crayfish for the Critter Crawl, but they aren't usually good contenders."

"*What* is the Critter Crawl?" Parker asks.

"Every week we'll have a contest where each group finds an animal to compete in a race," Eric replies. "Like granddaddy longlegs and beetles and worms. We put the animals in a ring and whichever one escapes the ring first wins."

Parker sets her hands on her waist. "I am so calling PETA."

• • •

I had forgotten all about hobo packs.

I loved them when I was a little girl. It's Sunday evening, the day before camp is to start, and we're preparing to cook over the campfire.

"It should taste like beef stew if you make it right," Megan tells us. "Everyone watch how Carlie does it. Her hobo packs are always delicious!" Megan has a bright smile on her face.

When her back is turned, Carlie sticks a finger in her mouth, fake-gagging herself. "I wish she'd stop sucking up to me. As if I have any control over who my mom hires."

"We should use Megan's brownnosing to our advantage," Ian says. "Tell her we need a karaoke machine!"

Matt asks, "I really want a hot tub."

I laugh, making Matt grin. "I want a fountain soda machine," I say.

We all gather around the picnic tables to assemble our hobo packs. First we each rip off a long strip of aluminum foil. I take pieces of beef and spread them across my foil, then pile mushrooms, carrots, potatoes, and green beans on top. Add salt and pepper to taste. Wrap it up like a burrito and place it right in the fire, on top of the logs.

And of course mine immediately starts falling apart. The foil splits open. The veggies and beef fall onto the wood. I groan loudly. I spent twenty minutes preparing that!

"Try wrapping it tighter," Megan tells me, clucking her tongue.

"Like a burrito," Eric interrupts.

"I'm sorry," I say. "I'll start over."

"You have to be able to show campers how to do this right," Eric says, pushing the skewer into me even deeper.

"Like a burrito," Megan repeats.

"Like at Just Tacos!" Matt calls over his shoulder to me. He's already feasting over at the picnic table.

I snort. "Did they have hobo packs at Just Tacos?"

"Probably. They had everything in the world there," Matt replies. "It wasn't just tacos!"

Ian and Brad just pulled their hobo packs out of the fire and are moving back to the picnic tables. Carlie turns hers over, using tongs. The fire crackles and hisses as she nestles her pack back down in the embers.

I go back over to my cutting board and start slicing beef, carrots, and potatoes all over again, to make a new pack. I'm not even hungry, but if I just say to heck with it, Megan will probably get angry with me, and I'm sick of that blasted whistle.

At the table beside mine, Andrea and Matt are whispering as they eat.

"Please?" she says, pushing a chunk of beef around with a plastic fork. "Let's do something during free time tonight."

"I think I'm gonna work on this new dodgeball court thing I want to build," he replies, popping a cooked carrot into his mouth. "Do you want to help me?"

"I was hoping we could take a hike or go down to the lake. Alone? Together?"

He goes quiet for several seconds. "I really want to get started on my dodgeball idea."

"Fine."

I want to ask him about his dodgeball court idea, but I stay silent, so that maybe Andrea will forget I exist.

I mix all of my hobo pack materials, taking more care this time, and then wrap up my aluminum foil as tightly as I can. The last thing I want is for my hobo pack to disintegrate twice in one night.

Can a person get banned from camping?

This time my hobo pack stays in one piece as it cooks, and Will fishes it out for me with tongs. He drops it onto my tin plate. Careful not to burn my fingers, I rip the aluminum open and the smell of beef stew wafts up to my nose. Okay, so I was hungry.

Matt, Ian, Brad, and Will finish up their food and decide to go play a game of two-on-two up at the basketball court. I pick at my dinner and eavesdrop on Andrea and Carlie.

"Give it time. If you really like him—" Carlie says.

"I *do* really like him." Andrea's voice is hard.

"Then you can wait for him to work stuff out," Carlie whispers.

"He's getting even more distant." Andrea shuts her eyes and sucks on her bottom lip. "I wish I'd get the sign this year. I wish God would show me how I'm supposed to work things out with him. I wish I'd never fallen for him in the first place."

"You can't help how you feel. He needed somebody, and you were a good friend to him," Carlie says quietly, putting an arm around Andrea. "You're a great person."

Carlie looks up at that moment and catches me staring. "This isn't your business," she says.

My face heats up. I wad my aluminum foil into a ball and throw it in the garbage bin, then stand and just walk. I have no idea where I'm going. I could go get my knee brace that's made of more steel than a skyscraper and see if I can do some jogging in it, to try to get used to it. Maybe if I go out and roam the trails, God will give me the sign. Sorry to act selfish, but I feel like I need the sign more than Andrea does.

I pass by Parker, who's telling Eric (Camper Extraordinaire), that the Critter Crawl is "an unbelievable act of cruelty and must be called off immediately."

I shove my hands in the pockets of my jean shorts and make my way up the trail. If Emily were here, I bet we would've died laughing when my hobo pack fell apart in the fire. Then she would've shared hers with me.

The sunset looks like a rainbow. Stars are beginning to peek through the colors. I pass by the basketball court, where the guys are playing shirts versus skins. Will and Matt are on skins and Brad and Ian are shirts. Matt takes a jump shot and makes it—nothing but net. When his bare feet hit the ground, he looks up. He drags a hand through his shaggy blond hair, then waves at me.

I wave back.

Will playfully shoves Matt's shoulder, and Matt grins, continuing to look my way.

I smile at him and keep walking toward Cardinal.

What was Andrea talking about? What can't Matt get past? How did I save him?

• • •

Past midnight, someone knocks on the screen door of Cardinal.

I'm tired. I'm sweaty. It's been a rough two days of learning how bad I am at everything outdoorsy, like fishing off the docks. Only I could manage to knock an entire can of bait into the lake.

Only seven weeks of camp to go.

My bed screeches as I roll over and peer up to find Matt standing outside. The moon casts a glow around his body. I swing myself out of bed and go open the screen door for him. He's wearing a pair of light blue scrubs as pajama pants, and no shirt. I already saw him shirtless playing basketball and swimming at the lake, but still, my stomach flips and flops.

"Hey," he says, checking out my XXXXXL T-shirt. Note to self: wear cuter pajamas in case boys drop by randomly after midnight.

"What are you doing here?"

"I don't like the idea of you sleeping in here all by yourself." He stifles a yawn.

"I'll be fine," I say, my shoulders tensing. "I can't let you sleep in here with me."

He waves a hand. "I'm gonna sleep out on the porch." He steps past and begins dragging a bed through the door. The metal frame creaks and groans.

"This isn't necessary," I say. My heartbeat races and races.

He drops the bed with a clang on the porch and stretches his sleeping bag out on the thin mattress. "What if the bogeyman is out here?"

"The bogeyman?" I laugh. "A myth."

Matt fluffs his pillow. "How about that dude with a hook for a hand?" He drops the pillow and makes a claw with his fingers and growls.

"Are you saying that you're the bogeyman?" I ask.

He smiles. "I'd already have captured you if I was."

"What if you get eaten up by mosquitoes? Or a black widow spider?"

"Eh, it's worth the risk." His mouth stretches into another yawn.

"Thanks for sleeping out here."

He nods and yawns again. "I'm about to pass out."

Where has he been all night? Has he been hanging out with Andrea up until now? I play with the hem of my long T-shirt. "See you tomorrow?"

"It already is tomorrow," he groans, flopping down on the bed. It screeches and wobbles.

I go curl up in my sheets.

"Sweet dreams, Kate," he calls out.

"You too."

Seconds later I hear him snoring up a storm on the porch and it makes me laugh. Didn't he say that Will is the bad snorer? Matt sounds like a bulldozer. I bring two fingers to my lips, laughing, and smile myself to sleep.

sketch # 346
what happened last night

Before campers start arriving at 9:00 a.m., I walk up to the cafeteria. The entire area is hilly and mountainous, but the building rests at the highest spot of the camp. From here, you can see everything. I sit Indian style on a bench, where I can stare at the valley full of cedar trees. I can smell their sappy smell.

I pull my pencil from behind my ear and open my sketchpad to a blank page. Chewing on the eraser, I think about last night. How Matt slept outside Cardinal. It was the first time in a long time I didn't feel alone.

I begin with the bed and mattress that he pulled through the door onto the porch, sketching the legs and beams that support the steel. I make thick lines across the mattress, to denote the blue stripes. After taking a quick glance around me to make sure I'm alone, I outline what Matt's body looks like without a shirt, showing him wearing only blue hospital scrub pants. I pay careful attention to his muscles. Not because I'm being a pervert or anything, but because the human body is the hardest thing to draw. It requires precision and patience and a steady hand.

That's when I hear footsteps. I snap the book closed against my chest. I look up to see Will, Brad, and Matt running together. Will and Brad are huffing and puffing, trying to keep up with Matt the marathoner.

I lift my hand to wave. All three wave back, which makes my heart swell.

"Come run with us," Matt calls out to me. "Get that knee in shape."

Can my knee handle running again? I'm not sure, but I'm willing to take the risk to spend time with Matt. "Okay! Meet me at my cabin in ten minutes."

He disappears down the dirt steps, heading toward the art pavilion. I walk as quickly as I can back to Cardinal and throw on a sports bra, shorts, a tank top, and sneakers. Carefully, I put on my steel knee brace that makes me sound like a walking indus-trial paper slicer. I step out onto the porch, where Matt is waiting for me.

"Where are Brad and Will?" I ask, tightening my black ponytail.

"They gave up already." Matt stretches out a hand to me and I take it. "You got this."

We walk, my hand lightly tucked inside his. I don't think I can handle running on trails full of hazards like rocks, sticks, and tree roots, so we go to the big field.

"Nice and slow," Matt says, and I lurch into a jog, keeping my breath steady. Thanks to my exercise bike, I've saved some of my endurance.

"You've still got your form," he says, looking me up and down while running. I hope he's seeing me as I want to be seen: black hair flowing in the wind, smiling, moving swiftly and gracefully.

We run five laps around the big field, hardly speaking a word. When I look over at his face, I find his mouth shut in a tight smile.

"What were you doing this morning? In the notebook?" he asks.

"Drawing."

"I'd love to see your work sometime."

I don't share my sketchpad with anybody. "Maybe," I say softly, not meaning it.

He must sense this. "It's okay…I don't share most of my lyrics and writing with anyone."

"It would be like letting someone inside me." I immediately regret my choice of words and feel my face go hotter than the sun.

"Exactly," he replies, glancing away.

After the run and a shower, my sketchpad catches my eye. I smile, pick it up off my bed, and finish what I was working on before.

Maybe the Chickasaw Tribe was right. Maybe this land is where heaven meets the earth.

The last things I draw before going to meet my campers are the laugh lines around Matt's eyes and mouth.

first day of camp

The sun is boiling me to bits by the time campers start arriving.

Mark my words. By the end of summer, freckles will have won the battle against my skin.

Megan checks campers' names off on a clipboard and sorts them into groups. Since I'm at Cardinal this week, I'm waving a red flag. Several girls head my way, carrying satchels and sleeping bags. Campers range between eight and twelve, but this week I have a group of ten older girls. All twelve-year-olds.

Some of them are chatting a mile a minute and others look nervous, like they are about to sing a solo during the school musical.

I swallow the frog in my throat. "I'm Kate," I tell them, and I begin passing out nametags. The nametags haven't changed since I was little: they are circular wood chips, and campers write their names in permanent marker right on the wood. Then we string colorful plastic cords through the holes in the chips, so the nametags can hang around necks.

I glance over at Parker. She's sitting with two adorable younger girls, both of whom are playing with her plaited hair.

"Look, it's the King!" a boy says, rushing toward Matt.

"The King?" I mouth at him, and he grins and shrugs. He shakes hands and gives high fives to his fan club. Like, twenty boys have gathered around him to talk.

"Matt is sooo cute," a girl named Sophie says. She used purple marker to write her name on the wood chip. She also took the opportunity to draw big purple hearts on the backs of her hands.

"Why do they call him the King?" I ask her.

She slings her satchel over her shoulder. "I dunno. He's just the King."

Ian appears next to me and whispers, "Last year, kids started calling me the Princess. It was humiliating."

I burst out laughing.

Brad and I lead our group back to the Cardinal cabins. The boys are checking out the girls and the girls are checking out the boys.

Brad rolls his eyes and whispers, "I prefer working with the younger kids. Puberty scares me."

I smile and climb the porch to Cardinal and open the screen door so my campers can file in. Much squealing and screaming ensues.

The girls all fight over who gets the top bunks and start unpacking clothes and draping them all over the place. Claire, a quiet, tall girl with big, open eyes, stacks a pile of books next to her bed, then begins applying lip gloss. She and Sophie appear to be best friends, but while Sophie is loud and authoritative, Claire hangs back. They remind me of Emily and myself.

Brad and I go over rules with our group and play the introduction game. Brad is Bison Brad and I decide on Koala Kate this time.

At lunch, the campers form a long line in the cafeteria, where a humongous wall fan blows warm air throughout the room. It should be really hot in here, but somehow it's comforting. The counselors form a cluster behind all the campers and start gossiping.

"I've got that little hellion, Cara Dawson, again," Andrea complains to Matt. "Last year she got up, like, ten times a night to use the bathroom."

"Taj is in my group," Matt boasts. "And he's gonna teach me to play 'Stairway to Heaven' on guitar tonight."

"Wait," I say. "A kid is gonna teach you guitar?"

Matt plays with the cross hanging around his neck and scratches one of his feet with the other. I still haven't seen him in a pair of shoes yet. "You should hear this kid play. He's gonna be performing at the Grand Ole Opry one day."

Andrea ignores me and focuses on Matt. "I can't wait to hear Taj play again."

"Maybe you and Taj could be in the talent show together," I suggest to Matt.

He points at me. "Good idea. That's the only chance I'd have of winning." He puts two fingers in his mouth and whistles. "Taj, wanna be in the talent show with me?"

Taj adjusts his ball cap. It's turned around backward. "You owe me, King!"

Matt clicks his tongue and points at the kid, and I laugh. I pull the talent show sign-up list and a pen out of my back pocket and write their names down. In addition to being the arts and crafts director, I'm in charge of arranging the weekly talent show.

A boy with a tray of food passes by us. "Yum, we're having chicken o' rings," I say, peering at the ringed nuggets. "I remember those."

"They're a hot commodity," Matt says, moving to stand next to me. So close, I can smell him: a mixture of soap and sweat. It's nice. Andrea gets edged out and is now standing behind us. I don't want to look at her face 'cause I'm sure she looks like the Hulk when he's angry.

He goes on, "I was gonna see if you'd trade me your green beans for my chicken o' rings."

My stomach grumbles. "I remember loving those too."

"So it's a deal?"

"Absolutely not. I want both."

He smiles at me sideways. We take a step forward in line. "Do you use honey mustard or barbeque sauce?" he asks.

"Both," I reply. "I never can decide."

"Me too. I usually throw ketchup in there too for a little

excitement." He elbows me. "Watch this." Matt lifts his hands above his head, forms an O with his arms, and yells, "OOOO OOOOOOOOOOOOOOOOOOOOOOOOOOOOHHHH HHHHHHHHHHHHH."

The campers join in, and Matt mutters to me out of the corner of his mouth. "You're leaving me hanging here. Would you bow to the almighty o' rings already?"

I start laughing and lift my arms over my head and scream along. It feels good.

At the pool after lunch, Brad doesn't take off his T-shirt when we're in the water. Some people who aren't comfortable with their bodies wear a shirt over their bathing suits, but I can see Brad's six-pack through the thin cotton.

"Are you sure you're okay?" I whisper to him, nodding at the bruises on his arm.

"Drop it, okay? Please?" His eyes plead with me. He glances around. What happened to him? He seems like a very normal guy. He takes his job seriously and everyone likes him. Did he get into something bad? Does Megan know? Should I tell someone? Am I the only one who notices he's wearing a shirt in the pool?

I skim the top of the water with my hand. The regional conference wouldn't hire someone questionable. I decide to drop it, like Brad wants me to.

I peer up at Matt sitting in the lifeguard stand. He salutes me and smiles, and his eyes go back to scanning the pool.

"Are you going to college?" I ask Brad.

He scoops water up with his hands and wets his face. "Not sure yet."

"Did you just graduate from high school?"

"Yeah."

A boy from our group suddenly does a cannonball, making a huge splash, drenching me and Brad. When the boy comes up for air, Brad playfully dunks him under the water. The boy jumps on Brad's back, trying to dunk him back, but Brad doesn't budge except to pluck the kid off his back and toss him into the water as if he were weightless.

"What are you doing this fall?" I ask Brad, wiping water off my face.

He shakes his head. "If I manage to save enough money this summer, I'll take a road trip across the country."

"I've always wanted to do that!" I smile, skimming the surface of the pool with my fingertips. "I'd love to drive the entire California coast."

"I always wanted to see the Grand Canyon…and Yosemite. I maybe want to become a park ranger…"

"So working here is sort of like training to become a ranger?" I say with a laugh.

He chuckles. "I'd much rather deal with snakes and bears than kids going through puberty. Seems easier."

We laugh together.

Brad seems like a really good guy. A normal guy. So what's going on with him?

Before dinner, while the kids are forming a rowdy line, Megan pulls me aside. We sit together on a boulder outside the cafeteria. "How's your first day going?" she asks with a smile.

"Good so far," I reply.

"I really liked the candles you made in arts and crafts this morning. The campers' parents are going to love them. I took some pictures to send to the regional conference."

"Thanks."

"Keep up the good work."

I smile to myself, happy that everything feels a bit lighter today. Keeping busy keeps the bad thoughts at bay.

On Tuesday afternoon, when we're walking back from kayaking at the lake, a kid from our group, Marcus, falls and cuts his leg open on a sharp stick. He bites into his lip as blood gushes out, coating the blond hairs on his shin. The cut looks totally tetanus-shot worthy.

Brad picks the boy up and throws him over his shoulder. "I'll patch him up. Can you get the fire and burgers started?" he asks me.

I swallow and nod, not sure if I'd rather deal with burgers or blood. They both sound equally terrible. I lead the group of nineteen kids back to Cardinal by myself. While the campers change out of their bathing suits, I begin taking the spatula and frying pans out of the milk crates, and glance at the fire pit. Glance at the fire pit some more. I pick up sticks for kindling, narrowly avoiding a patch of poison ivy. Poison oak? Which is it?

I drop the wood in front of the pit. Set my hands on my hips. The sun is setting lower and lower, and I only have about an hour to get this fire started, cook the food, and get my campers to Great Oak before the talent show starts. Not to mention I have to set up for the talent show too.

I kneel in front of the pit, matches in hand, and arrange the logs and kindling the way Matt showed me on Saturday morning. Glancing to make sure no one's watching, I smash some paper towels up under the logs and light them.

Fire whips through the paper towels. I smile. But then the flame goes out and I have to start over. This happens three more times. I have no idea what to do. Where's Brad? Was Marcus's cut that bad? What if Brad doesn't come back in time for dinner?

Two boys from our group, Rick and Michael, walk out of Cardinal cabin and head my way, and then I see Sophie and Claire too. The four of them start talking about the sign. Sophie says that she heard that God spoke to a boy through a campfire last year.

Is God trying to tell me something here? Is that why the fire won't start? I doubt it. I just stink at all things camping.

"Is it time for dinner yet?" Rick asks me.

"Be right back," I tell him.

Matt is two cabins away at Bluebird. About a minute walk. I wring my fingers together and follow the path up to his cookout pit, where a fire is roaring. The kids are already eating burgers and sipping lemonade, and he's lounging in a lawn chair, plucking away at his guitar strings, playing classical music for them as if these woods are a cafe. He's like the epitome of the perfect counselor, and I can't even start a fire.

He sees me, sets his guitar against the picnic table bench, and hops to his feet. "What's up?"

"You're really good on guitar."

"Thanks." He loops his thumb around the leather cord hanging from his neck.

"Did you write that? I mean, the song you were just playing?"

"Yeah."

I nod and set my hands on my hips. "I've always loved your music."

He smiles and scratches the side of his neck. "Why'd you stop by?"

I mumble, "One of our campers got hurt and Brad went to get him first aid…I can't get my fire started."

He raises his eyebrows, then turns and starts pawing through a milk crate toppling with supplies. He pulls out a starter log the size of a Kit Kat bar, a roll of paper towels, a book of matches, and a can of Crisco.

"This oughta do it," he says, dumping the items into my arms.

"Matt! I found a toad," a tiny girl says, and he rushes to squat down next to her. They peer into the bushes. It's really cute.

I turn around and trudge back to my campsite, where I tuck the starter log inside a bunch of kindling and hold a lit match up to it. I stuff a wad of paper towels next to the burning starter log. The paper towels quickly turn to hot ash, so I drip Crisco onto the wood and a fireball bursts up.

"Whoa, cool!" a camper named David says, and the boys rush to surround me.

"Grab more skinny sticks," I tell them, and soon we have a blazing fire, and then we're saying grace before eating cheeseburgers hot off the grill. When Brad returns, carrying a heavily-bandaged Marcus over his shoulder, he smiles at my work and says, "Nice job."

I decide I like being part of Matt's Crisco cult.

A couple minutes later Matt appears at our campsite and salutes Brad. "Yo, Bumblebee Brad. How's it goin'?"

Brad winces and looks up from trying to get the knot out of a sparkly pink sneaker.

"Bumblebee Brad! Bumblebee Brad!" Rick and Sophie start yelling, laughing their butts off.

I cover my grin with a fist. Matt grabs one of the burgers I just cooked and slips it inside a bun. "Ow," he says, sticking his thumb in his mouth.

"The burgers are hot, you know," I say, laughing.

"Thanks for the warning."

"You've gotta pay for that."

He bites into it and chews. "Mmmm." He chews some more and swallows. "That's a good burger."

"Thanks," I say, proud. "But you still owe me for it." I rub my fingers together, indicating I want cash, and he grins.

"As payment, later, I'll play you a song I wrote, okay?"

"Okay," I say with a smile, remembering the girl whose beauty he compared to a redbird. I wipe my hair away from my sweaty face. "I need to go get ready for the talent show." I have to put out the microphones and speakers and make sure the popcorn is popped.

By the time I finish frantically running around trying to find the mike (it was under a chair in Megan's office) and then determining how to plug the mike into the amp, the sun has completely set. The campers take their seats on the grass in front of the Great Oak porch (the stage). Blazing tiki torches and laughter surround me as I step up to the mike and say, "Welcome to the thirty-second annual Cumberland Creek talent show!"

Everyone cheers, and I'm smiling because I got the fire going. I managed to cook dinner by myself. I say a quick thanks to God.

I introduce the first act: a girl named Taylor, who's doing a mime performance. Another girl sings songs while doing interpretative dance, and a boy juggles three bowling pins he found in a closet in the art pavilion.

I laugh so hard when Ian sings Aretha Franklin's "Respect" along with two of his boy campers. They use brooms as microphones and when Ian hits the really high notes, he falls to his knees and clenches his eyes shut. Ian's not a very good singer. At all. But he still gets a standing ovation.

When he hops off the Great Oak porch, I say, "And you want to get a camp karaoke machine?"

"Just wait until next week." He winks. "Maybe I'll do some Mariah Carey."

But the funniest thing—the sweetest thing, is that Matt plays guitar, accompanying six different singers on six different songs. My favorite is when an eight-year-old girl named Lizzie sings "Jesus Loves Me" in the purest voice, and when she gets scared and I think she might run off the stage, Matt sings along with her as he strums his guitar.

Leaning against a tree, as bugs chirp around me, as warm wind rustles the branches, that's when I know it for real.

I want him.

bonzo ball

Before my arts and crafts lesson, Megan calls me into Great Oak for a "counseling session."

"I understand you had problems getting your fire started?" she says. "And the talent show nearly didn't start on time because of it." She taps her whistle on her desk, eyeing me.

How did she find out about my fire problems? Did Matt tell her what happened?

"That was the first time I've ever had to start a fire without help before." I clear my throat into my fist. "But I got it going. All the kids enjoyed dinner."

"That's not what I heard. I heard they ate nearly forty-five minutes later than scheduled and were starving."

Maybe I ought to tell her most of the kids were either:

1. reading in the cabins;
2. having a water fight;
3. talking about members of the opposite sex;

4. flirting with members of the opposite sex; or
5. searching for critters for the Critter Crawl, which Parker is still trying to get banned.

Only a couple of the boys complained and, well, boys are always hungry.

"I will try my hardest not to let it happen again."

"Eric has offered to coach you, so next week you'll be co-counselors with him. Parents pay a lot of money for their children to come here, and we have to give them an excellent week, or the regional conference will blame me, understand?"

She wants that Bible education job bad.

"I understand."

She taps her whistle on the desk some more. "You can go."

I swivel around to face her again. "How did you hear about what happened?" I ask softly.

"I heard from Andrea. I believe Matt told her."

I nod and leave the cabin, holding my nose so it doesn't start running, because I want to cry.

Matt told Andrea about my cooking issue? The backs of my eyes burn as I head toward the art pavilion.

How humiliating. I get where Megan's coming from, but she said it herself: the conference hired me for my artistic skills, not for my camping abilities. How could she expect me to be Camp Counselor Extraordinaire after three days?

I got the fire started! The kids scarfed their burgers and lemonade down like warriors after an epic battle. They loved it!

I can't believe Matt blabbed to Andrea.

My eyes are still burning as I step into the pavilion, where thirty campers are waiting for me. Using the most cheerful voice I can muster, I explain that we'll be doing decoupage today. Decoupage is where you use clear paste to glue bits of paper to any ole piece of junk, to decorate it. You can use crepe paper or construction paper. Newspaper and magazines work great too. I have piles and piles of junk and magazines.

"Decoupage is a chance to show who you are as a person," I explain to the campers. I hold up an old glass Coke bottle covered with pictures of footballs from sports clippings. "What do you think the person who made this likes?"

"Sports!" a boy calls.

"Coke!"

"Football!"

"The Titans!"

When the kids have stopped yelling their thoughts, I muse, "They might be very patriotic." I turn the bottle from side to side so everyone can see it. "Coke and football are totally American, right?"

"Right!" a bunch of laughing kids yell.

I hold up the music box I made and lift the lid. The campers go silent. It took me a while to repair the speakers, but now it plays "Moonlight Sonata" and the little ballerina slowly spins in wobbly circles. I covered the wood in pictures of white flowers cut from various newspapers and magazines.

When the music stops, I say, "What do you think the owner of this music box likes?"

"Gardens," Claire says.

"The outdoors?" replies a boy.

"Music!"

"Art!"

"Life," says Sophie. "Being alive."

I give her a small smile. "Moonlight Sonata" is one of Emily's favorite pieces. And the ballerina reminds me of being little. Some white flowers symbolize innocence, but white lilies mean death. To me, the music box is a symbol of the day I went against my beliefs and helped a friend, going against God.

"Is it about beauty?" Claire asks. "The person who made the box loves beautiful things?"

"That's what's great about decoupage," I say. "You can make something that says something on the outside, but maybe only you understand what it really means inside. To you, you know?"

I look up from the music box I decorated to find Parker standing in the doorway.

I set the box down and clap my hands a few times. "Okay, everybody, start looking for an object that most defines you!"

The kids scramble away from the picnic tables to dig through my boxes and crates of junk I hauled here in my trunk.

With a smile on her face, Parker navigates past the kids, seeing what they pick out. Holding my nose again, so I don't cry, I watch her make her way across the pavilion.

"What are you doing here?" I ask.

"I'm on my break." She picks up the music box I made using decoupage. "This is incredible," she says, turning it over in her hands.

"I can get you started on making something," I tell her, slipping my paint brush behind my ear. I lead her over to my milk crates full of junk just begging for a makeover. I love going to yard sales and finding piggy banks and cracked bottles and dusty vases and even scratched records. I love painting new life into them. Part of me wants to tell her this, but it also feels too personal.

This week had started out great, and now I'm back to where I was. Can I trust anybody here? Yes, this is a job, and yes, it's important, but did Matt have to sell me down the river?

I shut my eyes for a sec, praying to God, and then focus on Parker, remembering how she called me judgmental and nasty on Friday night. Then I remember how I thought about college and how I need to figure out my life so I don't stay lonely. But if I open myself up to new people, like I have with Matt, and then they go and betray me, is it worth knowing people at all?

Will told me that everyone left Parker, and now she's standing right here in front of me.

"Pick something out," I tell Parker, and she sorts through the junk until she finds a tiny wooden box.

"I could put earrings in here," she says.

"Sure." I hand her a pair of scissors and sit her down near the toppling stack of magazines with the kids. "Cut out anything that you think looks cool and then we'll decoupage them to the box."

"Decoupage?"

"It's like a clear glue."

Parker licks her lower lip as she clips pictures: roses, dogs, kittens, lips, a softball glove. She cuts out words: him, me, run, fly, you, touch, kiss.

When she's done I show her how to layer the words and pictures on top of each other, and then use patches of cloth and velvet to give the box some texture. I test out *kiss* next to *him* and *me. Kiss him* seems more interesting.

"I had no idea you were so artistic," she says, watching me arrange her words.

I use my fancy scissors that cut shapes to make a red felt heart. "Thanks." I still haven't gotten over what she said on Friday. But I'm going to try. "I'm sorry I upset you the other night," I say quietly. "Um, what I wanted to say came out wrong. I worry about people."

"You worried that we'd all have sex and get pregnant?"

I touch my throat. "One thing generally leads to another."

She cocks her head, thinking. "Yeah, sometimes…"

"I'm not sorry I said what I said, but I could've explained what I meant better. And I'm sorry I wasn't there for you before, you know, um, when your mom left."

Parker's eyes meet mine. She plays with a long strand of her messy hair.

That's when Megan appears in the art pavilion and lightly toots her whistle. "What are you doing, Kate?"

"Showing Parker how to do decoupage." I wipe my hands on a dishtowel.

"Shouldn't you be working with the campers, not another counselor?"

"I'm available if anyone needs help—"

"Shouldn't you be working with the campers?" she repeats, making my face flush. A few campers notice me getting reprimanded and look from me to Megan and back to me again. Nothing like your boss embarrassing you in front of everybody, eh?

"Yes," I say quietly, and move to observe Claire and Sophie decorating vases, but I feel like I'm in their way. That's the thing about art. You can't force it. You can't tell someone else how to do it. You can let them watch you, you can show them examples— like I just did for Parker—but you can't do it for them, or it's not their art.

Art can't be shared in that way.

I spend the rest of the art session moving around and watching the campers, feeling like a nagging cough that won't go away.

Parker finishes her little jewelry box, and looking pleased, she sets it to dry on the picnic table in the sun.

"Thanks for helping me," she says.

I nod slowly and start collecting paint brushes so I can wash them in the rusty sink.

"I didn't mean to get you in trouble," she adds.

I lift a hand. "It's okay. I should've been working with the campers."

Parker scrunches her eyebrows. "Megan's not very understanding sometimes if you ask me."

I don't respond.

"It's like, everything has to go exactly her way. She's like a crazy OCD perfectionist or something."

"Isn't that redundant?" I ask.

"In her case it fits," Parker says with a laugh. "She lectured Will 'cause she didn't like the consistency of the homemade ice cream the other night. And she yelled at me after I refused to participate in the Critter Crawl."

It makes me glad she's not specifically targeting me.

Parker goes on, "Everything has to be perfect or Megan loses it. Carlie's right. Megan is doing everything she can to make sure she gets that job. Either that or she wants to impress Eric baaaaad." She makes a kissy face and kissy noises.

I start to smile along but then I wonder if I would be just as bad as Megan if I was in her position. Would I go out of my way to make sure that everyone does their job exactly right and follows all rules no matter what?

• • •

Following Parker's lead, I decide to take an afternoon break while most of the campers are doing field events with Brad and Andrea.

I hope someone knocks Andrea down during the three-legged race or hits her in the head with a whiffle ball or something. I clench my eyes shut, mad at myself for being so mean.

I carry my sketchbook up and down the trails, wishing I could calm down enough to draw, but it's not working.

Breathing in and out, I storm up the path into the clearing where the basketball court is and find Matt squatting on the asphalt beside a pile of wood planks.

"Kate," he calls out, waving a drill.

I ignore him and decide to go back to Cardinal for my break. There, at least, I can sit beside the box fan and cool down a bit. I secure my sketchpad under my arm and stride off.

"Kate!" I hear him yelling.

Ignore, ignore, ignore, like the times Paul Markwald would taunt me at school, calling me the Jesus Freakazoid. You'd think the one place I'd fit in is a Christian camp. It's like, the older people get, the more they change.

I feel a tug at my elbow and stop walking. Matt turns me to face him.

"Want to help with my Bonzo Ball court?"

"Bonzo what?"

"A game I invented." He points over his shoulder with his drill. "Wanna check it out?"

I gaze at the planks of wood. I catch his eye for a sec, then shake my head. "No, thanks."

His forehead crinkles. "You okay?"

My eyes start to burn again. "This job is harder than I thought it would be."

He nods quickly. "It is, but you're getting the hang of it pretty fast. You're smart."

Is he lying? I narrow my eyes at him.

"What happened?" he asks quietly, sliding a hand onto my shoulder. It feels warm.

"Megan got upset with me for taking too long to feed the kids last night. 'Cause I had problems starting my fire…" His face doesn't change from concerned to guilty, like I expected it to. He just looks concerned. "Why did you tell Andrea about it?" I whisper.

He lifts a shoulder. "Because I was impressed."

"What?" I ask, surprised.

"You impressed me last night. You got your fire started and made dinner for twenty people. There's a reason why new hires are paired up with the most experienced counselors, you know. This is hard work. And Brad's been camping for forever."

"So you told Andrea about it?"

The corner of his mouth lifts into a mischievous smile. "I might've been bragging about my Crisco Cult. You proved it works!" I playfully smack his forearm, and he keeps on smiling. Then it fades. "Did something happen with Andrea?"

"She turned me in to Megan for not doing a good job at dinner."

He shuts his eyes and runs a hand through his hair. "I'm sorry. That's not what I intended to happen…"

I touch my lips. What if I hadn't asked Matt about what happened? What if I had just assumed the worst about him?

"Hey," Matt says softly. He reaches out a hand, as if he's going to touch my jaw, but then stops. He quickly drops his hand, and I see his Adam's apple shift as he swallows. "You all right?"

"What's up with this Bonzo Ball game you're inventing?" I ask, changing the subject.

He gently slaps his drill against his palm. "I thought you weren't interested."

"Need some help?"

The biggest grin appears on his face. "C'mon."

It takes us about five more minutes to finish building the Bonzo Ball court, which turns out to be a wooden pen of sorts. The pen has eight sides and comes up to the tops of my shins. The pen is about fifteen feet in diameter. Standing inside it makes me feel kind of cramped.

"So what I'm thinking is," Matt says, picking up a rubber ball and tossing it in the air, "is that we play dodgeball inside this wooden enclosure, but you only go after people's feet. Like, you hit the ball at their legs, and they can slap it away and try to hit someone else. If you get hit in the legs, you're out, just like in regular dodgeball."

I step inside the pen. "Okay, let's try it."

Matt drops the ball to the ground and squats like a football player right before the snap. Using his hand, he slams the ball toward my legs and I jump out of the way. The ball bangs against the wooden pen and ricochets toward the right.

"This game of yours involves a lot of geometry," I say with a laugh.

"Right?" He laughs too, and moves to slap the ball toward me again. This time I block it with my palms and nudge it away from me a bit, then bomb it at him.

He leaps out of the way and the ball rolls to the other side of the Bonzo Ball court. "That one had some heat on it!" Matt says.

We keep playing for a few more minutes until Brad appears with a group of campers. Field games just ended, apparently.

"Taj!" Matt says, sounding like a little boy. "You gotta try out my new game. Y'all, get in the ring."

Matt and I demonstrate for the boys and girls, and the game gets a whole lot more cramped but a whole lot more fun as we bat the ball around the pin. Kid after kid is disqualified until it's down to just Matt and me again. I squat down low, moving from side to side, jumping to avoid the ball.

The boys are screaming, "Get her out, King!"

Then the girls start calling me the Queen. "Queen of the Ring!"

Before Matt slaps the ball toward me, he looks up and finds my eyes, grinning like a madman.

I'm grinning too.

making music

On Wednesday evening, the activities are night swim and s'mores.

Matt is up in his lifeguard stand, and I keep sneaking glances at him. I'm not the only one—Andrea's doing that too. It's quickly turning into a one-way staring contest. Luckily Matt doesn't seem to notice either of us.

To distract myself, I grab a Nerf football and throw it to Brad, yelling, "Catch!"

We start tossing the football back and forth.

"What church do you go to again?" I ask Brad.

"Summitville. You?"

"Forrest Sanctuary."

He chews on his lip before speaking. "You guys get to go on all the mission trips, right? Like to Mexico and the Caribbean?"

"Yeah, every year."

"Our church doesn't have money to finance stuff like that."

I ask, "What kinds of stuff do you do in youth group, then?"

He throws the ball to me. "We have a pool table and some old arcade games. I used to go there every day after school. We just hang out."

I love church, but even I don't go every day.

I toss the ball back to him. "Are the people there nice?" I ask, thinking of Parker and how she thinks everyone at our church turned on her.

He smiles as he catches the football. "Yeah. Been going there since I was little. That's how I got this job—Megan goes to my church and helped move my application along. My mom's the one who got me hooked on God and church." His expression suddenly changes, but I don't get a chance to ask if he's okay because Megan screeches her whistle at me.

"Kate, Brad, no talking."

I forgot.

Megan has this new ridiculous rule that counselors aren't allowed to talk to each other while campers are in the pool. It makes sense that she'd want us to keep an eye on them, but (1) we have a lifeguard; (2) this rule doesn't apply when campers are canoeing or kayaking, even though the last time I checked, lakes, creeks, and pools all have water; and (3) the only reason she made this rule is so kids won't go home and tell their parents that us counselors spend time socializing.

It's like a gestapo up in here.

But it is pretty cool that Megan got Brad this job. I wish she'd show off more of her good side here, but I guess she can't let her guard down.

I wade off through the water to grab a seat on the pool steps with Claire and Sophie.

Claire asks, "Are Parker and Will dating?"

Parker and Will aren't allowed to talk to each other during pool time, so they are settling for staring across the shallow end and waving at each other.

"Yep," I reply.

"Aww," Claire says quietly. Then she and Sophie whisper to each other.

"Do you have a boyfriend?" Sophie asks me.

"Nope."

"How old are you?" Claire says.

"Eighteen."

"And you don't have a boyfriend?" Sophie asks.

I groan quietly under my breath. "I don't."

"But you're eighteen!" Sophie says.

"That doesn't necessarily mean I have a boyfriend."

Sophie and Claire whisper some more.

"Do you like anybody?" Sophie asks.

I splash water on my arms and neck, not allowing myself to gaze over at the lifeguard stand where Matt is holding a flotation device that resembles a giant hot dog. "Not right now."

Sophie and Claire roll their eyes at each other.

During the last three minutes of night swim, Megan allows the counselors to jump in the pool together while the campers dry off and put their sneakers back on.

Matt does a cannonball off the lifeguard stand, making a huge splash, making all the campers cheer and squeal. I stand on the edge of the pool, watching for him to emerge from underwater. I always worry people are going to crack their heads open on the concrete bottom. When he doesn't come up in the deep end, I flex my fingers, feeling panicky. Should I dive in after him?

That's when his head pops up right beside my feet.

"Ahh!" I scream, hopping.

He grabs the side of the pool and stares up at me, beaming. The campers are cracking up.

"Good one, King!" Taj yells.

"You scared me!" I say.

Matt shakes the water out of his dirty blond hair, which looks black under the night sky. The pool lights illuminate his glistening blue eyes. He lowers his face to focus on my ankle.

"I like this," he says, gently touching my ankle bracelet. Blue beads are threaded through the hemp.

"Thanks, I made it."

He glances up at me, wipes water off his face and focuses on the bracelet again. "Make me one?"

I touch my cheek, trying to hold back my grin. "Sure."

His fingers lightly graze my ankle, tickling my skin. I imagine him tracing my leg, dragging his fingers up and down. I breathe deeply, as shivers race along my spine.

"What color beads do you want?" I add, my voice shaking.

"Surprise me," he says, then yanks me into the pool. I crash into the water and fight my way to the surface, gasping for breath. Come up for air and hear the squeals and laughter from the kids.

"I can't believe you," I say, splashing water at Matt. I chase him over to the shallow end, much to the delight of the little girls. They laugh and yell, "Get him, Queen Kate!"

"Matt and Kate!" I hear Sophie squeal to Claire.

"Kate." Megan blows her whistle. "Counselor swim is over. Let's go. Get your campers ready."

I stop chasing Matt and stand up to my full height. Claire and Sophie look from me to Megan and back to me again. I squeeze the water out of my ponytail, embarrassed that she called me out like that in front of everybody. How will any of the campers respect me if my boss doesn't? I get that I don't know much about the outdoors or camping, but really?

Does she really think being hard on us will help her get that big education job?

Megan blows her whistle again.

"The Queen? Seriously?" I hear Andrea saying to Carlie.

I turn to walk up the steps and Matt comes toward me, scanning my bathing suit. No boy has ever looked at me this way. His eyes pause briefly at my stomach and chest. If I had one word to describe it?

Sinful.

But I don't want him to stop. I want him to drink me in as long as he wants.

"I didn't hurt you, did I?" he asks, stopping next to me. He lightly touches my elbow. "Your knee?" he asks again. "Did I hurt you?"

My elbow tingles. "I'm fine."

"Good. Can I stop by your cookout pit later? By your cabin? I'll play that song I owe you."

I scoop my towel off the deck and cover my grin with it, not looking at his face.

"Is it okay for you to leave your cabin when the kids are asleep?" I whisper.

He smiles. "I'll still be able to hear them. It's only two cabins away. Besides, Andrea and Carlie go smoke by the lake every single night. And don't even get me started on what Carlie and Ian do behind the cafeteria sometimes."

"Oh."

"So how about it?" he asks quietly.

"Midnight?" I dry my hair with a towel, trying to keep my voice steady.

"Perfect," he says. He smiles, then goes into the pool maintenance closet.

I walk back to our group and Brad shakes his head at me and

grins. "King Matt and Queen Kate, eh? Can't say I'm surprised you're already married—"

I swat at him with my towel, and he hops away, laughing.

Megan's giving me a look, but I don't care.

Matt wants to share music with me.

"Can you keep an eye on my cabin tonight?" I whisper to Brad. "At about midnight?"

He smirks. "You meeting up with Matt?"

I suck in a deep breath. My hands feel sweaty. "Yeah."

"You guys are together now?" He throws his towel over his shoulder and we start leading our campers back toward the Cardinal cabins, where we'll make s'mores.

"No," I whisper back. Sophie is right on my heels, trying to listen in.

"I think he likes you," Brad goes on.

I shake my head quickly. "Impossible. Andrea likes him."

Brad glances over at me and smirks again. "If he wanted that, he could've had her a thousand times by now."

"Maybe..."

"Trust me," Brad says quietly. "You've got all the power here."

I burst out laughing. I haven't felt powerful since soccer season.

"So you like him?" he asks, smiling.

After a few moments, I nod.

"Good for you." He smacks my shoulder with his towel.

It's almost like he's becoming a guy friend.

• • •

The night is cool, the girls are asleep, and all I can hear are the whirring box fan and chirping crickets.

I watch the clock tick down. 11:00 p.m. 11:21 p.m. 11:36 p.m. It's nearly midnight, and midnight means Matt.

I'm wearing short plaid pajama shorts and a fitted white T-shirt, something more revealing than I'd normally wear, because I want to show Matt that I can be cute like Andrea. I can act like a girl who wants a boyfriend. I have no idea what he does outside of camp, whether he sleeps around or smokes weed or drinks or what, but here he's sweet and funny and loves music and makes all the kids laugh.

And I want to know that Matt. I pray that Matt is the real Matt.

At 11:58 p.m. I step out of my cabin and tiptoe down the path to my picnic area, where he's already got a small fire crackling. He's sitting on top of the picnic table, barefoot (of course), strumming away at his guitar. With my heart pounding like mad, I take a seat next to him and listen to the soft crooning of the guitar.

He smiles and focuses on his fingers moving swiftly on the strings. He plays the tune over and over again, and I hum along. He softly works lyrics:

I know you can see, out of those pale green eyes.

He stops. Tunes his guitar. Tries out a few more notes. Sings more words.

But maybe you've seen too much, 'cause you're hiding behind that disguise. I shouldn't talk, 'cause I'm hiding too. So how can we meet? How can I find you? Will I see you on any other day but Christmas?

"That was insanely pretty," I say when he finishes, hoping the green eyes in the song are the same shade of green as mine. He scoots closer to me. Our hips touch. If not for the chirping crickets, I bet I could hear our hearts. I stretch my legs out and lean back on my hands. Our silence hangs on the warm air, but it's comfortable with him in the quiet.

"I'd better get to sleep," he says with a yawn.

"Me too."

He climbs off the picnic table and holds out a hand to help me up. His fingers are warm and I find myself wanting to run a thumb over his knuckles. But I let go.

Moonlight guiding us, Matt walks me back along the dirt path to my cabin. Once I'm safely back on my porch, he says, "That was fun. See you tomorrow."

He smiles, waves, and walks away with his guitar slung over his back. I don't know what I was expecting. A hug? A kiss on the cheek? Something?

Was it nothing?

But if it was nothing, why won't my heart stop racing?

I climb into bed, cuddle up under the covers, and imagine his fingers touching my ankle. My body tingles again, like it did at the pool. Heat rushes between my legs. My breathing gallops away from me. I want to touch myself. I roll over and clutch my pillow, praying for relief but also not wanting the feeling to go away.

• • •

My camper Claire and I are DJing the Thursday Night Dance. Claire's best friend, Sophie, has already danced with a couple of guys from our group.

It's less than a day until I get to go home for the weekend. On Sunday, I'm going to take Emily half of my paycheck, to see if she needs it. Unless I lose my courage. Thinking of seeing her makes me feel cold all over.

Claire picks out songs on iTunes, clicking away on my computer. I never really went to school dances in middle school and high school because Brother John railed against secular music all the time. I didn't even go to senior prom.

"Claire, are you about to start your first year of middle school?" I ask.

"Yep," she says. The computer screen casts a blue glow on her face.

"Will you go to dances this year?"

She shrugs, looking uncomfortable. "Maybe I'll go if they let me DJ."

I missed out on a lot because I was scared other kids would be drinking or doing drugs or having sex, and I didn't want to be around that.

And because no boys ever invited me.

"No one would ask me to dance," Claire mumbles, echoing my thoughts. She clicks around on iTunes.

I sip my lemonade. "That's not true. You're really kind and pretty."

"You can say that again," Matt says, striding up to our table. He says to Claire, "You're gorgeous."

She giggles and plays with her earring.

Matt has a mortified-looking boy in tow. He nudges him. "So, ladies, Jackson and I were wondering if you'd like to double date."

"Double date?" I ask with a laugh.

"Right," Matt says, looking at me. "Jackson wants to dance with Kate and I want to dance with Claire."

Claire's mouth falls open.

"But we're DJing," I say, gesturing at the computer.

Matt looks around the streamer covered pavilion. "Quincy! Get over here." A tiny boy no older than nine comes sprinting over to Matt. "You know how to work iTunes?"

Quincy's head bobs up and down quickly.

"Great, you're DJing for a couple songs while Jackson and I take these lovely ladies on a date." He stretches out an elbow to Claire, who takes his arm. I raise my eyebrows, smiling, and follow them out onto the dance floor with Jackson.

Jackson sets his shaking hands on my waist and avoids my eyes. Sweat forms on his forehead and he rocks back and forth. I'm slow dancing with a penguin.

I've gotta start living.

I look over at Matt, who's twirling a laughing Claire. Jackson keeps glancing at her. Almost as much as Megan keeps glancing at Eric, who is sitting on a picnic table, whittling yet another stick. Pretty soon this entire forest is gonna be out of sticks if he doesn't stop whittling.

"Do you think Claire's pretty?" I ask Jackson.

"Matt told me that if I dance with you first, he'll get her to dance with me."

I'm laughing now. Matt smiles at me and I return the grin. "Do you want to dance?" I mouth at him.

Matt raises his eyebrows and steers Claire toward us. He asks, "Hey, Claire, do you mind dancing with Jackson so I can dance with Kate?" Matt whispers to her.

"Uhhh…" she says, glancing at Jackson.

"For me?" Matt asks. "I really want to dance with Kate."

"Yeah, no problem," Claire says, rolling her shoulders.

I wrap my arms around Matt's neck and he pulls me in close. Over his shoulder, Megan gives us a disapproving glare, and Andrea looks like she wants to stab me, but whatever.

He's the perfect height for me. Only a few inches taller. His body fits snuggly against my curves. This is the first time I've experienced his cologne. It's woodsy. He smells like walking in a forest.

"Your dress is pretty," he whispers in my ear.

"You dance well."

"You feel good."

He thinks I feel good?!

"You do too," I mumble, nearly choking on the words.

"I love your hair," he says, clutching a clump of it.

"I love your invisible shoes." We look down at his bare feet, and laughing, we look up at each other. He shakes the dirty blond hair out of his eyes and holds my gaze, pulling me closer. My heart pounds against his chest.

I can barely think. All I can concentrate on are his skin and warmth and how I want to press my mouth to his. Like seven years ago. I want him to pull me behind the pavilion again.

Megan appears behind Matt and clears her throat. "I need you two to chaperone the dance now, got it?"

"It's just one dance," Matt says, letting me go. When he's out of my arms, I feel like I've lost a limb.

"This is a job," she says under her breath, throwing me a dirty look. "You aren't paid to socialize with each other."

So Andrea and Carlie are allowed to go smoke cigarettes by the lake every night, but I can't share one dance with Matt?

"It's fine," I tell Matt. "I'm sorry," I tell Megan, then head over to DJ again. I change the music to rap and all the kids start jumping around in a mosh pit.

Matt goes back to pouring punch. He talks to Andrea, Ian, and Carlie, laughing with them, but Megan doesn't seem to mind. It's okay for *them* to socialize on the clock. If Megan pisses Carlie off, Carlie could put in a bad word with her mom, ensuring Megan doesn't get the job at the regional conference.

Maybe it's a good thing they're trying to keep me away from Matt. It's not like I've had the best judgment in the past. What if I end up sinning again? I don't think I'm the kind of girl who'd ever end up pregnant, but like I told Parker, one thing leads to another.

Last night when I thought of Matt, my skin flushed. The thought of his woodsy cologne makes my stomach leap into my throat. Being around him makes my body go hot everywhere.

That dance with Matt just might have been the best moment of my life.

• • •

On Friday morning, before the campers leave for home, we all go to Woodsong Chapel for morning devotion. Megan tells the campers we have twenty minutes to sit and think about God and pray or do whatever we want, so long as we're silent.

I decide not to go to the altar, but to bury my face between my knees and stare at the ants marching through the dirt between my flip-flops. To God, we're all ants.

I stare up at the sunlight filtering through the trees and wonder how Emily could question whether God exists. This place is perfect. How could any of it be possible without a God?

He speaks to people here.

I examine my hand. It's perfect. Five fingers that allow me to touch, grasp, feel, move, hold, rub, test. How could something so perfect have come into being without God making it so?

None of the campers have approached the altar—no one wants to be first, but then I see Matt stand and make his way past the log benches. He tips onto his knees and his cross necklace swings like a pendulum as he bows his head. I really want to know what he prays about. Who does he pray for?

After morning devotion, we walk the campers back to the welcome pavilion, where we'll see them off. Everyone is exchanging email addresses and signing T-shirts and hugging good-bye.

I wrap my arms around Claire. "Go to some dances for me this year, okay?"

"I will," she whispers. "Jackson asked for my email address!"

"Nice!" I say.

When I hug Sophie good-bye, I tell her how much her decoupage vase impressed me. "Stick with art, okay?"

She smiles. "I will."

Then I spot Matt on one knee, speaking quietly with Quincy, the boy who played DJ last night. Matt takes off his wood chip nametag and hands it to him. The little boy puts it around his neck, smiling. I quietly step toward them and see that a phone number is written on the other side. I have no idea what they talked about this week, what sort of bond they formed, but I want to bottle the look on Matt's face.

By noon, all of the campers have left to go home and I'm standing here, looking at the empty green field. Thinking about how some parts of this week weren't that great, but a lot of it rocked. I smile, reliving the dance with Matt, remembering the cheeseburgers I made all by myself, thinking about how Claire grew more confident this week.

I ran outside again. On actual grass!

All in only a week.

Megan toots her whistle. "Everybody gather around me… You need to be back here by six p.m. on Sunday evening, to prepare for Monday. Kate and Parker, if you could please be here by five p.m., Eric will give you some pointers on starting fires and first aid."

Parker and I catch each other's eyes, and we nod at Megan.

"Great first week, guys," Megan says with a smile, and everyone cheers.

Everyone goes to pack up their cabins and clean. By the time I get my suitcase back to my car beside the tree line, to get ready for my forty-five-minute drive home, nearly everyone else is gone. Andrea's Camaro and Matt's Jeep are still here, and so is Brad's little blue Datsun, but I don't see him anywhere.

Andrea and Matt are talking quietly beside his Jeep, so I avoid their faces and pop my trunk.

"Kate," Matt calls out to me, even though he's still standing with her.

She gives me the Death Stare to end all Death Stares.

"Can you hold up a sec?" he asks me. I nod, and he turns his attention back to Andrea. I lift my suitcase into the trunk of my car, shut it, and then stand here, jingling my keys. I can't hear what they're saying.

A minute later, she climbs in her Camaro and shuts the door. The car bolts up the dusty road out of camp. Matt stares after her for a few heartbeats before walking my way.

What was Andrea talking about last week, when she said to Carlie, "You think he'd be over it by now"?

Matt stops right in front of me, taking in my eyes, ruffling his hair. "See you Sunday."

I twist the purity ring Mom gave me around my finger. "Looking forward to it."

"Yeah? Me too. You can make my breakfast on Monday."

"I'll try," I say, laughing.

He glances around, I guess to make sure we're alone, and then pulls me into a bear hug. His touch makes my knees buckle. His breath is warm on my ear as he whispers, "What's your last name again?"

He doesn't know my last name?! And we've been dancing and splashing in the pool and sitting in the darkness together? He was my first dance, my first kiss. Him not knowing my last name makes me feel embarrassed and nervous and excited all at once.

"It's Kelly."

"Kate Kelly?" His blue eyes look happy as his hands settle around my waist. "That's pretty."

"See you on Sunday."

"Yep," he says. He lets me go, then jogs over to the Jeep with no doors and hops in and buckles his seat belt. Matt looks back over his shoulder at me and grins and waves.

"You need doors!" I call out. "That Jeep is a death trap."

"It's an adventure!"

The real adventure is waiting for Monday, when I'll see him again.

• • •

I let out a loud groan when I reach my room and collapse onto the bed. I power up my laptop and shut my eyes, trying to relax. I never knew how important air-conditioning and Diet Coke were until now. *Thank you, God, for AC and Diet Coke.*

I check my email. Lots of junk. Two emails from Emily that I'm afraid to open. I drum my fingers on my laptop. I will go see her this weekend. I will. I bite down on my thumb, trying to ignore her voice running on repeat in my mind.

"You're being a judgmental bitch," she'd said.

I resolve to go see her on Sunday before heading back to camp—I worry she doesn't have enough money to buy food.

An email from Facebook pops up. Matthew Brown wants to be my friend. My hand shakes as I accept the friend request. I'm scared to check his profile, for fear of finding pictures of him with other girls or something, but I can't help it.

When I see his picture, I grin. It's of him and a woman that must be his mother. She has the same dirty blond hair, blue eyes, and warm smile. He's kissing her cheek and she's laughing.

I can't stop staring at his blue eyes.

Heat rushes through my body as I remember him wading up to me in the pool, his eyes taking in every bit of me by moonlight.

Another Facebook email pops up. "You have a message from Matthew Brown."

Can I get your number?

I gasp, shove my laptop off my thighs, and rush to make sure my door's locked. Should I write back now? Or wait a little while so he doesn't think I'm a desperate loser? I peer around my room. Wait, I am a loser.

Framed sheet music hangs on the wall. Mom put it up after I pulled the pictures of me and Emily down. Books I read in middle school still line my shelves, and my bedding is pink and yellow with ruffles. I need to buy new, adultish bedding immediately. Part of me wants to call Parker, to ask for advice. What does her room look like? I doubt she has a stuffed cow resting on her pillow.

I walk to my mirror. How could a guy like Matt Brown

possibly want my number? Why would a boy like Matt visit my cabin at night?

Is God testing me? Seeing if I'll hang out with Matt, a guy who's in a frat, a guy who has done questionable things with a banana and maybe has fooled around with Andrea?

But Matt's mom is a youth minister. I've seen him praying and he wears that cross around his neck. Brother John said we should only date other Christians. Does Matt worship somewhere in the middle? And is that okay?

I pinch my thigh. Stop thinking so much, I tell myself, and before I can change my mind, I write back to Matt and give him my number.

I pace around the room, slapping my cell phone against my hand. I stop in front of the mirror and turn sideways, to examine my figure. I am thin, but my boobs aren't that big. Why does Matt stare at me the way he does?

The cell rings. I swallow and answer.

"Hey." I thought I'd be scared, but I'm calm like a soft breeze.

"Hi," Matt says. He goes silent for a bit, then says, "You busy tomorrow night?" He sounds nervous.

"Nope."

"Can I take you to dinner?"

"Me?" I exclaim.

"You're funny," he says with a laugh.

I lick my upper lip. "Yeah, I'd love dinner."

"I can pick you up at seven-thirty."

He lives in Bell Buckle, which is forty-five minutes from here.

"You don't have to pick me up. I could meet you—"

"My father would crucify me if I didn't pick you up."

"Wouldn't want that."

"Yeah, because who'd take you dinner then? Bumblebee Brad?"

sketch #351
what happened on april 18

Every time I get my hopes up about Matt, I think about how I made a fool of myself in front of Will Whitfield last spring.

Using my blue coloring pencil, I shade in the outline of my prom dress.

One evening in April, I had rested my chin on my fist and clicked through the website again and again until the pictures of children burned my eyes. Planned Parenthood. I was trying to figure out options that Emily might consider instead of abortion.

A knock sounded on the door and Mom came in, dressed for church in a white blouse, slacks, and loafers. I quickly exited out of the site before she could see it.

"Sweetie." She tsk tsked. "You need to get dressed for youth group."

Mom never let me miss a day of church.

Normally I didn't mind that, but today I just wanted to bury myself under the covers and wallow in my own humiliation and sadness.

She adjusted my curtains and fluffed my pillows, and I sat there staring at the blue prom dress hanging on my closet door. Mom and I had picked it out a couple months earlier because she always thinks the best will happen.

Brother Michael and Brother John often say that forcing relationships is against God's will, that if He wants us to be with someone, He'll make it happen. But He only wants us to date other Christians.

For years, I'd waited and waited for the right boy to come along, watched as Emily and Jacob fell in love and grew up without me. Sitting there in my room, I knew I should've waited for a sign from God, but I had done it anyway.

I had asked Will Whitfield to prom.

It was my last chance for high school, and I couldn't seem to forget about him. He seemed like a good match for me: Christian, a gentleman, friendly.

Emily used to comb her fingers through my hair and tell me, "You're beautiful. You just have to let guys know you're interested in them. Ask Will out already!"

So I approached him in AP Chemistry, and cracking my knuckles, I said, "Can we talk after class?"

"Sure," he said with a brief smile, then went back to checking over his homework. I should've noticed that was the sign I'd been waiting for all that time. If a guy would rather triple-check some chemical equation he balanced, he's just not that into you.

Later, in the hallway, he seemed distracted as Parker walked by, giving him a long look. He scratched the top of his head and followed her with his eyes.

"What's up?" he asked me.

I adjusted my backpack straps. "I was wondering if you'd go to prom with me. If you don't have a date." I studied my loafers for the longest time, waiting. Waiting.

Finally he cleared his throat. "I don't have a date."

My head shot up.

"But…" He gazed up and down the hallway before refocusing on me. "I'm interested in somebody else," he whispered.

His response sucked the air out of my chest. "You're going to prom with her then?"

"No." His face seemed conflicted. He felt bad, but I also saw pity there.

"Oh." I needed to get out of there before I started crying, so I stalked off down the hall without even saying bye. Daddy would be so disappointed that I'd be home on yet another Saturday night.

"Thank you for asking," Will called out.

It's not that I hadn't had a chance to get with guys before. Besides Bruce Wilson, the creepy captain of the math team, I mean. One time Daddy's partner came over for dinner and brought his nephew, Scott. The two of us ended up watching a movie in the basement, laughing and talking about school. Emily asked why we didn't make out or anything, and I told her I just wasn't feeling it. She said, "Nothing wrong with that. If there's no sparks, there's no sparks."

"Such a pretty dress," Mom said that evening before church, smoothing the silk with her fingers.

I make shadows on the paper, to show the folds of the silk. It is a pretty dress. I hope I can wear it one day.

i'm thinking chili's

I have Will Whitfield's phone number because we once did a Culture Fair project together in high school. I take a deep breath and call him.

So much has changed since I asked him to prom.

He answers on the second ring. "What's up?" he asks.

"I love air-conditioning," I groan, making him laugh.

"Me too. I've never sweat so much in my life. So how are you?"

"Good. Listen, could I get Parker's number?"

"She's right here—"

"Wait!" I say. I wasn't prepared to talk to her yet. I don't even know what I'm gonna ask. But Will's already put her on the phone.

"Hey," she says.

"Um, I could use your help."

The next evening, Parker and Will show up at my house. He's carrying a box under each arm and she's got a bunch of outfits draped over her wrists.

I bring them in through our side door because Daddy has

all these animal heads on the wall in the foyer and I don't want to upset Parker. Daddy's hunting dog—our old bloodhound, Fritz—is lounging in the mudroom when we come in. Parker practically has a coronary because she loves the dog so much. She kisses him and pats him all over and Fritz closes his eyes and wallows on the floor, enjoying the attention.

Will loves it too—he can't stop grinning at how much fun Parker is having.

"Fritz can come upstairs with us if he wants," I say.

Parker gets to her feet. "C'mon, Fritz. Let's get to work on making Kate as beautiful as you," she says, following my dog to my room. I shake my head, smiling. Will flops down on my bed.

I sit at my desk and she starts rummaging through her boxes before approaching me.

"Is this your first date?" she asks, aiming tweezers at me.

"Yeah," I whisper. "But what if it's not a date? What if it's just us being friends, getting food together?"

She gives me a look. "It's a date. Trust me."

I stay silent.

"I only had my first real date a couple months ago," she says, throwing Will a smile.

"Really?" I exclaim.

She examines my eyebrows and then begins to pluck. *Ow, ow, ow*, I think, but I stay cool. I don't want to be a loser.

"Will's my first real boyfriend too."

He's grinning and typing on his iPhone. "How long do you think this'll take?"

"If you guys have somewhere to be…" I say.

"We're good for now. But we have plans tonight," Parker replies, sounding nervous.

"Oh?"

"We're going out with Drew Bates…and his boyfriend, Tate," Will says carefully.

"Drew Bates is gay?" I ask loudly. I had no idea.

"Yeah," Parker replies, stiffening at my reaction. "But they're my best friends."

"Oh."

"God made 'em that way. Who are we to question it?" Will asks, acting nonchalant. He taps on his iPhone some more.

"Where are y'all going?" I ask, trying to get rid of the tension.

"To a Nashville Sounds game and dinner," Parker says softly, her eyes avoiding mine as she brushes eye shadow on me. It seems like she and Will are disappointed in me. Again. They've been nothing but nice and supportive. Drew Bates has never once called me a Jesus Freak.

You're being a judgmental bitch rings in my head.

Maybe what Parker said at camp is right. It's none of my business.

"Sounds like fun," I say. "Listen, I'm sorry I was so surprised about Drew and Tate. I hope things are working out for them."

"Thanks for saying that," Parker replies quietly, comparing two colors of blush. "It hasn't been easy for Drew."

Will hugs his girlfriend from behind. He kisses her neck and stares at her with such love.

If things go well with Matt, will he kiss my neck like that?

• • •

"Who's this boy coming over?" Daddy calls out from the screened-in porch.

"Matt Brown," I reply, carrying my sketchbook into the room. I told Mom about the date earlier today but left out that Matt is twenty and in a frat. I can't tell my parents that! Not yet, anyway.

I kiss Daddy's cheek and sit down next to him at the table.

"What do we know about this boy, Irene?" Daddy asks Mom. He winks at me, showing he's just kidding. He eyes the too-short dress I borrowed from Parker.

"Matt's mom is the youth minister at Bell Buckle Chapel," I say, pulling a pencil from behind my ear.

"I've heard wonderful things about that program," Mom says, swiveling a vase of tulips and lilies, trying to catch the petals in the best light.

One thing I've always loved about my parents is that no matter what they're doing, they like being in the same room. So if Daddy is doing paperwork on the patio, Mom is usually sitting there beside him with a pitcher of iced tea and a home deco- rating guide or the Bible. Today she's flipping through a brochure because Daddy is taking her on a cruise to Spain in a few weeks for their twenty-fifth wedding anniversary.

"Don't forget we're doing food baskets tomorrow after services," Mom says to Daddy.

"You know you won't let me forget," he says, smiling at her. I swear, she could ask him to enter a beauty pageant and he'd slap a big grin on his face and go forth and conquer. Mom and Daddy have always been big churchgoers and care about God, just like I do. Mom leads a weekly Bible study for elderly people at church and Daddy plans (and usually wins) the annual Chili Cook-off.

"I saw that the Belmont registration booklet came today," Daddy says, licking his finger before turning a page in his case file.

"Yup," I reply.

"Do you want to go over it together? Pick out some classes?"

Technically I have another three weeks to register. I need that time because I have no idea what I want to study. Law, like my family? Physical therapy? Psychology? Art? When Emily came back from D.C., she told me she had met a girl there who was planning to major in *The Simpsons*.

Maybe if God doesn't give me a sign about forgiving me for helping Emily, he will at least tell me what to do with my life. "Can you let me go through the catalog a few more times first?" I ask.

"It makes sense to be well-prepared. Good girl." Daddy puts

his pen back in his mouth and pores over his paperwork. It amazes me that he really enjoys reading all that mumbo jumbo. It's so…black and white? Where's the color?

I open my sketchbook and draw the tulips that Mom can't seem to get situated. She keeps adjusting the vase and arranging the flowers. How does Daddy handle all that racket Mom makes while he's trying to work?

If you hang out with a person for a long, long time, do you just get used to the differences?

"I ran into Bill Mansfield down at Foothills this morning," he says. Foothills is this diner where he reads the paper every Saturday morning.

Bill Mansfield is Emily's dad.

"Did he mention Emily?" Mom asks.

"Not a word," Daddy says, putting his pen back in his mouth.

Mom turns to me. "Have you talked to her?"

I bow my head and shake it.

"Are you ready to tell us what happened?" Mom asks me. All my parents know is that Emily had a fight with her parents and that she moved out. They know we had a fight too, but I can't say anything without betraying Emily.

Without telling my parents what a horrible person I am.

"No, thank you," I say quietly. The shame erases the excitement I had about my date.

My parents look at each other.

"I'll keep praying for her," Mom says, and I focus on filling the paper in front of me with tulips until the doorbell rings.

Daddy leaps to his feet with a pen in his mouth and a case file in his hand, and rushes to the front door. I groan inwardly. From the hallway, I listen as Matt introduces himself to Daddy, then I shuffle over to find Matt standing there with hands in his pockets. He has on flip-flops! This is the first time I've seen him in shoes since he was thirteen. He's wearing holey jeans and a wrinkled, weathered, white polo. The leather cord holding a silver cross hangs around his neck.

"Hi," he mouths at me.

"Hey," I mouth back, giving him a wave.

He grins and it's so cute, I have to catch my breath.

But I wish he'd dressed up more to meet my parents. And for me, for that matter. Maybe I've got this all wrong? Maybe he only wants to be friends? Why would I be so boastful as to think he'd want something more with a girl like me anyway?

He glances around at our marble foyer and swallows.

Before I can even say hi, Mom is brushing past me to shake Matt's hand.

"Tell your mother I said hello," she says to him.

"Yes, ma'am," Matt replies. His eyes flash to the moose head on the wall (Daddy shot it last year), then he focuses on me again. "Are you ready to go to dinner now? Or did you want to hang out here for a bit?"

"Whatever's best for you," I say, wringing my fingers together. Should I go change out of this dress into something more casual? Should I call Parker to ask? How could I have been so stupid as to think this was a date? He didn't even bring flowers.

"I'm starved," he says with a laugh.

"Y'all have fun," Daddy says, kissing my forehead.

"What time should I have her home, sir?" Matt asks.

"Kate doesn't have a curfew. We trust her."

"We have church in the morning," Mom says.

"Just call if you're gonna be real late," Dad adds.

"Okay," I reply, and give Mom a kiss bye. Matt leads me outside and I laugh. "You put the doors on your Jeep?"

He smiles. "I didn't figure your mom and dad would appreciate it if I put you in danger."

Him putting the doors on his Jeep is kind of like giving me flowers.

"You look really pretty, by the way," he says, jingling his keys.

"You look pretty too," I say, smiling.

He looks over his shoulder toward my porch. I think our house with its eight white Corinthian columns freaks him out. "Where does your dad work?"

"He's an attorney."

"He must be cutthroat, eh?"

"Depends on the situation, I guess."

"That would explain Vincent Moose on the wall in there."

"Vincent Moose?" I smile.

"Yeah, I just named him Vincent."

He opens my door for me and I climb in, trying not to flash my undies at him. Parker's dress is way short. But I loved seeing myself in the mirror, and I wanted Matt to love the way I look too.

Three things stick out in the Jeep: (1) it smells like cinnamon, (2) the ripped seats have been patched up with duct tape, and (3) when I pull down the visor to shield my eyes from the setting sun, I lift the mirror to check my makeup and a picture of Matt and a girl floats into my lap. She's beautiful. Brown curls. Perfectly white straight teeth. He's kissing her cheek.

He jumps into the driver's seat and thrusts his keys into the ignition. I bite my lip, trying not to tear up. He has a girlfriend? He said he was a one-girl kind of guy. He said nothing's going on with Andrea. Is it because he has this other girl?

As he pulls out of my driveway, I slap a hand on the door handle. "Wait."

"What's wrong?" he asks, furrowing his eyebrows.

"Maybe we shouldn't go to dinner," I say, breathing slowly. I touch my forehead.

He slams on the brakes. "Are you sick?"

"No. Yeah. Kinda."

He looks concerned. "Which is it?"

"Who's the girl?" I ask, handing him the picture, suddenly

feeling courageous. "It fell out from behind the mirror in your sun visor."

Matt puts the Jeep in park. He stares at the picture for a sec, then passes it back over.

I cradle the photo in my hands. "You love her."

"I did," he says, turning to face me. He tucks a foot under his other leg. "Honestly? I forgot about the picture. It's been there forever."

"How long is forever?"

He stares through the windshield. "We dated for three years… from when we were fifteen until we were eighteen."

"What's her name?"

"Sarah."

"You broke up?"

Matt drums his fingers on the steering wheel. "You really want to hear all this? Before our first date even starts?"

"This is a date?"

His mouth edges into a smile and he gives me a withering look. "No, it's not a date. You're gonna be my wingman when we go out clubbing later."

"What?"

"Of course it's a date." He reaches over and squeezes my hand, but I remove it from his grasp.

"I still don't understand who Sarah is," I say quietly.

He lifts a shoulder. "She was my first girlfriend. My only girlfriend.

After high school, she wanted to see other people for a while so she could make sure I was the one. I figured we'd get married."

"And?"

"She's going to marry my best friend, Tom, instead. Well, my former best friend." Pain creases his face as he plays with his guitar keychain.

We sit in silence. I don't get the feeling he wants my sympathy. I get the feeling he wants to get this explanation out of the way so we can go on our date already. Andrea wondered why he hadn't gotten over this, right? That must've been it. But he asked me out. Maybe he wants to get over Sarah.

I slip the photo back where it was, in its spot under the sun visor. I quickly squeeze Matt's hand.

He gazes over at me for several seconds. "I'm thinking Chili's."

"We're not going to Just Tacos?"

"I guess we could." He puts the car in drive. "I bet Just Tacos has everything that Chili's serves anyway."

• • •

The minute we step into Chili's, I'm worried again.

"Matt!" the hostess squeals, skipping into his arms.

"Haircut, huh?" he says, fluffing the tiny girl's blond bob. She's a real-life Tinkerbell.

I'm on a date with a guy who's fluffing another girl's hair. He's such a flirt, it's really hard to believe he's a one-girl kind of guy. Really hard.

He releases her, then turns to me. "Ellie, this is Kate. Kate, this is Ellie, one of my best friends."

I shake hands with the girl, who seems very surprised to see me. She glances up at Matt in shock.

"Want your table?" Ellie asks him, grabbing two menus.

"Yeah," he says, rubbing his palms together. Matt explains that he comes here all the time as we follow Ellie to a table right next to the kitchen.

"Nice meeting you," she tells me, handing me my menu. She points at Matt. "You. Me. We're talking later. Call me."

Matt shakes his head, laughing, and stares down at his menu. "Fine. Now go away."

She grins and skips off.

"I don't even know why I'm looking at this." He tosses his menu to the other side of the table. "I always get the same thing."

"Oh yeah? I usually get the bacon cheeseburger."

"I like the ranch burger. I think ranch has nicotine in it, you know?"

"Nasty. You smoke?"

He sips his water. "Naw. But there's gotta be something in the ranch that makes me so addicted. It's either that or cocaine."

"You'd better not be doing cocaine."

"You ordering me around?" He lifts an eyebrow, smiling coyly.

"Maybe."

"You can't order me around."

"Have fun bailing yourself out of jail," I say, laughing. He laughs along with me, his blue eyes lit up. I twist my ring around my finger.

"I'm gonna kick you out of my Crisco Cult if you don't behave," he flirts.

"It's our first date and we're already arguing."

He studies my face, smiling. "That's a good sign, I guess."

"It is?" I laugh.

"My parents fight all day every day. This morning they got into it because Dad thinks the toilet paper roll should unravel from the top and Mom thinks it should unravel from the bottom."

"Sounds serious."

"Very serious."

"I think it should unravel from the bottom."

"The top."

We laugh, and he ruffles his dirty blond hair and looks at the little appetizer flipbook sitting on the table. "We're getting the bottomless chips with ranch dressing, right?"

I smile. "You're as bad as my dad. He's got serious blood pressure issues because he overindulges and now you're all eating two helpings of ranch in one dinner."

"Well, there's nothing I can do about that," he says. "Ranch dressing exists. Therefore, I must eat it."

A waiter takes our drink and appetizer order, then a guy carrying a beer struts up to our table. "Brown!" He and Matt shake hands and do a guy hug, slapping each other's backs.

"Who's this?" the guy says, sipping his beer and staring me down.

"This is Kate."

The guy squeezes Matt's shoulder and grins down at him. "Nice, bro."

Matt's face goes red. "Nick, I'll catch up with you later, okay?"

"You want to come to this party later? There's supposed to be a nude Jell-O wrestling contest."

"What?" I exclaim.

"Good-bye, Nick," Matt says with a stern voice.

"Okay," the guy says, heading back toward the bar. Beer sloshes out of his glass onto the floor and he nearly slips on it.

"Sorry," Matt says, scratching his neck. "One of my frat brothers."

"Is Nick a big drinker?" I ask quietly.

"It's Saturday night. Everyone drinks on Saturday night."

"Even you?" I ask. "I'm not really into that." And I'm really not into the idea of nude Jell-O wrestling parties. He takes in my face and I find his blue eyes.

"I've had a beer before, sure," Matt says. "But I like lemonade and hot cocoa too."

"Me too…"

"Listen, I take it it really bothers you I'm in a frat, right?"

I nod slowly. I take my napkin off the table, unfold it, and stretch it across my lap. "I don't know much about any of it. I've never been to a frat house or anything."

He plays with a coaster, thinking. "Last month? My older

sister, Leigh, had a flat tire on the interstate. My parents were on a mission trip and I was crashing for a final. Nick went and changed her tire and made sure she got back home safely. No questions asked."

Last night, when I called Parker to ask for help, she didn't ask any questions either. She showed up and did my makeup and gave me a great outfit.

"It's good to have friends you can count on," I say.

He points at me with a fork. "Our frat also raises money for charity. We do car washes."

"Let me guess. Without your shirts on?"

"Uh…yeah. Obviously."

I laugh. "What charity?"

"The ASPCA. You know, all those commercials on TV? With pictures of sad dogs and cats?"

"Awww," I reply, making Matt laugh. He takes his napkin off the table and opens it in his lap.

"It's weird," I say. "I don't know what to think about frats or other churches. I've never gone to another church besides Forrest Sanctuary and the only thing I know about frats is that they have wild keggers and sometimes people get naked and jump in pools. I saw that on TV."

"Well, those kinds of things do happen occasionally, I guess, but you can't judge all frats and people based on TV. All that really matters is what you think. And I care what you think."

"You know what I'm thinking?" I say.

"What?" He leans across the table toward me.

"Maybe I'll get the ranch burger too."

"Copycat."

We laugh, and that's when another guy stumbles up and slides into the booth next to Matt. He whispers in Matt's ear and gropes his chest.

"Stop," Matt says, slapping the guy's hand away.

"But I want your body," the guy slurs. I can't believe how drunk this guy is. It's only 9:00 p.m. and he's feeling up Matt!

"Dude, can't you see I'm on a date?" Matt says.

The guy pinches Matt's chest. Then he glares over at me. "Come on, man. She's not your type. I'm your loooooooooovvvvvvvvvvver."

A group of guys at the bar are cracking up and pointing at us. I rub my face, hardly believing this is happening. Another boy comes over, sits down, wraps his arm around me, and checks out my cleavage. I shove him away, regretting wearing this dress.

"Can I get you a beer?" he asks.

"She doesn't want a beer," Matt blurts, looking horrified. "Come on, guys. Get lost."

"But I want your body!" the guy whines again and rests his head on Matt's shoulder.

"Ellie!" Matt hollers, and she flits over and forces the two guys back to the bar. For a girl who weighs a hundred pounds, she sure has a lot of control over those two.

The waiter brings our Cokes and chips. I'm so nervous, I suck down a bunch at once and stuff two chips in my mouth.

"What's goin' on, Brown?" Nick yells from the bar. "You gonna lavalier this girl?"

"Quiet, you!" Ellie says to him, and all the guys shut up real fast and focus on the Braves game.

Matt groans. "I shouldn't have brought you here. My stupid friends…"

I eat another chip. "They seem…interesting," I offer, laughing nervously. I slurp more Coke.

"They are, but I'd trust all of them with my life."

"Do any of them go to your church?"

"Not a one of them. They're all in my frat."

"Oh."

"I trust the people at church too, but I have plenty of friends who don't go to church at all." He dips a chip in ranch and eats it. "I swear these things have nicotine in them," he says again, shaking his head.

I grin and pop another chip. "What does lavalier mean?" I ask through a mouthful.

Matt stuffs a chip in his mouth. "It means that you give a girl your letters. Like, your frat letters?"

"And?"

"If you let a girl wear your letters, it means you love her as much or more than your brothers. It's a big deal."

"It must happen a lot, right?"

"No way." Matt laughs. "The last time one of my brothers lavaliered a girl, some guys tied him to a tree, naked. Then they threw eggs at him."

"Wow. That's terrible."

"Yeah, it was over the top."

I gaze over Matt's shoulder at his friends. Half of them are laughing and messing around, but a bunch of them are staring at me. Like they're sizing me up or something. I play with the napkin in my lap. If my car broke down on the side of the road, I wouldn't have that many people to call. My parents. Maybe Will or Parker, but it's not like they'd ask me to hang out afterward. At this point, I doubt I'd call Emily. I guess I'll have to rely on AAA the rest of my life.

"Your friends are staring at me," I tell Matt.

He looks over his shoulder. "They're worried about me, I guess."

"Worried?"

He sips Coke from his straw. "I don't date often. Hardly ever, really."

"But you hook up, right?"

He smirks and shakes his head. "Are you always this up-front?"

"Sorry…"

"Naw, it's okay." He swirls his Coke with the straw. "Hooking up isn't the same thing as a date, you know."

"I wouldn't know," I say, deciding to tell the truth. "This is my first real date."

"And I brought you to Chili's?" he exclaims. He cracks up. "I'm such an asshole. I can't believe I've ruined your dreams of a first date at a real restaurant. I'm not even wearing shoes."

I peek under the table to find he's kicked his flip-flops off.

"It's kinda like I'm on a date with you and your frat."

"I'll do better next time," he replies. A pause. "Tell me about your friends."

Emily's face flashes in my mind. I pull a deep breath. I don't know that I want to talk about her right now, especially when I'm so happy. At that moment, cheers erupt from the bar and Matt swivels around to catch the TV for a sec. One of the Braves hit a homer.

When he turns back to me, I stretch a hand across the table. It's comfortable, intertwining our fingers. It's like it's where they belong. Our eyes meet.

Another of Matt's friends approaches us, and this time, I shake the guy's hand and ask if he wants to join us, which makes Matt smile the brightest smile I've seen in a long time.

• • •

After Chili's, Matt takes me to the Fun Tunnel at the mall, where we battle it out over Skee-Ball. He wins like a hundred tickets and I only get five.

"Wow, you are terrible at this," he teases, and I swat him.

"I played soccer. I wasn't a bowler."

"Clearly." He gestures at my five tickets. I use them to buy Matt a mini Tootsie Roll, which he pops in his mouth, smiling.

He uses his tickets to buy me a temporary tattoo of a fairy and a sparkly plastic mood ring, which he slips onto my pinky finger. It barely fits—my skin swells around the plastic.

We go over to the basketball free throw game where we take shot after shot, laughing and bumping into each other as we shoot. My hip brushes against his, and every so often, he'll stare over at me like it's hard for him to look away from my face.

"Another game?" he asks, slipping two quarters into the slot. Basketballs roll toward us and the game timer starts counting down from two minutes. The timer reminds me of life, and that I've never been on a real date before. I'm eighteen years old. The timer ticks down. Matt shoots while I stand there, not wanting to stay still, wanting to take a shot. The timer's ticking.

I turn to face him. He takes a jump shot. The ball swooshes through the net. He grabs another ball, but before he can shoot I drag a finger down his arm, from his shoulder to his wrist. He drops the ball and twists to face me, his blue eyes finding mine. And before I can second guess myself or lose my nerve, I get up on tiptoes and steal a kiss. A quick peck on the lips.

He grins and sets his hands on my waist, pulling me closer. "That was a nice surprise," he murmurs, then leans back in and kisses me more deeply. His lips are soft, moving gently, exploring. I wrap my arms around his neck and he digs his thumbs into my hips. I taste Tootsie Roll on his tongue.

A buzzer goes off when the game timer hits zero.
But we just got started.

sketch #358
what happened last night

Brother Michael is giving a sermon about caring for the elderly
and Meals on Wheels or something, but I've got an itch. I grab
a little offering envelope and one of those tiny pencils you only
seem to see at church and on golf courses. Mom sniffs when she
sees what I'm doing.

I start sketching Matt's hand.

Under a full moon and a sky full of stars, we sprinted out of
the Fun Tunnel, laughing and holding hands, jumping in circles.
When we reached his Jeep, Matt gently leaned me against the
door and kissed me so fully, the whole world went dark. It was
just me and him and our bodies and a spark that flicked on and
wouldn't go out. His fingers traced from my ear to my chin, from
my chin to my cheek, from my cheek to my lips.

I take care to draw the creases of his hand. I make his nails
rugged but clean.

He dragged his fingers along the back of my neck as he pulled
me forward so his mouth met mine.

I grin as I shade the dip between his forefinger and thumb.

Mom keeps sniffing and Daddy keeps looking at me sideways and smiling, so I carefully fold the drawing and stick it in my Bible.

I put the little pencil back into its holder and try to focus on the sermon.

tell me what you want from me

Part of me is still giddy about my date with Matt and can't wait to see him again in a few hours when counselors return to camp. To be honest, he and I didn't talk much the rest of the night. He drove me home, where we sat in the driveway and kissed and kissed and kissed. His fingers explored every inch of my face and I couldn't stop touching his strong shoulders and dirty blond hair. Mom and Daddy were asleep when I finally dragged myself inside. I stayed awake for hours, thinking of Matt, and overslept and nearly missed Sunday school this morning. I kept thinking, *Matt, Matt, Matt,* and I felt so good inside it felt wrong.

But the other half of me is terrified to see Emily today. We haven't spoken since graduation, when we told each other good luck and walked away without even a hug. And according to Mom, Emily hasn't contacted her parents since they kicked her out of the house.

The only reason I know where she lives is because Mom got

Mr. Munroe, the mailman, to spill the beans about where Emily's mail is being forwarded to, and maybe I'm invading her privacy, but I need to give her part of my paycheck. To make sure she has enough to eat. It's the right thing to do.

Before driving to Nashville, I stop at Sonic to get a cherry limeade, to soothe my nerves, and find Will Whitfield there when I pull into the parking lot. He's lounging at a picnic table, talking to Sam Henry and Drew Bates.

I order my drink, then watch the guys chat until Will looks over. He grins and beckons me. In high school, I never would've gotten out of my car at Sonic to talk to people, but I slowly open my door and make my way to him. Drew narrows his eyes while Sam shakes his Styrofoam cup, rattling the ice around.

"Hey," Will says, standing up. "Want to join us?"

"Thanks, but I'm on my way to Nashville to see Emily Mansfield before going back to camp."

"What happened to her anyway? I haven't seen Jacob around in weeks. Are they okay?"

I clear my throat. "I guess they're both sad about the breakup," I lie.

Will tilts his head. "Oh."

"We had a class together, right?" Sam asks me, chomping on his ice.

"Yeah," I reply. "Art."

He points at me. "That's it." He grins like he's seeing me for the first time, and I don't know what's more embarrassing—that I'm forgettable, or that my artwork is forgettable.

My face flushes and I'm turning to climb back in my car when Will touches my elbow. "How was the date?"

I can't stop my smile. "Fun. Unexpected. Crazy."

Will laughs, nodding. "That sounds like Matt. You gonna see him again?"

"I'll see him tonight at work—"

"I know that. But another date?"

I bite my lips together and sneak a peek at Drew, who's still staring at me. "I hope so, yeah."

"Nice," Will says, patting my shoulder. "You look happy."

Did Will and Parker tell Drew that I was surprised he's gay and now he's pissed? My face goes hot when Drew rolls his eyes at me. Will catches him doing it and leans over to whisper in my ear. "Don't worry about him. He's really protective of Parker because they've been friends forever."

"Oh?"

"Yeah," Will whispers. "And you go to Parker's church, therefore Drew believes you are evil."

I laugh a sad laugh.

"Don't worry about it," Will says, patting my shoulder, but I know I will.

A roller-skating waitress brings me my cherry limeade, so I say good-bye to the guys and get back into my car.

I sip my drink through the straw, wondering if Sam will forget about me again. I want people I can call if my car breaks down on the side of the interstate. Judging by the way Drew treated me, he only seems to associate me with bad stuff. At the stoplight, I close my eyes and lean my forehead against the steering wheel. I don't know where I get off thinking I deserve to be remembered.

In Nashville, I park outside Emily's new apartment. A few pieces of trash litter the parking lot, which has been overrun by cracks and weeds. I climb two flights of metal stairs to reach her door. A rip runs down the screen. She's definitely here—I can hear a violin crooning inside. I ring the doorbell and try to figure out what to do with my hands while waiting. I settle for sticking my thumbs in the pockets of my jean shorts.

I hear locks unlocking and the door whips open to reveal Emily standing there in a white tank and khaki shorts. Her auburn hair is pulled back into a messy ponytail. Darkness rings her eyes. But they brighten a little when she sees me.

"Hey. Want to come in?" She pushes the screen open. I step inside. I had no idea her living room, bedroom, and dining room would all be merged into one. It's so small. I turn in a circle. A piece of cardboard covers a broken window. Bits of linoleum are flaking away from the floor, like sunburned skin. I bite the inside of my cheek when I see a mousetrap.

I spin around to find the butterfly painting I painted for her sixteenth birthday hanging over a sagging couch. She remembered my art. My eyes burn.

She relocks the door, slides the security chain into place, and eyes my shorts. I wore the short ones Mom bought me because I think Matt will like them. Now I wonder if I shouldn't have.

"How did you find me?" she asks.

"Mom found out. From the mailman."

Her mouth forms an O. "What are you doing here?"

I pull my lower lip between my teeth and reach into my back pocket and grab the money. "I wanted to bring you this. You know, in case you needed it." I cough into a fist. "For your rent or groceries or whatever."

Her eyes grow dark. "Why would you think I'd want your money?"

"I thought I could help—" I thrust the money toward her hand. She steps back.

"You haven't answered my calls for a month and now you show up and give me money?"

"I want to help."

"If you want to help, you could call me once in a while. Or maybe pick up when I call you?"

I don't know how to tell her that just seeing her reminds me of what we did. I put the money back in my pocket and stand in front of the butterfly painting.

"You kept it," I say quietly.

She appears beside me and studies the purple butterfly, its wings bursting open to reveal orange, yellow, red, and white. "This painting gave me the courage to play for the Youth Philharmonic."

If I hadn't painted this butterfly for her, would she have still gone to D.C.? Because last summer is when she started changing.

I touch my throat, staring down at the stained linoleum. Mom would have a fit if she knew Emily was living here. She'd insist on redecorating it, that's for sure.

"Do you, um, want to sit down?" Emily asks. "Maybe we can go out for something to eat? I can't afford much, but I get fifty percent off at the diner where I'm working nights."

"I'm not sure," I reply. "I have to be back at camp early."

"How's that going?"

I swallow. "Not too bad. Um…" Now that I'm here, I know how much I miss her. The pain is deeper, rawer than it is when she's not around. I want to tell her that. But I need to know something first.

"Did you ask for forgiveness?"

"Ask who for forgiveness?" Sadness rings in her voice.

"God. You know, for what we did."

"I want to move on already. Can't you forgive me?"

"You care about *my* forgiveness but not God's?"

"I care more about yours."

The tears start to well in my eyes. Is my friend going to Hell? And will I be there with her? I wipe my cheek with the heel of my hand.

"Your shorts are cute," she says.

"That's all you care about? My shorts?" I'm pissed, but part of me wants her to know why I'm wearing the shorts. Matt. How he can make doughnuts over a campfire and how he invented a new kind of dodgeball.

"Do you want something to drink?" she asks, gesturing at her tiny kitchen. "I have water, and, um…" She looks over her shoulder, blushing.

I shake my head.

"Look…" she says. "I'm sorry about what I said that day."

"I don't want to talk about it." I find myself crossing my arms across my stomach and inching away from her.

"I was so angry," she adds. "I can't even explain what I felt like. I mean, my parents…it was like I killed part of them by doing what I did…And I needed you."

"I needed you too. I still feel bad about what I did…Maybe if I hadn't agreed, you wouldn't have gone through with it," I mumble, wiping my nose.

"It was my decision," she says. "Only I should be allowed to regret it."

"Do you?"

Her eyes close. "You really won't forgive me for this, will you?"

"I forgive you, but we need God's forgiveness too. It's not about you—"

"That's just it," she exclaims. "It *is* about me. About me and

Jacob." She covers her face. "I wish you hadn't come here—I was finally starting to calm down and get into a rhythm and now you're back and I feel terrible again and—"

"I'm sorry," I say quickly. "I just need time and to talk and some help and—"

She peeks at me from behind her fingers. "I want my friend back."

"I do too—"

"Kate," she says before laughing bitterly. "You are so far gone I don't think I can get you back."

These are my beliefs, my feelings, what I know to be true, and she thinks I'm too far gone to be helped? "If you were my friend, you'd understand what I'm trying to say," I cry.

"Well, maybe we can't be friends then," she says. "I don't want your money. I don't want your pity." She points at the door and I quickly let myself out. It slams behind me. I dash down the squeaky staircase and slip into my car.

I turn the ignition and, before reversing, I look over my shoulder, out into the world.

• • •

I arrive at camp earlier than expected.

Will I get in trouble with Megan for being here early?

I park my car at the tree line right next to Brad's. It's in the exact same place I left it on Friday. Did he stay here? That's against the rules. Maybe he just parked in the same spot?

I have time before my *super special* campfire lesson with Eric, and I need to de-stress, so I pull on my knee brace, sports bra, running shorts, sneakers, and a T-shirt, and take off down the trails. I haven't tried running anywhere except for the big field yet and I should feel scared that I might trip on a tree root or a rock or something, but I don't. I hurl myself as fast as I can go. The speed keeps the pain away.

I jog for an hour—for four miles, and by the time I slow down and rest my hands on my thighs, my knee is throbbing and I'm panting, but somehow I feel better.

I pass by Matt's Bonzo Ball court and bend over to the spigot to slurp some water. When I look up, I find Andrea stalking toward me.

"I heard," she says with a shaking voice.

I wipe my mouth with my T-shirt. "What?"

"I heard you were at Chili's last night with Matt." She bites her lips together.

"Yeah," I say quietly. I ran for an hour to de-stress and now my heart is speeding right back up.

"You knew I liked him. I don't understand why you'd go out with him, knowing that."

"You didn't even talk to me last week except to yell at me or tell on me to Megan," I mumble. "It's not like we're friends."

"It's not like he'll stay with you. He'll never get over *her*."

Andrea storms off toward Great Oak and I bend down to

the spigot again, slapping water all over my face, trying to make myself look sweaty so no one will suspect I'm crying, that I've been crying all afternoon.

I'm not sure which cabin I'm staying in this week, so I grab a change of clothes from my car and head to the bathhouse over in Birdland. There, I stand under the hot water and try to clear my head. I pray to God, thanking him for my date last night. Deep down, I can't help but think what happened today is what I deserve.

But is Emily right?

If I'm doing what the church and Bible and God tell me to do, then why am I so far gone in her eyes?

It's time for me to meet Eric and Parker for extra training in starting fires (too bad they don't have flame throwers at camp). I get out of the shower and look in the mirror as I dry my red, puffy face.

What am I supposed to believe?

• • •

After the never-ending campfire training with Eric aka *the Best Camper Ever,* I stand waiting by the tree line. When Matt's Jeep pulls up, I see he's taken the doors off again.

He climbs out and I say, "That thing is a death trap."

He grins. "Nice to see you too." He glances around, I guess to make sure we're alone, and presses a kiss on top of my head. "I had fun last night."

"Me too." I want to ask if we're dating now or what, but I'm way nervous. We walk together to Great Oak not holding hands, but his hip bumps against mine. He glances over at me, a small smile on his face. Last night we couldn't keep our hands off each other and now I have no idea what's next.

While waiting on the staff meeting to start, we sit together on the porch swing—prime real estate. We're still not holding hands or anything. Our thighs aren't touching. It's hard to keep my breathing steady. I sneak a glance at Andrea—her eyes and cheeks are red. She's been crying. I'm pretty sure Matt notices because he keeps tapping his bare foot and biting his lip.

After the meeting, I approach Brad and ask him to walk with me. He runs a hand through his short brown hair, glancing over his shoulder. "Yeah, okay."

Matt is watching me; I hold up my pointer finger, telling him I'll be a minute.

"What's up?" Brad asks when we're away from the group.

"Did you stay here over the weekend?" I whisper.

He swallows and places a hand on my forearm. "Please don't say anything. Please."

"Can you tell me what's wrong? Did you do something?"

"Me? No! Of course not." He rubs a hand over his head again. Looks around. "I can't go home, okay? My father and I—"

He pauses.

"Your father...?"

"I just can't go home."

I furrow my eyebrows.

"Kate?" Matt calls.

"Trust me," Brad says, sliding his hands into the pockets of his khaki shorts. His eyes are begging me.

"I won't tell," I say. "But be more careful with your car. Park it in a different spot or something."

"Thanks," he says quietly.

"I'm worried."

"Don't," he says, smiling meekly, and turns toward Treeland.

I head over to Matt. He wraps an arm around me and whispers in my ear. "You okay?"

"Fine," I lie.

"I don't buy that," he replies, leaning his forehead against mine. "What were you talking to Brad about?"

"Just making sure he's okay. He seemed upset tonight."

"Oh. I didn't notice 'cause I was too busy thinking about last night."

I smile, stretching my arms around his waist.

He says, "Want to roast some marshmallows? I'll nick a bag from the cafeteria."

I glance up to find Parker and Will grinning at us while the rest of the counselors are staring. In disbelief? Does wrapping his arm around me in front of people mean we're official?

"I can't believe this," Andrea mutters, loud enough for everybody to hear.

Ian gives her a nasty look before shooting me a look of sympathy. Then mischief breaks out on his face. "Let's hear it for Matt and Kate! Woooo!"

"Oh my Lord," Matt says, shaking his head at Ian, who starts dancing a very inappropriate dance, grinding his hips in our direction.

"Gross," Carlie says, sticking out her tongue. "I've told you so many times that guys should never, ever grind."

"I totally agree," Parker says, disgusted. "Guys' bodies are just not meant to work that way." Will starts moving his hips, which earns him a prompt slap on the chest from Parker.

Matt is cracking up, as Ian keeps right on doing strange things with his pelvis.

"Ugh," Andrea says.

"Ugh, indeed," Brad replies, making Andrea snort with laughter.

"How about we get those marshmallows now?" I say to Matt.

"Please!" He takes my hand, leading me away from the group. I go quiet for a bit because I can't believe how rude Andrea acts sometimes.

"Are you okay?" he asks when we're out of earshot. He rubs his thumb along the back of my hand.

I hold my chin up. "Um, are you friends with Andrea? Or just acquaintances, or what?"

"Friends, I guess." He drags a hand through his messy blond hair. "Why?"

"She's not nice to me, really."

"What did she do?" he mumbles.

I don't want to bring up how she said he'd never get over her. Her meaning Sarah, I guess. It would be terrible dating a guy who doesn't completely want me. Wait. He hasn't even asked me out officially.

"It's fine," I say. "Forget it."

The sun is setting into a gorgeous pink puddle in the sky, as Matt takes me by the shoulders and turns me to face him, his warm breath breezing across my face. He lightly touches my cheek. I get up on tiptoes and wrap my arms around his neck.

"I don't want to forget about it," Matt says. "Did Andrea hurt you?"

"She's mad I went to Chili's with you. She must really be into ranch dressing," I say with a nervous laugh.

"Ranch is serious business."

I play with the hair at the nape of his neck.

"I'll talk to her, okay?" He hesitates before leaning in to kiss my forehead. "It's nothing to do with you. It's between me and Andrea."

I don't like the idea of anything being between him and Andrea. Not even friendship. "Have you, um, ever been with her?"

He shuts his eyes. "She's tried to make out with me before, yeah, but it was nothing." He gently moves fingers up and down my arm. "She was a good friend after Sarah dumped me...I really needed someone to talk to, and she made me laugh and kept me company. We played a lot of Scrabble and did crossword puzzles together...And even though she didn't mean to start feeling this way, she ended up wanting a lot more from me. But I've never felt anything special with her."

I nod, stepping closer, wrapping his T-shirt in my fist. No wonder she was crying. Something inside me breaks a little for her.

"You know what I think?" he whispers in my ear.

"What?"

"It's marshmallow time."

Matt snags marshmallows and Crisco from the cafeteria and gets a fire blazing up at Redwood, the cabin out in the middle of nowhere. Flames burst into the air when he throws a glob of Crisco onto the wood. We jump back, laughing.

It's a gazillion degrees outside but we cuddle together next to the fire, spearing marshmallow after marshmallow with our skewers. He feeds me one and I feed him one, and we both gag. Turns out he likes his golden brown and raw on the inside, while I like mine gooey and burnt to bits.

"I really like you," he whispers, bumping his knee against mine, staring at me. He leans over and gently kisses my lips.

"I like you too."

"You're funny and you can paint a mean watercolor painting of apples in a barrel and you've got a great body."

I accidentally snort and blush, and when I peek over at him,

I begin to understand that he probably won't forget me, that he thinks there's something inside me worth knowing.

"You've been looking in my art closet, eh?" I ask, thinking of my apples in a barrel painting.

"It's like a little art gallery in there."

He picks a piece of gummy marshmallow off my lower lip, and my stomach flips.

A few minutes later, I yawn. He extinguishes the fire, and we go get our bags from our cars. I'm staying in Pinecone cabin this week, in Treeland, so I say good night and start to head that way.

He takes my hand, looking around. "Why don't you come sleep in Dogwood with all of us tonight?"

I shake my head.

"Is it Andrea? Don't worry about her. She'll get over it. Maybe Bumblebee Brad will strike her fancy."

I giggle nervously. "It's not Andrea…"

"Then what is it?" He kisses my knuckles.

"It's not right for guys and girls to share a bed before marriage," I mumble.

Will and Parker walk past, carrying their sleeping bags. Will is moving his hips like Ian did earlier and she is laughing hysterically, trying to sidestep her boyfriend and his grinding.

"They shared a bed last week," Matt says.

"So? We've been on one date."

"A great date." He grins down at me and wraps his arms around my waist. "The best date ever."

"You're just saying that because you beat me at Skee-Ball."

"And basketball."

"You have to rub it in, eh?" I say with a grin.

"It's fine," Matt says, pressing his forehead to mine. "You don't have to sleep in Dogwood."

"Thank you," I reply, sighing a little. But what if he goes to sleep in Dogwood with everybody else? Andrea's in there...

"Want to go running in the morning?"

I nod, even though my knee is sore. Matt grabs my bedding and suitcase and leads me to Pinecone, where we share a long, passionate kiss good night on the porch. I make my bed and unpack my clothes. I read from the Bible and pray for Brad and his father and whatever's going on there, then spend some time sketching and studying my work.

Fifteen minutes later, a knock sounds on the door and I shove my sketchbook under my covers. I look up to see Matt standing outside.

"Can I come in?" he asks.

My heart goes wild. Does he want to make out or something? If I let that start, will he want to spend the night? Will he want to sleep in my bed like Will sleeps in Parker's?

"It'll just take a second," he says, grinning.

"Okay."

Matt walks in, and like last Sunday night, he drags a bed from inside onto the porch. I watch through the screen as he unrolls his sleeping bag and crawls inside.

"Good night, King Crab Kate," he says softly.

"Good night," I say, laughing. I turn out the light and lie down. I focus on the gap between us, wanting to fill the space between. I can't help it.

"Sweet dreams," I say, and face the opposite wall so I won't give in and invite him inside.

I flip my pillow over to the cool side.

• • •

Monday morning, after a run with Matt and after my new group of campers have arrived, I spend my break praying in the Woodsong Chapel. I kneel down in front of a splintered log serving as an altar and bow my head, trying to forget about what happened yesterday with Emily, but it recycles over and over in my mind. Minutes later I hear pine needles and sticks crunching beneath feet. I glance up to find Brad making his way down the path.

"Hey," I say.

He nods back at me and kneels a few feet away. What's he praying for? I say a prayer for him, and then go back to thanking God for my date with Matt and asking God for forgiveness for helping Emily. When I'm finished, I stand carefully, so I don't mangle my knee. Brad stands too and gives me a smile.

"Where you off to?" he asks.

"Art pavilion. I've got a group coming in a few minutes." We hike up the trail together and I reach out to drag my fingers across pine needles dripping from trees.

"So you and Matt, huh?" He grins, slipping his hands in his pockets.

My face blushes and I grin back at him, not saying a word.

"I so called it."

"Are you seeing anyone?" I ask.

He digs his hands further down into his pockets. "Nah…"

I furrow my eyebrows. Brad is cute, sweet, and nice. Granted, I don't feel a strong pull to him like I do with Matt, but I am sure plenty of girls could feel like that toward him.

"I want to get out of here after this summer," he says quietly. "That'd be hard if I had someone."

"What are you trying to get away from? Why did you mention your dad yesterday?"

He runs a hand over his head and focuses on his feet. "It's just me and him. He drinks…he's gotten worse ever since Mom left."

"Your mom left?" I exclaim. "Why?"

"'Cause Dad is a nasty drunk, that's why." His eyes shift to his upper arm, where I saw the bruises last week.

"Where did she go?"

"Not sure, don't care," Brad says quietly. "She left before Christmas. She missed my graduation." His voice is soft.

I can't imagine my parents missing my graduation. They'd buy a bong before that would happen.

"That's why you stayed here last weekend?" I ask.

He shrugs. "I can't afford to live anywhere else but at camp this summer. I need to save my money so I can leave…I want to take my road trip and get a job at a park."

"Does your dad hurt you?"

He touches his bruised bicep. "That's not what scares me," he whispers, staring off into the trees. A bird chirps above us. "I'm scared that"—he pauses to take a breath—"If I stay, I'll end up like him. And my grandfather."

He looks over at me, his eyes begging me not to tell.

"Have you talked to Megan? She got you this job, right? She might understand—"

He quickly shakes his head. "You know how strict she is. And I don't want my church involved. It'll just piss Dad off more."

If I keep this a secret and Megan finds out, Brad would get fired. If she finds out I knew, I'd get fired too, and my church and parents would be disappointed in me for lying. Can something like this stay a secret for five weeks?

I'm tempted to invite him to live with us, but Mom and Daddy would get all nosy and try to fix the situation between Brad and his dad, and it seems like Brad wants to leave.

"Can you do a better job of hiding your car?" I tell Brad.

"I will." He squeezes my shoulder. "Hey, I'm glad about you and Matt. You deserve it. You're a good person."

A good person.

I shut my eyes, smiling a sad smile. Should a good person lie?

I trudge over to the art pavilion and start pulling out paint brushes and paper for my lesson, but I can't stop thinking of Brad and how's he's a good Christian, but he's willing to break a big rule like this. It's a good rule. If Brad got hurt bad on a weekend, nobody would discover him until Sunday night.

I've always heard that saying, "Some rules are meant to be broken," but no one ever says that even if the rule is meant to be broken, usually something bad happens when you break it.

Brad needs more help than just me covering for him.

He needs a real family and friends and love.

But I guess not all of us get that.

Sometimes we get a mess. Like Emily did. And then you have to work past that or drown where you stand.

* * *

Before Tuesday Talent Night, Matt takes my elbow and pulls me behind Great Oak. I tiptoe around the bushes, in case of poison ivy.

"What?" I whisper. "It's almost time to start the show."

"I can't wait."

"Wait for what?"

Sticks snap under my feet as he shoves me up against the wooden wall and presses his mouth to mine. Kissing me hard and fast. My skin prickles. I'm panting. He pulls my hips against his.

"What if Megan hears us?" I ask. Her office is on the other side of this wall.

"Sometimes you just can't wait," he says between kisses. "Like at Just Tacos."

"I'm not a taco," I reply, playfully pushing him.

"Yummy," he says against my lips. I run my fingers underneath the hemp necklace I made for him, caressing his collarbone.

I can hear Ian and two campers practicing Madonna's "Material Girl" for tonight. And apparently he enlisted Will for some additional harmonies.

I gently nudge Matt away. "To be continued?" I whisper.

"Can't wait." He grins and sneaks another kiss. "By the way, will you be my date to the dance on Thursday?"

"Sure," I say with a smile, and kiss him again.

After the girls are in bed that night, I climb the hill to the cafeteria. It's the only place besides Megan's office with a phone. And it's a pay phone, at that. I drop two quarters into it and dial Emily's cell number.

She picks up on the second ring. "Hello?" She sounds confused. Probably has no idea whose this number is.

"Hi. It's me, Kate."

I hear a click. And then a dial tone fills my ear. And then a voice comes on, saying that if I'd like to make another call, I have to deposit more change.

That's when I hear the noises. I hang up the phone and sneak around the side of the building. So Matt was right about Ian and Carlie doing it behind the cafeteria. Ew. I hustle away, cringing.

At midnight I sit on my porch and open my sketchbook to start writing her a letter, trying to explain what I feel. She hung up on me. She kicked me out. Why can't she understand I only want her to pray with me? I wipe a tear away with the heel of my hand.

When I had surgery, Emily sat in the waiting room the entire time. Afterward, she drove home with me and my parents and curled up in my bed with me. She poured my favorite candy, Milk Duds, into my palm. For days she kept my water glass full and read aloud from trashy Hollywood magazines and told me how, at school, Will Whitfield had asked how I was doing. She played P!nk songs as we lay in bed, singing so loud Daddy told us to shush because Fritz kept howling along.

I tear the sheet of paper out of my sketchbook and crumple the letter in my fist.

Why say anything if the person you're talking to doesn't get what you're saying?

Is our friendship over for good?

• • •

"This is inhumane."

Parker has said that, like, eighty gazillion times, but after she didn't show up for the Critter Crawl last week, Megan warned her that if she skipped it again, her pay would be docked.

Therefore, while the rest of us counselors are grappling with the campers, Parker is standing with her arms crossed. Glaring.

"Dude, your girlfriend looks pissed," Ian mutters to Will.

One of my boy campers waves a glass jar containing a gigantic spider.

"That poor animal," Parker says. "He might never see his family again."

Ian is in charge of the Thursday afternoon Critter Crawl, so he takes a stick and draws a big ring in the dirt road. Then he makes a smaller circle inside it. At the same time, Megan walks over to Parker. And even though Megan's talking quietly, I can tell by Parker's expression that she's done something wrong.

Will nudges Ian, pointing at Megan. Ian rolls his eyes and turns his back so the kids can't see, and makes a jerking-off motion with his hand. The guys speak quietly to each other, then start laughing.

"Attention, Critter Crawl participants, attention," Ian yells, sounding like an announcer in a boxing ring. "The first critter to make it out of the ring will win eternal glory!"

The campers roar and jump up and down, hollering.

"You're going down," Matt tells a girl carrying a plastic cup, her hand covering the top so her butterfly won't get free.

She makes a face at Matt. "I beat you so bad last year, King."

Ian says, "Team Sparrow's lizard and Team Dogwood's cockroach, please come forward."

"The cockroach's name is Harry!" a kid says.

"You let your kids capture a cockroach?" Andrea blurts at Eric, who shrugs and keeps on whittling a stick.

Ian goes on, "There's been a last minute change to the Critter Crawl roster. The lizard and Harry have been disqualified."

"What?" yells a boy. "You've got to be kidding me!"

"Noooooo," another boy screams, raising fists in the air.

"On what grounds are they disqualified?" Megan asks, rushing forward to inspect the critters in their glass jars.

I bite down on my thumb, trying not to laugh. These kids are acting like it's Armageddon. I walk over to Parker. She runs a hand through her plaited hair, staring at the ground.

"You all right?" I ask.

"Fine. If I didn't need the money so bad, I'd be so out of here…" she mutters.

"Never fear!" Ian calls out to the hundred campers surrounding the circle. "We have two new contestants!"

"A snake?" a boy asks, causing all the girls to start screaming and running around. Megan looks like she might murder Ian.

"It's even better than a snake," Ian replies. Will and Ian bump fists, and Ian comes running at me. He throws me over his shoulder and runs around in front of the campers. Will does the same thing to Parker.

"It's Critter Kate!" Ian shouts.

I pound on Ian's back, yelling, "Put me down! Maattttt!"

When Ian swings me around, I find Matt cracking up, and even Megan and Eric are laughing.

"I'm so breaking up with you," an upside-down Parker says to Will.

"I feel like I'm on a ride at the fair," I say, woozy. "I might throw up."

"Gah!" Ian says, plopping me down in the center of the ring.

Parker slaps Will when he lets her down, and then she goes and slaps Ian, and then she slaps Matt, I guess for good measure.

Ian claps his hands together. "It's Critter Crawl time. Let's get ready to rumble!"

The sun begins to set as the campers cheer for their critters. I catch my breath, sitting off to the side with Parker, watching Matt root for his team's beetle, feeling a bit of heaven inside me.

After the race is over (Harry the cockroach lost to Team Bluebird's granddaddy longlegs), I walk with Ian to let the critters go free. He has four glass jars in his hands.

"That was nice of you to take the attention off Parker," I tell him, as I release the lizard back into the woods. He scurries away.

Ian squats and places the jars at his feet. "Megan needs to get laid. She's so crotchety."

"Carlie said the same thing," I say.

"Sometimes I think she and I share the same brain," Ian replies with a small grin, which quickly disappears.

"What's wrong?"

"Are you and Matt going out now?" he asks. He opens a glass jar and coaxes the beetle out.

"Not yet," I say quietly.

"But you want to be, right?"

"Yeah."

He screws the lid back on the jar. Stares at it. "Maybe seeing you with Matt will make Carlie want to try it with me."

"You guys aren't dating?"

"Not officially."

"But you guys, um, are like, behind the cafeteria all the time."

"You know about that, huh?"

"Everybody knows about that."

He pauses, his eyebrows pinching together. I squat down next to him.

"So Carlie doesn't want to date?" I ask.

Ian releases a granddaddy longlegs, thinking. "We went to the same high school and church, but different colleges. I hadn't seen her in over a year until we got jobs here last summer..." He glances at me. "I've always liked her."

"Go on," I reply.

"Last summer I told her I wanted a relationship, but she didn't want that with anybody, you know, right in the middle of college and all. I guess she doesn't want to get tied down. I was hoping she might want to try for real this summer...but—"

"But?"

He looks up at my face. "I'm not going to pressure her. I'd rather it just happen naturally if it's going to."

"Um, why are you sleeping with her if it's not serious?"

He laughs a little, seeming even sadder. "I just can't help it."

"I just don't get that."

"You and me both." He stands, wipes off his hands, and grabs the jars, motioning toward the cafeteria. "Dinner?"

"Yeah."

We walk together back up the hill. "Thanks for listening," he says quietly. "I've been praying about it…but sometimes it's good to say it out loud."

I nod slowly. If I said what I helped Emily to do out loud, would it change things? Make me feel better?

I don't see how it could.

sketch #361
what happened last night

The campers are showering and getting ready for the dance, so I grab my portfolio and a pencil.

Last night, Eric made me start the fire and get the hobo packs going all by myself. He basically ignored me while he played with fishing lures. I had no Crisco and no starter log and no hope.

I sketch the patch of kindling I stuffed under the logs. Bits of hay and grass.

I used a match to get it going. My flame went out three times, but I kept trying and finally, on the fourth try, the kindling got hot enough to catch a few sticks on fire. From there, the logs didn't have a chance.

"Nice," Eric said to me, smiling, and went back to his tackle box. I grinned to myself and told each camper to tear off a piece of aluminum foil.

"Wrap it like a burrito!" I told them.

I smile to myself as I draw the scene: a fire blazing next to a bunch of campers stuffing their faces.

It's nearly time for the Thursday Night Dance. I hide my sketchbook under my pillow and use the rest of my time to pray, to say thanks for helping me start my fire.

nothing's set in stone

I'm making cheese and crackers when Daddy comes into the kitchen and tells me to meet him in his study to discuss college courses.

I carry my snack down the hall and step over Fritz, who's napping in the entryway, and take a seat in a stiff armchair. Mom redecorated this room in January, so the cushion isn't worn-in yet. Not like Daddy's chair. I swear, the thing must be from 1965. Mom hates it. It's orange, has multiple ink and coffee stains, and a big rip runs down the back of the upholstery. But she lets him keep it 'cause she loves him.

Pictures of me, Mom, Fritz, and Daddy's hunting escapades fill the bookshelves and walls. Every other space is filled by dusty plants and gigantic law texts.

Daddy steps over the dog, carrying the Belmont registration booklet and an ice cream sundae covered with chocolate syrup, chocolate chips, peanuts, and cherries.

"You know you're not supposed to eat that," I warn.

"I know," he says, smiling as he flops down in his orange chair.

"But you only live once." He crosses his leg and jiggles his loafer. "So which classes have you picked out?"

I pull a deep breath. "None. I have no idea what to do."

"What about the pre-law track we talked about?"

"It just sounds…boring to me."

He scoops some ice cream into his mouth. "Is that your way of saying you think I'm boring?"

I laugh. "No, no. I'm just not sure what I want to study."

"That's fine. You've got time."

"Aren't I supposed to pick out a major before I start school?" I bite into my cheese.

"Kate," he starts. He stops to take another bite of ice cream. I give him a look and mutter "blood pressure" before he speaks again. "You don't have to know right now. You can change your mind about what you want to do two years into college. Or after college. You could go back and study something else if you wanted to."

I tap my sandals on the floor. "I love art, but I'm not sure I want to do it as a career. It's just something for me."

Daddy nods. "Why don't we pick out a bunch of random classes and talk again after next semester?"

"Isn't that a waste of your money?"

"Learning is never a bad thing. And neither is changing your mind about things…It's always good to reevaluate. To think and consider all sides."

I bite into a cracker and stare out the window. I don't like that Matt's in a frat. I don't like how Emily's been treating me. I don't see how I could ever change my mind about those things. But at the same time, I love everything else about Matt. I love that he wants to run a marathon barefoot and I love that he can't seem to get enough ranch dressing. I like how he touches my jaw and stares deep into my eyes, like I'm the only girl he's ever seen.

He drinks beer and I know he wouldn't mind sharing a bed with me.

But this week, when I asked him if he believes in God, he said, "What a silly question. Just look at that." He turned me to face the sun setting above the rolling hills beyond camp.

If I were to ditch Matt and wait for a guy who's 100 percent devout, I might end up with a guy who doesn't stare at me like I'm the only girl he's ever seen.

But living with an ugly orange chair is a lot different than putting up with a fraternity.

"Can we wait to register for classes?" I ask. "I need more time."

Daddy smiles. "Let's hold off for another week or two, okay?"

"Okay," I say quietly.

"Can I ask you something?" he says, and I nod. "Can you tell me what happened with Emily? Why you've been so out of it?"

Care fills his voice. I don't want to lie to him. "We had an argument about church and God."

He raises his eyebrows. Takes another bite of ice cream. "And?"

"She doesn't believe in God anymore."

"And you do."

"Of course, don't you?"

Daddy leans onto his armrest, propping his jaw up with a fist. "It doesn't matter what I believe. What matters is what you believe."

"I believe in God. He loves us."

"And Emily doesn't believe that anymore…but she's still your friend."

I slowly shrug and stare down at the plate in my lap.

"Your truth isn't everybody else's truth. Your beliefs matter, right?" he asks.

"I think they do. Not everyone else thinks they do, though."

"But you wish they respected your beliefs?"

I nod.

"So don't you think Emily wants you to respect what she thinks?"

I set my plate on the coffee table and cross my arms across my stomach. Fritz wakes up and drags himself across the room and plops down at my feet. I pat his head.

"Tell me what's going on with this boy," Daddy says, smiling coyly. He scrapes the bottom of his bowl. "Matt."

I bite my lower lip, smiling. "I like him. He invited me to dinner tonight to meet his family."

"I'm glad. I can tell he's something you're serious about."

"How can you tell?"

"He makes you smile when not much does anymore. Even drawing doesn't make you smile like that."

My face grows hot.

"Is he treating you right?" Daddy asks, looking down at the dog.

I clear my throat, thinking of how many times we kissed in the past week. I lost count after fifty. "Everything's perfect."

We sit in silence for a few moments. Something is nagging at me, and I just have to ask. "I care what you believe," I say quietly. "When I asked if you believed in God a few minutes ago, you looked away."

He leans back in his chair, shaking his loafer. Our eyes meet, but he says nothing.

I ask, "Why did you always make me go to church?"

"I've never made you go to church, Kate. Never. You've always enjoyed it...up until Emily left. I know you've been upset."

"But you don't really believe?"

He sets his bowl on the coffee table and leans over onto his thighs, peering up at me. "I've thought for years about this, Kate. I just don't know. Part of me believes that a higher being created evolution."

My chest burns. Is he saying he doesn't believe in God?

Has he just been going through the motions all this time?

"Why do you go to church?" I whisper.

"I have friends there. It makes your mother happy. I like organ music."

I can't help but laugh.

"Do you pray?" I ask him.

"Doesn't everybody pray sometime?"

He is fifty-two years old and still hasn't figured this out. He's right that my beliefs matter.

But why does no one else seem to share them anymore?

• • •

Matt ushers me through his back door and we climb a short flight of steps to enter a madhouse.

His mom, a thin woman with bags under her eyes, is trying to make room on the table for dinner. She removes a tutu from the table and replaces it with a whole chicken.

"Jere," she says. "For the tenth time, put away your tennis racquet. Please."

A cute boy about my age doesn't stop looking at his phone as he yanks the racquet off the table and stashes it under his chair.

"I don't want lima beans!" a girl yells. This must be his littlest sister, Jenn. I remember Matt saying she's six, about to turn seven in August.

"But beans are yummy," Matt says, sweeping her up in his arms and kissing her cheek. He gives her a raspberry, blowing air against her face, and she's giggling and squirming. "Jenn, I want you to meet someone special, okay?"

That's when Matt's mom and Jeremiah look up and see me. His mom pushes her damp blond hair off her forehead and wipes her hands on a dishtowel before coming to shake mine.

"Mom, this is Kate. Kate, this is my mother."

She pats my shoulder and beams at Matt.

Jeremiah manages to put his phone down for approximately five seconds to say hi to me, but then goes right back to texting. Then Mr. Brown comes into the kitchen and moves a bunch of schoolbooks so his wife can set the bread and water on the table.

"It's really nice to meet you," he tells me, pushing his glasses up on his nose.

Mom would have a heart attack if she were to see their kitchen. Every visible surface is covered by toys, newspapers, and kitchen appliances. Why is an umbrella on top of the fridge? Why is a sock hanging from the ceiling fan? I don't think the room has been redecorated in years, judging by the faded blue-and-yellow-flowered wallpaper. But I love it. It's cozy and homey.

Matt wraps an arm around my waist and pulls me closer. Jeremiah watches Matt holding me and raises his eyebrows, then goes back to texting. That's when five girls strut into the kitchen. One of them must be his sister, Lacey, who's twelve.

I figure out which one she is pretty quickly because she pinches Matt's arm and says, "You brought a girl home!" Then proceeds to tease Matt.

"You're just jealous 'cause Dad won't let you date," Matt says to Lacey, and she scowls.

"Not until you're ninety," Mr. Brown says, placing a roll of paper towels in the middle of the table.

"Who'd want to date me then?" Lacey asks, plopping down in a chair. "I'll be all wrinkly. Gross."

"My dad says I can date when I'm sixteen," one of Lacey's friends says, looking pointedly at Jeremiah, who keeps right on texting.

Matt whispers in my ear. "Slumber parties freak me out. Last time she had one they played Truth or Dare and someone got dared to launch an Apple Pie Water Gun Kissing Attack at me."

"What's that?" I whisper back.

"You don't want to know." He shudders. I laugh softly, and he kneads my lower back.

I catch his mom and dad watching us. They share a meaningful glance before focusing on dinner again.

"Kate, Kate," Jenn says, patting the table. "Sit by me."

That's when I notice nearly every seat is filled. "Oh, um, I'm not sure there's room."

His parents' heads pop up. I watch them count the chairs.

"One second," Mr. Brown says. He comes back and squeezes an eleventh chair in for me. He moves a pile of Barbies and a pair of shin guards so I can sit down between Jenn and Matt.

Holding hands, we say grace, and I'm grinning as Matt rubs his fingers back and forth across mine.

• • •

After dinner, Matt and I grab a seat on the couch in the basement. Finally alone.

Our mouths move together slowly, grazing, testing. He massages the inside of my thigh.

While he was in the bathroom, I studied the pictures sitting on top of the grand piano in the living room. I was learning the faces of several generations of Matt's family when his brother came up behind me.

"Please don't hurt him," Jeremiah said quietly, as he texted on his phone.

"What?" I asked.

"My brother. You're not messing with him, right?"

"I think that's the last thing I'd ever do."

He peeked up from his phone, smiling slightly. "Good. So do you have any sisters? Or cousins?"

I laughed, and that's when Matt appeared and gave me a piggyback ride down to the basement.

"I love your family," I tell Matt, leaning over to press my lips to his.

"I love them too," he says back. "But let's not talk about them right now."

I dip my head and our lips meet again. I can feel him smiling against my teeth.

That's when Jenn comes running down the stairs, screaming at the top of her lungs. She's wearing *Little Mermaid* pajamas that look so comfortable. Matt breaks away from me as his little sister launches herself into his arms.

"Attack of the killer Jenn!" he says, tickling her. She escapes, but he chases her until she falls onto the floor. She howls and laughs and kicks at him as he tickles her. I'm getting exhausted just watching them play together, but I love that they have a connection. It makes me happy that she invited me to sit next to her at dinner.

When the Great Tickle Fest is over, he drags himself up onto the couch. Jenn climbs onto Matt's lap and squeezes his nose. He stares back at her and that's when I notice their eyes are an identical grayish blue, the color of Normandy Lake. If I ever have a little girl, I want her to sit on my lap and love me like that.

Was Emily's baby a little boy or a little girl? Would she have had Emily's straight auburn hair and green eyes? I find myself reaching out and touching Jenn's elbow, to feel the skin, the reality.

"Jenn," Mrs. Brown calls from upstairs. "Time for sleep."

Jenn's bottom lip begins to quiver and Matt wraps her up in a hug and kisses her cheek. "No tears," he says. "I'll see you first thing in the morning. You'll wake me up, right?"

"Right," she replies, bopping his nose with a finger.

"Good. How would I ever wake up without you?"

"An alarm clock, silly," she says, rolling her eyes.

"Ohhh. Right. An alarm clock." He knocks himself in the forehead, and she giggles again.

I smile at them.

"Jenn!" Mrs. Brown yells. "C'mon!"

"Night, Munchkin," Matt says. His sister jumps off his lap and runs up the stairs.

I clear my throat and will my tears to dry up. Matt weaves his fingers with mine and we watch TV together, and I want nothing more than to be here with him in the now, but I can't stop thinking. If I hadn't agreed to take Emily to the clinic, she would've found another way there. If I had done that, would I feel so guilty now? Would I feel guilty just because I know what happened? Maybe if I hadn't gone, Emily would've realized I didn't support her whatsoever and would've come home and decided to keep the baby. Maybe by being there, I somehow validated her decision. Or maybe Emily would have felt abandoned and refused to talk to me after the abortion and sunk into depression and who knows what.

And now my own father questions the existence of God? I don't know what to make of that.

I touch my cheek and focus on my lap.

"What's up?" Matt whispers, taking in my face.

I lean my head against his shoulder. I can't tell him what I've done. What kind of person I really am. "I'm just a bit down, is all."

He squeezes my hand and kisses my hair. "Anything I can do?"

"Nah." Just be with me, I want to say. But I'm not ready to let on how much he means to me yet.

"What did you mean that day at camp?" I ask. "When you told me I saved you?"

He leans his head back against the sofa and pulls me against his chest. "Mom was pregnant with Jenn when I met you. And Jeremiah was ten and wouldn't stop trying to set things on fire, and Leigh was seventeen and wouldn't stop asking Mom and Dad for a new car…Lacey was five and threw temper tantrums that would scare the devil…Dad worked all the time, teaching drivers' ed on weekends to earn us extra money. Mom was busy with church and my brother and sisters, and I wanted to make things easy for her, so I kept my head down."

"You were lonely?"

"Really lonely. And I didn't get along with anybody at school really. I wasn't very popular and no one cared about my music. No one read books as much as I did."

I press my face against his chest, and he tucks my head under his chin, holding me tighter. "I know what you mean," I tell him.

"Kids at school were picking on me about my clothes from yard sales and my songwriting. I didn't want to give up my music but people kept making fun of me. And I didn't know what to do…but that week at camp, you wanted to hear my music."

I smile and shut my eyes.

"And then Jenn was born and I was the only one who could get her to stop crying," he says. "And she made me feel good again. I figured if Jenn liked me…and you liked me, I could like me too…So I started living for me. I joined the track team because I love running, and I kept writing music. And then in high school, I started making friends who liked the same stuff I do."

But what if I would rather have a relationship with God than friendships with people who don't believe in him like I do?

Why is it cool for some people to do what they want to do, but uncool for others? Why is being on the football team considered cool while being on the math team is not?

"I'm really happy you figured that out about yourself," I tell him.

He holds me closer. "I'm just glad I met you." His voice is filled with emotion. "I'm not sure I'd be where I am today," he whispers.

We kiss gently, a fire blazing in my lips as I try to keep this slow and steady.

That's when his sister, Lacey, appears in the basement with her friends, and they take one look at me and Matt cuddling and start going, "Woooo!"

He grins and blushes, and his mouth gently touches my earlobe. "We'd better escape before an Apple Pie Water Gun Attack happens. Want to see my room?"

Deep inside I know it's not right but I can't think of anything I'd rather do than see his room. Smell its smells. See if he puts his clothes in a laundry basket or leaves them scattered across the rug. Sit on his bed and hold his hand and be closer to him than to anyone else.

I nod slowly, and we make our way past the five giggling girls throwing popcorn at each other and climb three flights of stairs to reach the attic area. His door opens to reveal T-shirts and boxer shorts draped everywhere, dirty dishes sitting on the dressers and end tables, and Jeremiah lounging on one of the two twin beds with a car magazine in one hand and a cell phone in the other.

"Out," Matt says to Jeremiah, who gives us a knowing smile.

He points at Matt with his cell phone. "Annabelle's coming over tomorrow after church. I expect reciprocity." He tosses his magazine on his bed, stands, and struts out of the room.

"Reciprocity?" I ask.

"Jere likes big words…So, this is where it all happens," Matt tells me, flopping down on his twin bed. He knocks a pile of clothes onto the rug and pats his blue-striped comforter, indicating I should sit with him. I weave around teetering piles of books to join him.

"All what happens?" I ask, pulling my knees to my chest. "Do you have girls over a lot?"

"Nope." He gives me a mischievous grin. "I don't think I've had a girl here since high school. Since Sarah."

"Were you really close?" I glance around at the posters of women and cars on the walls.

"We never had sex, if that's what you mean," Matt says quietly, falling backward onto his pillow.

Is he a virgin? Did they really date for three years and manage not to have sex? Hearing that makes me really happy.

"Nah, I wasn't wondering that," I reply, even though I was.

This relationship (or whatever we are) will never work if we aren't truthful. I inhale deeply through my nose. "Okay, so I was wondering that."

Matt chuckles. "I know. I can see right through you."

"Great," I say in a sarcastic voice, laughing. I'm shaking as I lie down next to him.

"Can't you see through me too?"

I tuck a strand of hair behind my ear. "Sorta…"

"Well, if you can't see through me, here you go. I want you bad. Kiss me."

We're laughing as we stretch out on his bed. His hands are in my hair and I play with his T-shirt. He positions himself between my legs as we make out. All I can think about is how I want to press my chest to his, my skin to his skin.

Then the door opens.

"Oh!" his dad exclaims.

Matt suddenly rolls off me. "Dad! Why didn't you knock?"

"Sorry, son," Mr. Brown says, grinning. "Your mom sent me up here to make sure your brother didn't have any girls in your room." The door clicks shut.

"That was so mortifying," I groan.

"At least we have our clothes on." He chuckles, pressing his forehead to mine. "One time Mom caught Jeremiah and some girl completely—"

A knock sounds on the door.

"Who is it?" Matt yells, exasperated.

"Your father."

"What do you want?"

"Can you mow the lawn tomorrow after church?"

"Daaaaaaaad." Matt's shaking his head and laughing. My mouth has dropped open. "Couldn't you have waited until after Kate goes home to ask me?"

"I didn't want to forget," Mr. Brown says from behind the door.

Matt whispers to me, "This is his way of saying we shouldn't be in here alone together."

I nod.

Matt yells to his dad, "Fine, I'll mow the lawn. Now go away."

I smack his chest.

"What?" Matt asks, clutching my hands so I can't hit him again.

"You shouldn't treat your dad that way."

"I like her," Mr. Brown says from out in the hallway.

"Daaaaadd, stop eavesdropping!" Matt jumps to his feet and grabs his keys from the nightstand. "That's it, I'm taking you home. We'll never find any peace around here."

I can't stop laughing.

• • •

I get Emily's voicemail. Again.

"Hey, um," I say into the phone. "It's me. Again. I'm just calling to say that I miss you. Call me or my mom if you need anything. Really—anything. Okay, well, bye."

I push the end call button.

● ● ●

On Sunday evening, everyone's heading for Dogwood, and I suck in a breath when Matt sweeps me into his arms. I'm afraid he'll ask me to sleep in there with the other guy counselors.

I'm afraid I'll say yes.

"I got a surprise for you," he whispers.

"What?"

"Come on."

He leads me out into the big field where we do field games, where he and I run every morning. The stars shine brightly on the patch of grass where he's set up a campfire and has stretched the giant parachute across the grass. Two thin mattresses and our sleeping bags rest on top of the parachute.

"Thought we could sleep out here tonight," he says, squeezing my hand.

The air is warm and just right for camping. Our mattresses are about ten feet apart. I glance over at him. I want to lie close enough to whisper to him.

"You can move your mattress closer to mine if you want."

His face reddens, and he smiles. We move our mattresses, so near they are kissing, but I decide to lie down with him on his, and his hands are shaking and mine are shaking but we're laughing.

"You're awfully presumptuous," he says, as I cuddle up next to him under a sheet he brought. It smells clean and crisp and feels cool against my skin. I twine my feet with his; his blue hospital scrubs tickle my legs.

We begin kissing gently. More slowly than we did last night in his bed. He keeps touching my face and my hair and I find myself wanting to get as close to him as possible. I press my chest to his and kiss him harder.

"Wait, wait," he mumbles, pulling away, our sheet tangling around his body. He rolls onto his back and brushes the hair out of his eyes, staring at the sky.

"Did I do something wrong?" I whisper.

"No, no…It's just, what are we?" He looks over at me.

"Huh?"

"Are we, like, together? Or dating casually? Or what?"

A lump fills my throat. "Um, what do you think we are?"

"I guess I'm hoping this isn't just a casual thing for you…"

"For me?" I blurt. "Never."

He laughs and props himself up on an elbow to stare down at me. "You want to keep me around for a while?"

"Yes, please."

He drums his fingers on my rib cage. It tickles. "Are we giving a relationship a try?"

"Yes, please," I say, laughing.

He grins. "Okay, now that that's settled, I can permit you to have your way with me."

I flick his forehead. "Oh, whatever."

"Oh, whatever?" He starts tickling me and I squirm around. "Oh, whatever? You were the one all pushing up against me a couple minutes ago."

"C'mere," I say, pulling him in. He touches my bare stomach as we kiss. His fingers inch higher and higher until they reach my bra. I'm about to shove him away from me, but his blue eyes catch mine, and they are so warm and tender, and I just want us to be happy and close as can be.

He brushes his fingers across my breast and pushes my shirt up. Matt focuses on the little white bow between my breasts, taking it between his fingers. Then he's kissing me through my bra. He shrugs out of his T-shirt, pulling it over his head in one motion, and I can't stop touching his strong, smooth chest, and then we're moving in tune with each other. He presses himself against my cotton shorts.

"Does this feel nice?" he whispers, rocking his hips against mine.

I can barely nod because it's like every nerve ending in my body is primed to explode. And then they do and I feel like I'm falling away and I'm shuddering and gasping for breath.

We cuddle in silence until he falls asleep next to me, his warm breath tickling my neck as he snores softly.

The stars above me are blurry because my eyes are watering.

I don't know what makes me feel more guilty: that I love how he touched me when I should hate it, when I should have pushed him away, or how I couldn't hear God's warnings because of the way Matt made me feel.

sketch #362

what happened on june 19

I've always worked hard to control my temper.

I'm sketching a picture of every happy thing I can think of.
Fudge, sunshine, kittens.

Grandpa Kelly always says, "Never let anyone see your weak
point. It's the opening they're looking for, to do more damage."

So that's what I'm trying to do during lunch: Not get angry in
front of Megan or any of the other counselors. Earlier today, she
humiliated me.

"Is this really an art project?" she had asked in front of fifty
campers, staring at my decoupaged Coke bottle.

"I like the footballs!" shouted Liam, an eight-year-old.

"Art is about expressing yourself in whatever way you want,"
I told Megan, digging my thumbnail into my hand. "Self-
expression is an important thing to teach the kids."

"But this," she said, holding up my Coke bottle, "is not something kids can take home to their mothers as a gift."

"I thought that since I'm the arts and crafts director, I get to choose the program. I don't believe in censorship when it comes to art."

"I think the regional conference would be happier if kids could bring home presents to their moms. Why don't you make more candles or something?" She gave my boxes of junk a junky look and left the pavilion.

A little girl looked up at me, holding a baby food jar that she was covering with flowers. "Is this not really art?" she asked.

"If you think it's art, it's art," I replied, and breathed in deeply through my nose, trying not to shake.

Here in the now, I keep drawing suns and pinwheels and waves.

falling

I overdid it on my morning jog with Matt. With his help, I can run four miles again, but I don't think my knee is cut out for long-distance running anymore, and that makes me want to cry.

In high school, if I ever felt down about something, I would run and run and run, and now I can't do that. I can't clear my mind. I'm not part of a soccer team anymore.

I also keep thinking of what happened with Matt on Sunday night.

At first when I think of it, a smile flits across my face, but then I feel ashamed. These feelings confuse me, and I want to talk to Emily about it, but after what happened at her apartment, she hasn't tried to call even once. Besides, she might say I'm childish—that everyone does *that* with their boyfriends. Matt hasn't even brought it up.

How is it possible to have a great boyfriend but still feel lonely?

My art class with the campers just ended. We made candles by dripping wax into sand holes we dug, and then made stained-glass votives.

Ever since she made that jewelry box, Parker has been coming to my art classes during her breaks. She doesn't say much, because she doesn't want me to get in trouble with Megan again, but she stuck around to help me clean up today.

She sweeps sand into little piles while I store supplies on the shelves, hobbling back and forth from the tables to the cupboards.

"Are you okay?" she asks.

The moment she asks that, tears fill my eyes. The emotions just get to me. "I'm okay," I say, staying in the closet until I get myself under control. I will not cry in front of her.

Then she appears behind me and catches me wiping my nose.

"Is your leg hurting?" she asks, looking at my scar.

"Yeah…I've been running with Matt."

"Should you be running on it?"

"My therapist said it should be okay, but I'm still trying to figure it out."

"I'm so sorry about soccer."

I focus on my watercolor of White Oak. "I'm sorry about your parents."

Parker bites on her lower lip and drags the broom across the floor. "It definitely sucked when they split up."

"I know we weren't really friends before that happened, but I'm sorry."

She pauses. "It's not your fault."

"I could've reached out, but…I didn't understand why you

were acting like you were, you know…hooking up with guys a lot. It scared me."

"It scared me too," she admits, clutching the broom handle.

"Will said your friends turned against you?"

"Most of them, yeah. It was…hard. My best friend told everyone I was probably gay, like Mom."

My eyes water again. I don't know whether it's the pain from my knee or just my overall state of mind, but I can't control my tears today. At all. "I lost my best friend."

Parker's eyes grow wide. "Emily? From church?"

I nod slowly.

"What happened?"

I avoid her stare and walk out of the closet. I stop to drum my fingers on a picnic table, dipping my fingers into the chipped wood where someone named Lily carved her name. "I'm dating Matt now," I tell Parker, dropping the subject of Emily. "Like a real relationship."

Parker squeals and comes to hug me.

"And?" she says.

"And what?"

"Have you guys kissed? Made out or anything?"

I swallow and tell myself to ignore the other night. All of our clothes stayed on, but I could feel him through my shorts. It felt great. It felt wrong. "We've kissed, yeah."

She grins. "I'm so glad he picked you instead of that nasty Andrea!"

I burst out laughing. I can't help it. But I feel a little bit bad, considering Andrea helped Matt get through his breakup and ended up falling for him, even though she didn't intend for it to happen.

"She keeps going on and on about how she'll be in Cabo at the same time as him," Parker says.

"Cabo?" I say quietly.

"Mexico."

"I know where Cabo is, but what does Mexico have to do with Andrea and Matt?"

"I guess his frat is going with her sorority to Mexico over the Fourth of July."

We have that week off from camp, but Matt hadn't mentioned a trip. And he definitely did not mention a trip with Andrea!

"He hasn't said anything," I tell Parker.

"I'm sure that he just forgot," she says, lifting a shoulder. "He's a guy, right?"

"What if—"

Parker cuts me off, waving the broom at me. "He does not like her like that. Trust me. He could've had her already. He wants you!"

I step to the edge of the pavilion and peer into the woods. "I can't imagine a week with nothing to do," I mumble. Mom and Daddy are going on that cruise and I'm staying home with Fritz the dog.

"We can hang out," Parker says, starting to sweep again.

"With you and Will?"

She glances up at my eyes, looking just as nervous as I feel. "No, like you and me. Don't become one of those girls who's super dependent on her boyfriend, okay?"

I smile, and then she suggests we walk up to the cafeteria to get some ice for my knee.

Later that morning after our swimming session, my group is drying off by the side of the pool. The campers are slapping each other with towels and acting like buffoons.

"Kate," Matt calls out from beside the pool maintenance closet.

"Can you watch the kids for a minute?" I ask Ian, my co-counselor this week.

A grin stretches across his face. "Nice. The pool shed is a good choice. Not as great as behind the cafeteria—"

"Gross," I interrupt, making him laugh.

Ian goes back to scolding a boy for slapping girls with his towel. "When you get older," Ian tells the boy, "these girls will remember that you smacked their butts and won't want to date you. So stop it!"

Glancing around to make sure Megan isn't at the pool right now, I zip across the concrete to Matt.

He scans my two-piece bathing suit, smiling, and rests a hand on my shoulder. His thumb grazes my neck as he bends down to whisper in my ear. "I got you something."

"Oh yeah?"

He reaches for a shelf in the closet and picks up a four-leaf clover. "For you." Matt gently sets it on top of my ear, like how women sometimes wear tropical flowers.

"Thank you," I whisper, thinking about how he's like a four-leaf clover. Something you don't find often. I'd be stupid to mess things up with him just because he's in a frat, especially when everything else about him fits just right.

He looks from the clover to my eyes. Based on his smile, which is full of friendship and something more, I doubt he's thinking of Sunday night. He's thinking of today. Today and me and not necessarily what's next, but right now. Maybe he's right—maybe I can see right through him.

But if that's true, why didn't I know about Cabo?

"I love the clover," I say.

"Maybe in trade you could give me your green beans at lunch today?"

"Absolutely not," I say with a laugh.

He gives me a mischievous smile. "It was worth a shot."

"Hey, listen, can we talk?"

His face goes serious, like my voice. "Now?" He looks over my shoulder at the towel fight. Ian practically has this kid in a head-lock, trying to stop him from smacking another kid.

"You're right. Later is good."

He pulls me into the closet and rubs my stomach, dipping a finger into my bellybutton. "I'll come by your cabin at midnight."

I give Matt a smile and go pry Ian off the camper.

"You guys are fast," Ian teases me.

"Perv."

By the time midnight rolls around, I've bitten my pinky nail down to the quick. If I confront Matt about going to Cabo over the Fourth of July, will he think I'm one of those controlling girlfriends?

I check to make sure the girls are asleep, then slip my feet into flip-flops and pad down the trail to my cookout area. Matt's already there, playing his guitar. As soon as I walk up, he puts the guitar aside and then lifts me onto the table and stands between my legs. He kisses me deeply, exploring my mouth, his fingers grasping my knees.

"Are you trying to distract me?" I ask, weaving my hands in his hair.

"Is it working?" He kisses me again.

"Yep," I say, laughing.

"So what's up?"

"I heard you're going to Cabo? Parker told me."

He pulls a deep breath through his nose and hesitates for a second. "I can't decide if I'm going."

"What does that mean?" I ask quietly.

"I already paid for it. Before you." He shuts his eyes. "Before we reconnected—before we started dating."

"You don't want to go?"

"I want to spend time with my brothers." He means his fraternity. He continues, "I've always wanted to go surfing. But I don't want to miss out on a week with you." We kiss again. His lips are so warm and soft.

"Why didn't you tell me?"

"I kept meaning to bring it up but wasn't sure what to tell you..." He shrugs.

"Parker said you probably forgot to tell me because you're a guy."

"I take great offense to that. You are in big trouble."

I try to escape but he wraps me up in his arms. "You're like a straitjacket," I say, trying to break free.

"A straitjacket of love."

I slap his chest. "I can't believe you just said that. That's the worst thing I've ever heard."

Does that mean he loves me?

We are laughing and kissing and then he leans his forehead against mine. I drag my fingers across his lower back, beneath his shirt, and dip my fingers inside his shorts.

"You should go surfing and be with your friends."

"Being away from you for a week will suck," he whispers. He goes up my shirt while he kisses me, making me shake all over. My nipple hardens under his touch. My body feels like a rubber band ready to snap.

"Is this okay? Should I stop?" he asks.

The four-leaf clover he gave me pops into my mind. I take a deep breath.

"Don't stop."

• • •

The next two weeks of camp basically go the same way—during the day I hang out with Parker, and at night, after everyone's asleep, I spend time with Matt.

Every morning, I pray in the Woodsong Chapel, asking God to give me the strength to keep my hands off Matt. I haven't let him go further than touching my chest, but it's getting harder and harder to stop because I want him to touch me, because I care about him so much. And sometimes I get so sad thinking of Emily that Matt notices. He keeps asking, "Where do you go inside that head of yours?"

I can't tell him. "Nowhere."

Then he grins a sad, lopsided grin and kisses my cheek.

The good news is that the fun of camp totally distracts me. One afternoon, the girl counselors challenge the guy counselors to a game of Bonzo Ball. Well, all the counselors minus Eric, who decides to lead a small expedition of campers to look for snakes at the lake because he's still not convinced I saw one.

With a hundred campers surrounding us, cheering and stomping, Parker, Andrea, Carlie, and I take on the guys. Much trash talk ensues.

"You don't even know what Bonzo Ball is," Carlie says to Ian, fake sneering.

"I do so know what it is. Don't you remember me beating you five times last week?"

"Ooooh," the boy campers say.

Carlie sets a hand on her hip. "I let you win because you always cry when you lose."

"Ooooh," the girl campers chorus.

Squatting low to the ground, Andrea slams the ball at Brad's shins, knocking him out of the game. The girl campers cheer like mad, and I give Andrea a high five. Matt, Will, and Ian fake pout.

"Come on, girls!" a boy camper yells at us. He's twelve and clearly has the hots for us.

Matt points at the boy. "Oh, you're so going down, traitor."

The game comes down to Parker versus Ian, and they totally start showing off, doing fancy jumps in the air and rolling out of the way of the ball. But in the end, Parker manages to hit Ian in the ankle, and us four girls jump up and down, hugging each other. It makes me smile that Andrea and I are getting along, at least in the name of girl power.

Thursday night before our week off, after I've said good night prayers with the girls in my cabin, I'm lying with Matt in the big field, staring at the stars.

"Where do you think heaven is?" Matt asks.

"It's up there," I say, pointing past the Big Dipper.

Emily said she doesn't buy any of it anymore. Religion. God. Faith. Before I decided to help Emily get an abortion, my life was just fine. My parents love me. I have a beautiful home. All in all, everything was okay.

Since I sinned, life has been terrible and wonderful. I never had a boyfriend during high school. I didn't have many friends except for Emily and my soccer team. But after they were taken away, I found out how little I truly had.

Now I have Matt and my heart is brimming with emotions, with something that feels like love, but I'm not ready to tell him that yet. We've only been dating a month. Can you feel love in that amount of time?

What if he still loves his ex?

I snuggle against his chest. "No girls in Cabo, understand?"

"No guys in Franklin, understand?"

"I'm being serious," I tell him, using an exaggerated warning tone.

"You're in trouble." He rolls over on top of me and tickles me until I can't breathe. I'm screaming at him, probably waking up the entire camp. I try to push him off me but he's too strong. Then his mouth meets mine and for the first time, he rests his fingers on the button of my shorts.

I inhale deeply, grabbing his hand.

He rolls off me, shutting his eyes and rubbing his face. "I'm sorry. I don't mean to push you to move so fast I just get caught up in you—and I—"

I climb on top of him. "I get caught up in you too."

We move against each other and my mind goes away into nothingness and it's just our bodies, straining to get closer. My shorts are unbuttoned, unzipped, and so are his. He's wearing light blue striped boxers that I can't help wanting to touch. His hand gently grazes me through my shorts and then he runs a finger beneath the elastic of my underwear. That's when I remember I have on plain white panties. I can't let him see those. I bet Andrea doesn't even own white cotton underwear.

"It's late," I whisper.

"To be continued?" he asks, smiling. "When I get back from Mexico?"

Even though I'll miss him like crazy, I'm grateful for the break. For the chance to figure out how to balance the physical part of our relationship with the emotional. Andrea would probably give Matt whatever he wants. What scares me is that I want to give Matt whatever he wants. Not because I'm scared of losing him.

Because I want to show him how much I care.

Because I'm falling in love with all of him.

Because I kind of want it too.

• • •

"You want to go where?"

Parker and I spent the first few days of break riding bikes, swimming, and lying out in the sun, and that was really fun, but

I never imagined Parker would invite me to a Fourth of July party at Jordan Woods's house. Jordan is Sam Henry's girlfriend, and like him, she probably has no idea who I am. I, however, know exactly who Jordan is. Former captain and quarterback of the Hundred Oaks High football team.

Loud rap music rings through the trees. Lit torches with flames reaching toward the sky dot the yard, along with tables and tables of food and drinks.

"Uhhh," I say to Parker. "I've never been to a party like this."

"I don't like them much, either," she whispers back. "We'll just say hi and then come up with an excuse to leave, okay?"

"Then why are we here?"

She jerks her head toward Will. A bunch of boys from the baseball team rush up to surround him, talking about how the Braves blew a 3–2 lead in the ninth.

Will never lets go of Parker's hand as he talks and even kisses her knuckles from time to time. No one is talking to me, and I wish so bad that Matt were here, but he's not. He's in Cabo. What if Andrea comes on to him? What if he changes his mind about me while he's in Mexico?

Leaving Parker and Will with the baseball players, I make my way toward one of the many drink tables. On my way, a really cute guy catches my eye and smiles. He abandons the guy he was talking to and stalks toward me with a major swagger.

My breath catches in my throat. The guy must be six-four, and he has these ginormous muscles and gorgeous blond hair. "Hey," he says, checking out my jean shorts.

"Hi," I say, not sure of what to do with my hands.

"I'm Jake." He thrusts out a hand and I take it.

"Kate."

"Are you a friend of Jordan's?"

"No," I say, swallowing hard. "We're not friends."

"Oh, good."

"Why is that good?"

"Jordan gets pissed if I talk to her friends."

"Are you her brother?" He fits the mold. Tall, blond, Adonis-like. But not as Adonis-like as Matt.

He laughs. "Her brother's my best friend." He takes a step closer to me, where I can see a few freckles on his nose. "Want to go for a walk down by the docks?" he says quietly. He slides a hand onto my shoulder. It doesn't feel good or exciting. It only reminds me of how much I miss Matt. It scares me a little, to realize I am beginning to depend on him like I depended on Emily. I don't think I will lose him, but I can't help but worry about how much I've come to count on him being around.

"I have a boyfriend," I tell Jake.

"I can understand why," he replies, scanning my body again and taking a step closer. "Can I ask you a question?"

"Okay…"

He grins a lazy grin, then whispers, "Do you believe in love at first sight...? Or should I walk by you again?"

I open my mouth to speak, then shut it again. "Really? Did you really just say that?"

"Reynolds!" I hear a voice yell. Jake jumps away from me, eyes wide. I turn to see Jordan stalking this way. "Get away from her before I get medieval on your ass!"

Jordan walks right up and takes Jake by the bicep and yanks him over to another guy, who looks a lot like Jordan. He hands Jake a beer. She yells at both guys and points toward the house and basically makes a big scene. The guys laugh at her and go back to drinking their beers.

I need something to do with my empty hands, so I dip my fingers into a bucket of slushy ice to search for a can of Coke or a bottled water. But all I can see are beer, wine, wine coolers, and more beer. Where are Jordan Woods's parents anyway? Her dad is a famous football player, so he must travel all the time.

"Can I get you a drink?"

Jordan has reappeared beside me. She's wearing a bright gold Purdue T-shirt.

"Um," I say, turning my focus toward the grass. Jordan is like a foot taller than me and she's supermodel gorgeous and strong and well-respected by just about everybody. I've never actually spoken to her but I've always admired how she follows her dreams.

"I'm sorry about Reynolds," Jordan says, smacking some chewing gum. "He's a perv."

I nod slowly and consider calling Daddy to ask him to come pick me up. Parker and Will are still chatting with people.

"Did you want a drink?" Jordan asks again.

"I don't drink," I reply.

She thrusts her hand down into the bucket and whips out a root beer, which she passes to me. Then she pulls out another and pops the tab. "I don't drink either," she says, taking a sip. "I'm not messing up my body when I've got football to play."

"I don't want to mess up my body either," I tell her.

"Nice," she says, tapping her can against mine. "Cheers." She jerks her head toward a picnic table over by a lush garden full of cornstalks and sunflowers. Sam Henry, JJ, and Joe Carter are playing flip cup and slurping beers. "My boyfriend doesn't mind messing himself up."

"That stinks," I say. Sam's as popular as Jordan, and I've never heard of him being mean to anybody. He does have a reputation, though—Emily once told me he's fooled around with lots of girls at school.

I don't love that Matt's off in Cabo with his frat brothers right now, but I like him enough to live with it. I guess you can love a person without loving everything about them.

"I don't really know Sam, but he seems like a nice guy," I say.

She sticks out a hand. "I'm Jordan, by the way."

"Kate Kelly. We went to school together."

"Yeah, I know."

"You do?"

She winces. "I heard about your knee. That sucks major."

I slip a thumb through my belt loop and toe the grass.

Jordan goes on, "And you were in my art class last semester."

I smile. "I liked the collage you made with pictures of Brett Favre and a bunch of monkeys."

Grinning, Jordan pushes my shoulder. Ow! She's strong. "Dad liked my collage a lot too. He put it up in his office."

We sip our root beers.

"I liked that painting you did of heaven," Jordan says. "The one with the sailboat?"

Jordan Woods noticed one of my paintings? That one won first place at the fair. "Thank you."

"I would've told you at school, but I didn't want to interrupt you during art. I could tell it was serious for you. Not like the shit goof-off time it was for me and Henry, you know? He made that papier-mâché sculpture of a dog peeing on a fire hydrant." Jordan rolls her eyes, but she's smiling.

"I wouldn't have minded if you interrupted me," I say quietly.

"I don't like it when people bother me during weights or drills. I need to concentrate."

I don't need concentration, though. I like activity around me. It gives me ideas. Makes me think in dynamic ways. Makes the colors explode.

Jordan thought I didn't want to be approached when I did.

What did I look like in high school? A girl who lived in Emily's shadow, where it was safe. The only place I broke out of my shell was on the soccer field, and when that ended, I shrunk even further back into the shadow.

But Jordan saw me even when I thought I was invisible. And she's strong and does what she feels is right. And besides all the sexist jerks out there, no one has a problem with her going after her goals and dreams of playing quarterback in college.

But can I still open myself up to new experiences and new people while doing what I feel is right? Especially if other people don't necessarily believe what I believe?

Why is believing in football different than believing in God? Why is one more socially acceptable than the other?

I look up at Jordan. "Are you looking forward to college?"

"I'm officially moving up to Indiana next week. I've already been practicing with the team. And Henry's shipped his stuff up to Michigan." She gazes over at him and I can see the pain on her face.

"Are you guys gonna keep dating?"

"You're like the only person who's asked me that!"

"Really?"

"Yeah—everyone else is scared to ask, I think." She gulps her root beer. "But I know we'll be fine."

"Michigan isn't that far from Indiana, right?"

"Yup. It takes longer to drive across Tennessee than it does to drive from Michigan to Purdue. We'll still see each other plenty."

That's when Sam Henry walks up and wraps his arms around her waist from behind. He sweeps her hair back and kisses her neck.

"Bedtime?" he asks, grinning at her.

"It's like eight-thirty!" she replies, shaking her head.

"I know." He stretches his arms and yawns a fake yawn, acting all dramatic. "It's super late. I'm so sleepy," he teases.

Jordan glances at his face, then focuses on me again. I see the want written on her face. I used to see it on Emily's face when she was with Jacob. Is that the same look I wear when I want to be alone with Matt?

"Go ahead," I say.

"Nice talking to you."

"Thanks for what you said, about my painting," I say to Jordan. She nods. "Friend me on Facebook so I can see your other art."

I watch as she and Sam Henry walk across the yard, ignoring everyone trying to talk to them—it's like they are in their own little bubble—and go up the back steps into her house. A minute later I see a light flick on upstairs, and then it goes out again.

Jordan and Sam love each other, but they love their dreams too. They love each other enough that it's okay to risk being apart. I rub my throat, thinking of Emily and her dream to play violin for the National Symphony. Like Jordan, she wanted that same balance with Jacob. And she lost that balance.

Matt and I are still figuring out our balance.

Holding hands, Parker and Will stride up to me. "Ready to get out of here?" she asks me.

"I'm fine to hang out if y'all want to stay longer. Well, except for this guy used the worst pick-up line ever on me."

"Gross," Parker says. "What did he say?"

I point out Jake Reynolds and tell her what he said. He sees us pointing and blows me a kiss.

"He is so hot," Parker whispers to me.

"I know!"

"I can hear you," Will says, shaking his head and grinning.

"But you're eight times cuter than he is," Parker says to Will.

"Only eight times?" he replies. "I'm at least ten times—"

"Do you guys need me to drive? Did you drink?" I interrupt. I wasn't watching to see if they drank.

"We don't drink," Will replies, dragging a hand up and down Parker's arm.

"I'm starving," she says.

"I want a Monster burger," he whines to her.

"You are such a baby." She gets up on tiptoes and kisses his lips. "We'll get you your burger."

"You guys are making me ill," I say.

Will squeezes my shoulder and laughs. "You and Matt are just as bad."

I swat his elbow. "Let's go get Will's burger already."

• • •

I got home from Jiffy Burger after midnight.

Now it's two in the morning and my phone just rang, waking up Fritz, who's curled up in bed with me. Matt's calling for the first time all week. It's not like I expected him to call, considering you could buy a small island for what it costs to call international, but to call in the middle of the night?

I answer and hear music blaring in the background. I can feel the bass through the phone. He has to yell in order for me to hear.

"Are you having fun?" I ask.

"I'd be having a lot more fun if you were here." He sounds really tired or buzzed.

I hear a girl calling his name. Is that Andrea? The music is making my head throb.

I rub my eye. "Matt, I miss you." I don't want to be one of those girls who is totally dependent on her boyfriend, and I don't think I am, but it hurts so much to hear him at a party with girls.

"I miss you," I repeat. "And I don't want to keep you away from your friends, but I'm kind of freaking out that you're there partying with other girls."

He goes silent. Then the music begins to dim in the background. I think he's walking away from the noise. The phone line goes silent except for his breathing.

"Today," he says, "I went to this art gallery called Los Cabos. They have all these pieces made of amber…I bet you'd love it."

I pause. "Me too."

"I shouldn't have called you from a party. I'm sorry…I shouldn't even be at this party."

"I just worry that some other girl will hit on you or something."

He laughs. "And you don't think I worry about the same thing?"

I tell Matt about how that pervy guy Jake Reynolds hit on me at Jordan Woods's party and Matt starts laughing and yelling and screaming into the phone. Turns out that Jake Reynolds is some big football star.

"You have no right to be pissed at me," Matt says, chuckling. "I get hit on by some random girl in Cabo, but the number one pick in the NFL draft hit on you."

"Huh?"

"Never mind."

Matt and I are laughing together now. I'm not sure why we're laughing, but it feels good.

"The reason I called is 'cause I'm coming home early," he says. "The airline will change my ticket for the low cost of seventy-nine ninety-nine."

"Matt," I say, shaking my head. "You don't need to do that."

"But I do. All I've thought about since I got here is you."

I drag my fingers through Fritz's fur. "Eighty dollars is a lot of money."

"Money's just money."

I'm smiling.

He goes on, "I'll be home on Friday, okay? I'll call you then."

"Be careful."

"I will. I miss you."

We hang up. I let out a long breath and lie down on my pillow.

I remember this one time when I was little, Daddy and I were listening to a Beatles CD. He told me about how John Lennon had once said, "We're bigger than Jesus." And when I asked Daddy how John Lennon could say something so bad, he cleared his throat and said, "Well, it was kinda true at that time. The Beatles were more popular than Jesus."

For the first time ever, I'm beginning to feel like something—someone—is more important than anything.

giving

How is Emily?

That's what Jacob's text reads.

I'd been clutching my phone, waiting for Matt to call. I jumped when it beeped.

What do I write back to Jacob? That I have no idea? That she probably never wants to talk to me again?

I'm glad he's thinking about her, even after she dumped him with no explanation. I don't know what I'd do if Matt stopped thinking of me. Jacob truly loves her. Would he have understood about the baby? Would he have agreed with Emily's choice? Would his love for her trump his morals and beliefs, whatever they are?

Does being in love mean forgetting everything you know? Or is it about folding that love into your life? Because right now, I have no idea how to balance that.

Love weighs a million pounds.

Matt calls me when he gets home at about noon. "I gotta crash for a few hours. I had to get up at like three a.m. for my flight."

"Sleep tight," I tell him. I wish I could curl up with him and take a nap too, but I doubt his parents would go for that. His dad would totally interrupt us every two minutes to ask for help mowing the grass.

"Want to hang out tonight?" he asks.

"And do what?"

"My mom bought me *The A-Team* DVD collection for my birthday," Matt says. "We could watch that."

"What's *The A-Team*?"

"You've never heard of it? That's insane!"

"What is it?"

I hear him yawning. "It's this show from the eighties where these military people get in trouble for a crime they didn't commit and they are always on the run from the Man. And Mr. T is in it!"

"Who is Mr. T?"

"This big black wrestler dude with a Mohawk. He wears tons of gold jewelry."

"You really want to spend our night watching a big black wrestler dude with a Mohawk?"

"I don't care what we do," he says with a laugh. "I know this bridge that goes over the interstate and hardly any cars ever drive on it. We can go watch the traffic if you want. And by watch the traffic, I mean make out."

I laugh. "Traffic fumes sound romantic."

"I'm a very romantic guy."

"Hey, listen…"

"Yeah?"

"My parents are in the middle of the Atlantic Ocean right now. On a cruise."

"Oh yeah?"

"That means they're out of town tonight…"

He pauses. "Mine are *in* town tonight."

I laugh. "Want to come over?" I ask with a shaky voice.

"Depends. Are you making me dinner?"

I grin. "You bring the dinner."

* * *

I now have Parker's number programmed in my cell. She squealed when I called.

"Of course I want to go shopping!"

I had only been planning to get some new clothes for college, and new sheets and a comforter for the twin bed in my dorm room, but now she's leading me through the Green Hills mall on a mission to Victoria's Secret.

"I don't need underwear," I say. This is a complete lie, but whatever.

"Kate, you cannot go shopping with me and skip the underwear portion of the trip. It's like refusing to sing "Take Me out to the Ball Game" at a ballgame. It's not happening."

"You owe me."

She grins mischievously. "*Au contraire*. I think you'll owe me after we get done in here."

I navigate past stands holding skimpy lacy panties and racks wielding barely-there bras. I avoid looking at the lingerie. Lotions and bubble bath lure me over to a shelf. I pop the caps open and start smelling lavenders, vanillas, and sea salts.

Parker snatches Love Spell out from under my nose. "We're not here for lotion. We're here to revamp your underwear collection."

"Revamp my underwear collection."

She nods, scanning the room as if planning a siege. "I think you need a stable of cotton panties and bras, all that can be swapped out but will still match."

"A stable of panties," I mutter.

"You need lots of panties with patterns so you can wear them with different bras," she says, marching over to where colorful underwear stretch across a table. She holds up a pair to my crotch, as if to measure.

I smack her hand away and glance around.

"Don't be silly," she says, holding the panties to my crotch again. "You're not the first person to ever wear underwear, you know."

I feel my face growing hot. "But what if someone sees?"

She lifts a shoulder. "If someone sees, that means they're here shopping for panties too. Or buying panties for their girlfriends."

"Guys buy panties for their girlfriends?" I ask, imagining Matt in here trying to pick out something.

Parker ignores my question. "You also need a couple of lacy bras and matching panties."

"I don't need those kind," I say quietly, even though that's exactly what I need.

She raises her eyebrows. "How far have you and Matt gone, anyway?" She's practically running in place, she's so excited.

I bite my lip. Part of me is ashamed to admit I've sinned, especially since I've questioned people in the past. But I'm proud of Matt and I'm falling for him and I want to tell Parker all about him. How he loves his parents, how he puts the doors back on his Jeep for me, how he sneaks out late at night to make music for me.

"We've taken our shirts off together," I admit, examining a pair of boy shorts.

"And?"

"And…it was nice."

Parker smiles and leads me to a rack of lacy bras. "You need one of these black ones for sure. Will loves mine."

My face heats up, but I smile back at her. I ask, "What other colors does Will like?"

An hour later, and each holding a pink bag, we make our way to the food court, jabbering about anything and everything. She tells me about how her dad just started dating again and that it's kinda weird but she's happy for him. We see a poster for a new animated film about a hippo who wants to perform on Broadway and she says her favorite Disney movie is *Finding Nemo* and I say mine is *Beauty and the Beast*.

We each buy pasta, some garlic bread, and a Diet Coke, and grab a table in the middle of the food court, where sun shines through the windows above. I wipe a napkin across the sticky table.

Parker takes a dainty bite of garlic bread. The cheese stretches out into a long, floppy string and she pushes it into her mouth. "So is Matt a good kisser?" she asks, chewing.

"Yeah…"

"What?" She sips her Coke through a straw.

"A couple weeks ago? His dad walked in on us making out."

Her eyes open wide. "Holy mortifying. What did you do?"

"Matt took me home and we made out in my driveway instead."

She laughs and takes another small bite. She never eats much. "Will and I usually hook up in his basement, but his brothers are always accidentally interrupting us. Or his mom asks him to do some chore. Like, last Saturday? We thought we were home alone, so we were kissing and he took my shirt off, and then his mom hollered down the steps for him to come upstairs and hang her new curtains."

I feel my face going rosy, but I'm laughing along with her. I like talking to her. I like hearing about her experiences. But it makes me feel ashamed that Emily had tried to talk to me about this stuff and I never wanted to hear it because I thought it was wrong. It *is* wrong, but at the same time, everything about

Matt feels good and I want to talk about him with Parker. It couldn't have been easy for Emily. I want to tell her I'm starting to understand.

"And then this one time," Parker whispers, looking from Häagen-Dazs to the Greek Palace, "Will's hand was, you know—" She points down and I suck on my lower lip, waiting to hear what comes next. "And his brother, Rory—he's gonna be a freshman at Hundred Oaks this fall—walked in on us and then walked right back out."

"That sounds really awkward."

Her face scrunches up in embarrassment. "That was the first time we'd done that too."

I'm really getting into the girl talk, and I feel like I can trust her. "I haven't done that yet," I whisper.

"I had only done it one other time before Will."

I raise an eyebrow. "With who…?"

She sips her drink and plucks a bite of bread and pops it into her mouth. She looks around the food court, chewing. "Remember Coach Hoffman?"

I lean back in my chair, shocked. Last spring, Jacob told Emily and me that Parker had gotten caught kissing the coach of the school baseball team. We heard she seduced him. "The rumors were true?"

"It was a mistake…I mean, at the time I thought he was right for me, but he wasn't."

"He left, right? He moved away?"

Her eyes glaze over. "Yeah."

"You okay?" I ask quietly.

"I'm fine. It's just…he left and I haven't heard from him since. And I don't care that much because I'm really falling in love with Will. It just sucks I didn't mean enough to Brian—I mean, Coach Hoffman, for him to check on me after he left."

"That sucks." I sip my drink. "So you're in love with Will? Have you told him?"

"Not yet…But I will soon."

"He'll say it back." I want to reach out and touch her hand, but instead I cradle my paper cup.

"Even if he doesn't say it back, I still love him and want him to know."

"I'm sure he loves you too."

Parker looks up at me and chews more slowly. She swallows. "Thanks."

Her phone beeps and she checks the screen. She shakes her head as she types. "It's Drew. He knows I'm at the mall and he wants me to come see this pair of jeans he likes at Nordstrom."

"Oh," I say, my voice soft. Does she want to leave already?

Then Drew appears at our table and sits down next to Parker. He takes a bite of her pasta and sips her drink, and ignores me.

"Can we check out the pants I want?"

"You in?" Parker asks me.

"It's okay—I should go anyway." I grab my purse and Victoria's Secret bag and push my chair away from the table.

"Come with us!" Parker says. She nudges Drew, and he lifts a shoulder.

I find myself following them past Gap, Banana Republic, and the yummy Lindt chocolate store, and while I try to ignore their conversation, I distinctly hear Parker telling him, "She's my friend. Would you drop it?"

At Nordstrom, Parker stands outside the guys' dressing room while Drew tries on the black jeans he just has to have. Neckties lay fanned across a display table, like a rainbow. I drag my fingers across the silk. Daddy wears a tie every day to work, and when he's not working, he's usually in a button-down shirt. Does Matt even own a tie?

I smile to myself because I never want to see Matt wearing a tie. I like him the way he is, with his ratty T-shirts and tanks and weathered polos. I like that he knows his style.

Drew struts out of the dressing room in the black jeans, and well, they look terrible with the gray polo he's wearing. Parker is looking at the jeans and shaking her head, but then I get an idea. I head over to the girls' juniors section, where I find an extra-large red and black plaid shirt with ¾ length sleeves, and carry it back to the dressing room.

"Drew, try this on," I tell him, passing the shirt over the top of the door. "Roll up the sleeves."

"This is so not me," he replies, but when he comes out, he's beaming. The outfit really works. "Maybe I should wear girls' clothes more often," he jokes, checking himself out in the mirror.

"Kate's really artistic," Parker tells him.

"Oh yeah?" He flashes me a brief smile.

"Let me go find some shoes to match," I tell them, grinning to myself.

• • •

Matt showed up at my front door with a pizza. He remembered that I love pepperoni and mushrooms!

I kiss his cheek four times and whisper how much I missed him.

"I missed you too," he says, focusing on my eyes. He pecks my lips. "Sorry I'm late," he says, squeezing past me into the foyer. "Lacey's driving me nuts. She thinks I'm her personal chauffeur."

"Where's Jeremiah?" I ask, taking the six-pack of Coke from his hands.

He pauses to think and takes a breath. "Out with some girl named Erin?"

After a quick tour of the downstairs of my house (Matt is both excited and freaked out by all of Daddy's antique shotguns and animal heads. I fear his heart now belongs to Vincent Moose), we settle on the living room floor to eat by tea lights. Parker let me borrow her short yellow sundress, so Indian style is a no-go. I have to sit with my back up against the couch with my feet out in front of me. Matt scans my legs and bites into his pizza, smiling.

"What?" I ask, sipping Coke.

"Whenever we're not at camp, you wear these clothes that drive me nuts."

I smile at him. Candlelight flickers across his face. I pull my foot up next to us. "Look, I finally put on the fairy tattoo you won on our first date."

He grins, gently running a finger across the tattoo on my ankle. Tingles rush up my leg. "Remember how you kissed me first?"

"I do." I grin back at him.

"You scandalized me."

I smack his arm. "I did not. You loved it."

We dig into our pizza again until he asks what I did today.

"Went to the mall with Parker."

"Did you buy anything?"

"Maybe," I say, barely able to contain my smile. He raises his eyebrows.

I go on, "Her friend, Drew, showed up and we helped him pick out some clothes. And when I got home I had some ideas for more outfits " I reach up onto the couch and pull my sketchbook into my lap.

Fear rushes through me. I clutch my book to my chest. I've never shown anyone my sketchbook, and just now, it was so easy to reach behind me and grab it and open it in front of him.

How serious are we?

"Can I see what you drew?" he asks quietly.

Pulling a deep breath, I thumb through my sketchbook until I get to the picture of Drew wearing the outfit I picked out. I show the drawing to Matt, who takes another bite of pizza and talks as he chews.

"He's a decent-looking guy."

"He's gay."

"Then I'm glad you had a nice afternoon shopping with him," Matt says with a laugh.

I close my book and move to set it aside, but he speaks again. "Can I look at your other sketches? I'll wash my hands first. Promise."

"It's okay," I say, passing him the book, even though I'd rather lock it up in a safe. "You don't have to worry about getting it dirty." But he gets up and washes his hands anyway, and then flops back down on the rug with me. He opens my book carefully to the first page. He doesn't move an inch as he studies a sketch of himself. Is he breathing?

Then his finger turns the page, and a minute later, to the next.

"They're of me," he says, his voice full of awe. He leans down and presses his lips to my forehead, and then goes back to my drawings, looking at each one carefully.

When he shuts the book, I curl up against his side, slightly lift his shirt and touch his abs. He shifts under my hand, then pulls me onto his lap, so I'm straddling him. The rug digs into my knees. Beneath my dress he sets his hands on my waist, rubbing his thumbs over my hipbones. His blue eyes stare into mine. Every noise—the entire world, seems to silence around us.

Finally he breaks it. "How about a tour of the rest of your house?"

"Like, my room?"

"Especially your room," he growls playfully. I smack his arm and he smacks me back, and then he's up on his feet and darting toward the staircase with me chasing after him. Our laughter rings through the house. I dart up the stairs as he checks doors on the second floor.

"Is this Kate's room?" he asks, opening a linen closet. "Are you like Harry Potter? Do you live in a cupboard?"

I pinch his elbow. "I sleep on a shelf with the Q-tips."

He moves on to my parents' room, where a pair of Daddy's dress pants lay on the chest. "Are you cheating on me?" he jokes, strutting into the room.

"Get out of here," I say, pulling him into the hallway.

"Where are you hiding this guy who wears the fancy pants?"

"I'm hiding him in here." I walk backward to my room, pulling Matt by an arm. His face goes serious when I push the door open with my butt.

Silently, he spends a lot of time looking around my room. I'm so glad I got rid of my kiddy bedspread for the soft white duvet and matching pillowcases. I light a few candles while he studies each of my paintings and looks at all of my books, even the ones from middle school, and when he finds the pile of pictures of me and Emily, the photos I took off the wall, he turns each frame over one by one. He laughs silently at the picture of us sitting together in the Forrest Sanctuary dunking booth at Vacation Bible School.

"Who's this?" he asks, waving the frame. "Your friend?"

Not tonight. I can't tell him tonight. I take a deep breath, holding out a hand. "Matt. Please."

Then he's moving across the room toward me, sidestepping my laundry basket, a blazing look on his face, and then we're kissing and falling backward onto my bed. But this isn't like at his house or on the parachute at camp. This is completely unhindered. I can't even think as he lifts my dress up and over my head—static from my hair catching the fabric, leaving me in the lacy pink bra and panties I bought today. His eyes slowly scan my body and his breath catches in his throat.

He tosses his T-shirt and khaki shorts onto the rug, and lies on top of me, his fingers digging in my hair. Our feet twist together. His lips pepper my neck and I can't breathe. I try to focus on the ceiling fan, going round and round and round.

"Matt, Matt," I mumble, delirious.

He pulls away. His biceps strain as he holds himself above me. "Yeah?"

"Slow."

We kiss and kiss, pressing against each other until I can't take it anymore. I ignore the guilt. It's not strong enough to make me stop. I need relief. My body feels like a bomb. It's like he senses it, because his hand heads south and he focuses on my face and asks if it's okay and I say yes, even though I shouldn't let him touch me there.

I clench my eyes shut. Clutch the duvet. He gently kisses me through my underwear, and then his fingers move below until tingles rush through my body, leaving me out of breath. Relieved. Then I tug his boxers off and move my hand up and down until he comes. He breathes in and out, panting, his eyes shut tightly, and pulls me up against him.

"Wow," he says, smiling. Just that one word makes me feel so many things. I feel proud, I feel remorse, I feel tingly all over, I feel responsibility. I feel loved.

I breathe.

"What time do you need to leave?" I ask quietly, playing with his hair.

"I don't have a curfew. I'll call my parents later and tell them I'm sleeping at the DTK house...Is it okay for me to stay?"

I answer him with a long kiss that leaves us both breathless again.

We relax against each other, cuddling, and he begins tracing the freckles on my arms. He touches everywhere, as if worshipping my body.

"What happened here?" he asks, rubbing a thumb over the purplish bruise on my knee.

"Tripped on a rock in the driveway. I fell."

He drags a finger up and down my surgical scar. He talks against my lips, kissing me. "Clumsy."

"Look away, I'm hideous," I joke.

"Far from it. I'm the hideous one." He chuckles, but I can hear the emotion in his voice. Does he really believe that?

He dips a hand between my legs again and guilt courses through me. I clutch at the hair at the nape of his neck, and even though my parents aren't home, I try not to make noise.

"Why would you think you're hideous?" I whisper.

He kisses my chin. "It's not important."

"Yes, it is. Tell me." I trace the soft hair on his lower stomach and wait for an answer.

"Tom's a lot taller than me, and he got into a better school… Sarah, um, liked him more…"

"The guy who was your best friend?"

"Yeah."

He rolls over to focus on the ceiling, where candlelight dances. I let him think. He doesn't say anything, so I slowly begin kissing his neck, and that turns into us making out again.

"Don't think about Tom and Sarah anymore, okay?" I whisper. "I'm here."

He tucks my head under his chin. And we fall asleep in each other's arms.

• • •

"What is going on?"

I sit up straight. Emily's here. Standing in the doorway. Staring at me.

I grab my duvet up to my chest, to cover myself. I'm in only my bra and panties. She looks from the discarded clothes littering the rug to Matt, who lifts himself into a sitting position and rubs his eyes, then secures the sheet around his waist.

"Hi—" I begin, but Emily starts yelling.

"You hypocrite!" she cries.

I clutch my duvet tighter. My breathing races.

"I'm Matt," he says, stretching a hand out to her. When she doesn't take it, he ruffles his hair and reaches down to pick his boxers up off the floor. He doesn't seem all that concerned he's naked in front of someone he's never met.

"You've been giving me such shit for months," Emily exclaims, "And you're sleeping with some random guy—"

"I'm not random," he says, and I blurt, "We're not sleeping together."

"But it's okay for you to fool around but I can't? Jacob and I were in love and you were such a bitch anytime you found out we did something—"

She's right. I shouldn't have let him touch me. He shouldn't have spent the night.

"Emily," I try to interrupt.

"You are such a hypocrite. I can't believe I wasted my time coming over here."

I'm trembling. "Why did you come over?"

She looks at the ceiling, shaking her head. Tears pool, filling her lower lids. "I felt bad for how I treated you when you came by. I figured you were off work this weekend…I wanted to apologize… and maybe talk about everything. I knocked and rang the doorbell and you didn't answer. I noticed a strange Jeep was here…I got scared. I found the spare key." She glances at Matt, who's now trying to wrangle himself into his underwear beneath the comforter.

"This is my boyfriend, Matt," I mumble.

Her eyebrows furrow and lines zip across her forehead. "You didn't tell me about him…"

"Not y–"

"I was your best friend." She turns and slams my bedroom door.

I cover my eyes, letting the duvet fall to my waist. I let out a low cry.

"Hey, hey," Matt whispers. "What's wrong? What was that all about?" He tries to hug me but I shrug him away and pick my duvet back up, so he can't see my body. He shouldn't see any part of me. We're not married. What was I thinking? We didn't have sex, but last night was a sin.

We woke up in the middle of the night and started all over again. I touched him, and when I think about how good it felt when his hands explored my skin, I shudder. When he touched me with his mouth, my entire body relaxed, and I felt sensations I'd never felt before.

Tears begin to drip down my cheeks.

"Kate," he says gently.

"Please go," I say, wiping my face on my duvet.

He scoots closer. "No. Tell me what's wrong. Why didn't you tell your best friend about me?"

"She's not my best friend anymore."

"What happened?"

"I can't do this. Please, just go."

"What do you mean, go?"

"We can't be together."

"No—"

I stand up, pulling the sheet around me.

"Kate please."

"Just go! I can't do this. Date you, I mean." I can't think straight when I'm with him.

"Are we breaking up?" His voice shakes.

"Yes," I mumble, as new tears coat my face.

He bends down and picks up his T-shirt to slip it over his head. His face contorts in pain. He bites his lips together and his eyes gloss over. "Please don't—"

I go into the bathroom, still wearing the sheet around me like a beach towel, locking the door, sitting down on the toilet. He bangs on the door and says my name. Over and over. Fritz starts barking. I lean onto my knees and count the tiny sky blue tiles because it's the only thing I know to do.

After I don't know how long, the knocking ends.

His voice goes away.

When I come out of the bathroom, I pull on a bathrobe and find Fritz moving in circles. I discover a note written in Matt's shaky cursive, lying on my bed.

I care about you more than anything. What did I do wrong? Please, let's not do this.

I don't completely understand what that last line means. But it doesn't matter.

God tested my faith, and I failed.

something i can never draw
what happened on april 27

The sun was rising when I picked Emily up at her house.

She told her mom she was riding with me to school, but really we drove to the women's center in Nashville. I stopped at a Walgreens, to buy all of her favorite candies. Sour Patch Kids, Twizzlers, Jolly Ranchers.

She clutched the arm rest and her lower lip trembled.

I kept reaching over to squeeze her hand.

I turned on the classical radio station for her.

I listened to her sniffle. Watched the tears fall from her eyes.

I handed her Kleenex after Kleenex.

At the clinic, a nurse escorted us into an exam room, and I helped Emily take her clothes off and slip on a flimsy paper robe. I folded her shirt, bra, underwear, and jeans into a pile. I passed her more Kleenex and tried to ignore the smell. It was probably all in my mind but I felt like chemicals were burning the inside of my nose.

A woman came in and asked Emily if she was sure, if she had explored all her options.

"Did you think deeply about this? Did you discuss it with the father?"

"Yes," Emily lied.

I don't think Emily's responses would've changed anything, but the counselor had to ask the questions. I never stopped holding Emily's hand except for when the doctor made me. I couldn't stop closing my eyes.

I kept thinking of my butterfly paintings, how colors drip from the wings.

The doctor gave Emily a sedative and she finally loosened up. The tears dried up somewhat.

It was over in ten minutes.

I can't forget.

My weekend just got worse.

"Let's go over group assignments for this week," Megan says. "Eric, you've got the all-boys group. Ian, your partner is Parker. Will, you're with Carlie. Andrea is with Brad. Matt, you're with Kate."

I glance up. He looks hurt and pissed.

He must've called a hundred times since yesterday, and he wrote me ten emails, repeating over and over how much he cares for me, wanting to know what he did wrong, telling me he misses me already. On one voicemail he said, "Is this 'cause I haven't taken you to Just Tacos yet? Because we can fix that right now." He laughed softly into the phone and quietly said, "Seriously, though? I want to fix whatever went wrong between us. Can we talk? You're the most important thing, um…" He cleared his throat. Stayed silent. "Please call me back."

I saved the voicemail and started crying all over again.

I barely pay attention during the staff meeting. Everyone decides to grill hot dogs for dinner, but I'm not hungry. I excuse myself and haul my sleeping bag and suitcase over to Bluebird in Birdland. There, I turn out the lights, curl up in bed, and try not to think, even though the sun hasn't completely set. I can't even cry because I'm so confused and upset and my mind is whirring thoughts around like the box fan.

I'm a hypocrite.

I can't imagine living without Matt.

I couldn't imagine living without Emily, either, but I've survived the past two months.

It's nearly midnight when I hear the knock on the door. Is it him? I hope it is, but I hope it isn't.

"Yeah?" I call out with a faint voice.

"Can I stay with you tonight?" It's Parker.

I climb out of the rickety bed and pad to the screen door. A humid mist hangs around the porch light. She studies my face, which is probably swollen and covered in red blotches. I let her in, and she unrolls her sleeping bag across the bed next to mine.

"Where's Will?"

"Sleeping in Dogwood with everybody else." She fluffs her pillow and kicks off her flip-flops.

"Wouldn't you rather be with him?"

The corner of her mouth lifts. "I always want to be with him. But I thought we could hang out tonight."

"Why?"

"I'm worried about you. Will told me that Matt said y'all broke up."

I chew on my lip and crawl on top of my sleeping bag. Parker flips the light off and we lie down. Matt is the last thing I want to talk about.

"What are you majoring in at college?" I ask, watching a shadow dance on the ceiling.

Her bed creaks as she gets comfy. "Biology. I want to become a vet, I think...You?"

"I dunno." I play with the zipper on my sleeping bag. The fan blows warm air across my face. "I've been thinking of design. Or something."

"That sounds good. You've got the artistic skills."

My heart swells and I nearly reach to squeeze her hand. "Thank you," I whisper.

I listen to the crickets and try not to think about anything important. I always think about Matt when I have nothing to distract me. Tomorrow is Chicken O' Rings Day. It's so hot in here, I could go creek stomping right now, just to cool off. If I were the camp director, I'd get new mattresses for the cabins.

"What happened, Kate? Everything seemed to be going great for you and Matt. Did he do something wrong?"

"Nah...but I did."

She pauses. "He wants to work things out with you."

"I can't think about it right now, okay?"

"Okay." She rolls over to face the wall.

I fold my hands behind my head and bite down on my tongue to distract myself from the pain in my heart.

"Parker?" I say into the dark.

"Hmm?"

"What do you think of evolution? Do you believe in God?"

She goes silent for a bit. "That's a pretty personal question…"

I bite into my lip.

She adds, "I do believe in God, but my relationship with him is private…"

"Oh."

"It's nothing against you…I just don't like to talk about it anymore…with anybody. I don't even talk about it with my parents anymore. Or with Will."

I smile slowly. "Thanks for telling me that."

"I think that religion is a personal thing. It's hard for me to share."

Matt prays and wears a cross but still goes to parties. He hangs out with people who drink. He worships God but does it in his own way. Just like Parker. That isn't to say that what Brother Michael and Brother John preach at church is wrong, but what if it's different for different people?

I've wondered if it's okay to worship somewhere in the middle.

But can I fit these people who worship in the middle into my life?

Can I hang out with people who don't believe in God at all? It's not like they're that much different from me, really.

That's when I hear the noise. Another knock on the door.

"Park?" I hear Will say. "You okay?"

She sits up and a smile flits across her face. She goes to the door, where she puts a hand up to the screen and he traces her fingers as they talk quietly. I can hear her explaining that I don't need any guys hanging around tonight upsetting me, and I say a quick prayer, thanking Him for her. The friend who became a friend when I wasn't paying attention.

And like that night Matt slept on the porch, Will drags a bed through the door and drops it onto the deck with a thud. Then he comes back in and drags another bed through the door.

Parker asks, "Why do you need two beds?"

"One's for Matt. His idea, not mine."

I suck in a deep breath.

Matt doesn't speak, but he's out there. Soon everyone is settled in their beds, and all I can hear are crickets and frogs and other animals.

Parker speaks again. "I love you, Will."

"Love you too," he replies.

She must've told him this weekend. Or did he tell her first?

My stomach leaps into my throat. I want to hear Matt say those words so bad. I wish God would tell me what to do. If I should be with Matt or if I made a big mistake when I sinned.

Why would God give me Matt, someone who makes me feel so good, only to take him away? Would God really do something that selfish and mean to me?

I scrunch my pillow under my head, and the memory of our first kiss plays over and over in my mind.

When Matt speaks to me, it's not to tell me he loves me, but somehow it's even better.

"Kate, I'm here."

• • •

On Monday morning before the new group of campers arrive, I'm out jogging laps around the big field under a humid sunny sky when Brad runs up next to me.

"I'm sorry," he says.

"I don't want to talk about Matt," I reply.

"No." Brad shakes his head and even though we're running, he snaps his eyes shut. "I did something stupid…"

Honestly, right now, I don't care about anything except that I'm not dating Matt anymore, but the pull to be a good friend is greater. "What'd you do?"

"Yesterday morning I was down at the lake, fishing for my breakfast, and the guy who mows the grass saw me. He knows I was here on a weekend. He told on me to Megan. I told her that you and I were here together—"

"I might get fired!"

"You won't, you won't," he stutters. "I told her it was all my idea. I told her you wanted to learn to fish better, so I agreed to meet you here early to practice—"

"I can't believe you!" I touch my forehead. "You could have asked first—"

"I didn't have time—she put me on the spot and I'm telling you now."

"Did she fire you?"

"Not yet." He bites into his upper lip.

"You used me…" I fold my arms across my stomach.

That's when Megan appears on the trail. She blows her whistle, shouts, "Kate!" and beckons me toward her cabin.

I wipe the sweat off my forehead with my T-shirt and climb the Great Oak steps, then pull the screen door open and sit beside Megan's desk. She settles in her chair and twirls her whistle, regarding me.

I fold my hands in my lap.

"Do you want to tell me why you were here yesterday morning before camp started?"

I touch my chest. "Me?"

"Yes, you."

"I'm sorry. Eric had suggested I get some pointers on fishing," I lie. "Because I'm not very good at it—"

"Eric suggested this?" she asks, touching her lips. She looks at the wall, thinking.

"Yes," I lie again. Eric gives so much unsolicited advice, I'm sure he'd say he suggested the extra training if asked. Even though Brad broke the rules, I don't want him to have to go live with his drunk father. "I asked Brad to give me some extra training. I thought it would be okay since it was just a few hours before camp started and you made me get that extra help in campfires from Eric that time—"

She holds up a hand. "Okay, okay."

Am I about to get fired?

She fluffs her curly hair and stares me down. "You knew the rules."

"I apologize," I say with a strong voice. We have three weeks left. If Brad were to get fired, he would miss out on a thousand bucks. What if he had to live with his dad again? What if his dad hurt him bad?

Sometimes it's okay to do the wrong thing if you're helping someone, I guess. But I hate lying.

"It won't happen again," I say.

She twirls her whistle and takes a deep breath. "Because Eric had suggested the training, I'll let this go with a warning on your written record. But if you make any other mistakes this summer, I'm afraid I'll have to tell the regional conference to let you go. I won't risk my job or my future on employees who disregard everything I say."

My eyes burn. I've worked hard this summer. Hard. And it's not like she tells me I'm doing a good job very often. What if my church finds out Megan thinks I'm a bad employee? My parents?

With one lie, I let Brad ruin all my hard work. And even though I understand why he did it, he threw me under the bus.

I tell Megan, "Understood."

I rush out of Great Oak, storm past Brad into the bathhouse, and stare in the mirror as the tears streak my face. The paper towels feel like sandpaper against my skin.

Carlie comes in to use the bathroom and catches me wiping my cheeks at the sink. Red circles ring my eyes. She washes her hands, and in the mirror, I watch as she gives me a sympathetic look.

"I'm sorry about Matt," she whispers, stealing a glance over her shoulder.

I blow my nose. "Thanks. Me too."

Before she pushes the screen door open, Carlie says, "I know how much he cares about you."

I stay in the bathhouse until it's time for campers to arrive. When I push the screen door open, letting it slam behind me, I find Ian and Carlie talking quietly. He gives me a long hug and says, "I'm here if you want to talk."

As we walk together to the welcome pavilion, I peek at them out of the corner of my eye. They waited for me? They are better friends with Andrea than with me, but staying behind to make sure I'm okay is one of the nicest things anyone's ever done for me.

After the kids have checked in, Matt and I lead our group of eight-year-olds along the trails back to the Bluebird cabins.

It seems that all of the little girls packed way too much. It's like they were planning to be away from home for months, because Matt has tons of bags draped over his arms and shoulders. I can't help but smile at him carrying a Hello Kitty purse.

"Why did y'all bring so much stuff?" yells Charles, a little boy. I can already tell he'll be a handful.

"Hey, hey," Matt says to Charles. "You never say things like that to a lady. The reason they have so much stuff is so they have all the outfits they need to look beautiful every day."

"Awww," says Isabella, a girl with blond curls.

On the inside, I'm saying awww too. On the inside, it's killing me that I broke things off with him. But what else am I supposed to do? I can't control myself when he's around.

"Are you okay?" Matt asks me as he lugs all the bags and purses up the rickety wooden steps to my cabin.

I look over at him and nod, telling myself not to cry again.

Once the kids have unpacked their stuff, we sit Indian style on Matt's porch and play the animal introduction game.

"I'm Spider Scott," says a wiry boy.

"I'm Lizard Leslie," says a girl, chewing gum.

"I'm Miniature Poodle Matt."

The kids roar with laughter. I look into his questioning eyes. I pick at my thumbnail, ripping my cuticle, wishing I didn't have to be so close to him this week. Miniature Poodle Matt reminds me of our first kiss. It reminds me of how he said I saved him.

"I'm King Crab Kate," I say, and he glances away.

He says, "After we go over camp rules, who wants to play my special new dodgeball game?"

The kids start screaming, "Me! Me!"

I pull my knees to my chest. On the inside, I'm screaming "Me!" too.

At lunch, Brad scoots a chair up next to me. "You okay? Did you get in trouble?"

I deliberately turn to face him. "Written warning."

He blows air out, nodding. "Thank you. Seriously." His eyes dart around.

"Did you get a written warning?"

His mouth falls open, then he closes it. He shakes his head.

"What if I ever want a job referral?! I can't believe this," I say through gritted teeth.

"You're a good friend."

"I'm not sure why you care," I hiss. "Isn't your big plan to blow out of Tennessee in a couple weeks? You didn't want any connections, right? So why would hurting a friend like me matter?"

"I'm sorry," he mumbles. He gulps down some lemonade, peeking at me out of the corner of his eye.

"I'm sorry too." I stand, pick up my tray, and move to sit with another group of campers. I grab a seat next to a little redheaded girl who immediately asks if I love Barbies.

"Of course," I reply with a smile. "I also like American Girl. You?"

"Yes!" She pops a chicken o' ring in her mouth and chews with her mouth open.

A few tables away, Matt's talking with Andrea. She's up to her same old antics, touching his arms and laughing at everything he says. He smiles back at her, but it's a blank smile. It's not the smile I've seen so many times. His expression is dark and sad.

I can understand how Emily got pregnant. When I'm with Matt, I stop thinking about everything but him. It's just him, him, him, and me. It's only about us. It must have been the same way between Emily and Jacob.

I've been told my whole life that our God is a jealous God and that he comes first. I've done everything He's ever told me to do up until the past few months. And while following God always felt right, so did helping Emily. It felt right to help her, just like it feels right when I'm kissing Matt or cuddling with Matt or sharing myself with Matt. It felt right to help Brad too, but look at what happened. He betrayed me.

We're only on the Earth for a tiny amount of time. God says we're supposed to love our neighbors. But then my preachers at church tell me we're only supposed to fall in love with other Christians.

And it's all so confusing.

I want to tell Emily that I understand why she did what she

did with Jacob. I may never understand why she decided to get an abortion, but now I know what it's like to get swept up in love.

But if I were to try to talk to Emily, would she call me a hypocrite and never want to see me again? Because I wouldn't blame her.

I play with my chicken o' rings. I poke my green beans with a fork.

I look up at Matt, watching him talk quietly with Andrea, and I want to tell him I love him. But I'm still scared of being with him because my body does what it wants—my hands touch him all over and my lips roam everywhere.

Deep inside, I feel God's love in my heart, and I know I shouldn't be with Matt until I can control myself. But I'm not sure I'll ever be able to do that. Is it healthy to have a love like that anyway? A love where you throw aside all caution and dive right in?

I love him.

But I can't be with him.

I pick up my tray and approach Matt. Andrea gives me her patented death glare, and he stares out the window.

I scrape my green beans onto his tray. He looks up at me, scratching his neck, his eyes clouded with pain and confusion. I return my tray to the dishwashing window and head outside into the sun to think.

• • •

After the Thursday Night Dance, we take the campers to the Woodsong Chapel for devotion.

"Tonight we're doing something special," Megan says. "We don't do this every week, but I just felt like we should tonight. If you have something you can't let go of or can't forget about, write it down on the piece of paper I handed you and throw it in the fire. You can also pray for someone using this slip of paper. It's just between you and God."

I crinkle the paper between my fingers and thumb. I want God to take it all out of my hands and show me what to do already.

In front of me, the fire roars. A movement stirs out of the corner of my eye and I turn to see Matt strutting down the path toward the flames. He stands there a moment before wadding up his paper and chucking it into the fire. Then he kneels at the altar, shuts his eyes, and prays. His cross charm swings back and forth.

I write on my sheet of paper, *Please show me the truth.*

No one else has approached the fire yet except for Matt. I follow the same path he took and let my paper float into the flames. I watch it burn into nothing and listen to it crackle. I kneel at the altar and clear my head, focusing on the crickets chirping and the noises of other bugs. Listen to the sound of water running into the creek down by the lake. Smell the pine and cedar. Sometimes nature is the closest thing to God.

I raise my head and find Matt still bowing with his eyes closed. He scratches his ear. The movement reminds me of how fragile he is—that he put himself back out there after Sarah because of me. Wind whips through the fire. I pull myself to my feet. I kneel next to him and grasp his hands.

"Hey," he says, peeking up at me.

"Hey."

I bite the inside of my cheek. We shut our eyes, and he gently rubs his thumbs over the backs of my hands. The leaves stop rustling. I can't hear any kids. I don't even hear the crackling of burning wood. It's just me and him.

"Tell me what happened with Emily," he whispers.

"It's bad," I reply. "I did a really bad, bad thing."

He squeezes my fingers. "You can let whatever it is go."

"I can't. It's so bad." I swallow a sob.

"You can tell me what happened and I'll never tell anybody. It's all you and me. Right here. Okay?"

Heat flushes my cheeks and my eyes sting, but his hands are wrapped around mine. Tonight I burned the words *please show me the truth*. As long as I've known Matt, he's worn the clothes he wants to wear, he's sung the songs he wants to sing. He's friends with whoever he wants to be friends with, including judgmental Kate Kelly. Me.

He's the truth.

"Emily got pregnant," I begin, glancing around to make sure no one else can hear me. The nearest campers are several feet away. Matt's gaze never leaves mine as I talk. "She decided to get an abortion, which is something I would never ever do and I can't understand how she could do that. But I agreed to help her anyway because she's my friend."

Matt rubs my wrist.

I keep going, "I drove her to the clinic and helped her get an abortion…I even loaned her money…" I sniffle and wipe a tear away. "I can't stop thinking about the baby. I drove her there. I paid for it. I helped, you know, to end a life…"

Matt tucks my hair behind my ear. "You know what I think?" he mumbles, and fear rushes through me because his eyes move away. "You're a good friend. I'm glad you were there with her."

"But I sinned. The baby…"

"You were there for Emily. You did something you didn't believe in because you're strong. And you care. God definitely forgives you."

"Are you just saying that?"

He chuckles lightly. "I wouldn't lie to the daughter of the killer of Vincent Moose."

I wipe my nose, sniffling and giggling. We grow quiet again. Past Matt, I watch as Ian and Carlie follow our lead, kneeling together at the altar. Ian catches my eye and smiles.

"Are they official now?" I whisper to Matt, who looks over his shoulder at them.

"They're getting there, I think…" He squeezes my hand, giving me a mischievous look. "No changing the subject on me. You should call Emily tonight."

"No cell reception," I reply.

He gives me a look. "There's a pay phone."

"I'm not ready." I can't believe I told Matt my biggest secret. My biggest shame. But I don't feel like I'm standing on the edge of a cliff anymore. I feel like I'm standing on the edge of a cliff with his arms around me.

"Is that what you wrote on your paper?" Matt asks, nodding toward the fire. "The abortion? The baby?"

I nod. "Sort of. What did you write about?"

He glances up at the cross nestled in the trees. "I care about you," he whispers. "And for the longest time, I didn't date anybody. I didn't fool around with anybody—"

"But on our first date, you said hooking up is different from dating and—"

"I haven't hooked up with anyone," he mumbles. "I never really got over Sarah. I never got over her until that day I saw you again."

I exhale, wipe my eye, and then clasp my hands together.

His mouth lifts into a smirk. "Do you believe in the sign? The rumor that God tells someone something every year at camp?"

"I want to believe in it…"

Matt goes on, "I think God gave you to me, and he gave me to you, so we can both move on."

"Move on to what?"

"To each other."

"To get over what happened to us?"

He grins a little and takes my hand again. Flames flicker on his face as he looks straight in my eyes. "So we can live. You can forgive yourself and I can trust again."

I bow my head, praying to Him to tell me this is true.

"This isn't the time or place for this," Megan says, appearing behind us, interrupting.

"Megan, give us a minute," Matt says in a strong voice. "This is important."

"Quickly, then," she says, and goes back to her seat on the log bench.

Matt is the rock. He makes me want to stand up for what I think is right. Maybe all that matters is that he's right for me, and I'm right for him.

"I care about you too," I whisper.

"I'm sorry about what happened with Emily that day. I shouldn't have stayed the night."

"I wanted you there."

He leans his forehead against mine. "Remember when I told you about how you saved me when we were younger?"

"Yes," I whisper.

He sighs deeply. "I didn't tell you the whole truth. Before I met you, I was so sad. I wanted to end it."

Is he saying what I think he's saying?

"But then I prayed here at camp. I hoped I would get the sign.

And then I met you. And you were so nice, and you liked my music, it gave me a reason to keep on for a while. Then Jenn was born and I felt like I had a reason to exist."

Tears are flowing down my cheeks now.

"I guess what I mean is," he says, "I'm here because of you."

sketch # 378
heaven

That night after the kids are asleep, I decide to take a walk out to the big field, to look at the stars. I sit down on the grass and sketch by moonlight, drawing the constellations. My paper looks like a game of Connect the Dots.

Ever since Matt asked where Heaven is, I've thought about it when I'm outside at night. Staring at the stars reminds me of how tiny I am, how I'm just one person. Being in the darkness makes me wonder if there really is a God and a Heaven and a Hell. Even though I can feel God inside me, a small part of me still worries that when I die, nothing will be there.

The Earth existed before I was born, and it will exist when I die. What if all that is me is just gone?

The thought of that makes me feel more alone than ever. I miss Emily. I miss Matt. I can't imagine spending my time on Earth without them. Because eternity is a long, lonely time.

I connect the dots of the Big Dipper. Then I hear the sound of feet crunching grass.

I look up to find him. I stare and he stares back, and then we're together.

I'm kissing him so fast and hard I get dizzy. Before I got my first real boyfriend, I thought about the kissing, but I never imagined the details—how his lips would be warm and wet and how his calloused fingers would feel rough yet soft against my skin. His hands settle in my hair, weaving through the strands. I hug him tight to me, trying to ignore the feelings building in my body. We kiss again and I can tell his body is buzzing like mine.

When I get back to Bluebird later that night, I finish connecting the dots of the constellations.

Is Matt right? Did God connect us together?

What will Matt say when I tell him I can't move this fast? I'm falling in love with him, but I can't let myself get into a situation where he and I could have sex. I just can't.

Will is grinning at me.

Today I'm using my break to work on an acrylic painting of the big field. And Will just showed up in the art pavilion out of nowhere.

"What's up?" I ask him, wiping the hair out of my face and going back to my painting.

He comes toward me, dipping his hands into his khaki shorts pockets. "I was just thinking about how if I didn't have Parker and you asked me to prom now, I definitely would say yes."

That statement hurts, but it's a good hurt. "Why?"

He lifts his shoulders. "You're more relaxed. And confident. You're pretty. I don't know if it's Parker's makeover that she's *always* bragging about—"

"I'm happy," I interrupt.

"That's probably it then, eh?"

I tuck my hair behind my ears. "I'm kinda glad you didn't say yes to prom, you know?"

"I get that. Matt's a good fit for you."

"Like Parker is for you."

"Damn straight."

I point at him with my paintbrush. "No cursing in my art pavilion."

He grins. "Yes, ma'am."

At lunch, I'm sitting with my campers, talking about how we'll make friendship bracelets later, when Matt leans over my shoulder.

"Boo," he says, making the girls laugh.

I smile at him, feeling the heat from his cheek warming mine. "What's up?"

He holds his tray above mine and scrapes his green beans onto my plate. "Don't you want them?"

"I know how much you love them," he replies with a smile.

"Thank you."

"No problem." He squeezes my shoulder and begins to walk away.

"I love you, Matt," I tell his back. Completely out of the blue. I cover my mouth. Wait for this eternity of a silence to end.

Slowly he turns around and leans down to quickly kiss my cheek in front of all the campers, who all start going "Wooo!"

"I love you too."

We smile at each other. He throws his backpack over a shoulder, puts his tray away, and heads toward the pool. I'm still beaming when I look up to find Megan staring my way, shaking her head. Whatever.

On Wednesday, Parker and I are sitting on the dock taking a break, dangling our feet in the lake. She's wearing a white bikini and I'm wearing a new navy blue one I just bought.

"I don't want camp to end," I tell her.

"You're not looking forward to college?"

"I am…but I'll miss you and Matt and Will."

"Even if we're at different colleges, Will and I will be in Nashville with you, and Matt's less than thirty minutes away, right?"

I nudge a bit of algae with my toe. "Yeah…"

"I can't wait for camp to be over. Will and I want to take a road trip to Florida the week before college."

"With his parents? Or your mom or dad?"

She steals a breath before answering. "Just us."

"Oh." I jiggle my feet, splashing. "Sounds fun. I kinda wish I could've gone with Matt to Cabo during the Fourth of July break. He told me about this art gallery he found there and now I really want to see it."

Parker narrows her eyes at me, her mouth arranged in a knowing smile. "You've changed a lot this summer."

I sit on my hands. "Is that a bad thing?"

"Not at all. I feel like you're getting to know yourself better, and that's a good thing."

"Oh."

She swings her feet back and forth. "I spent too long worrying about what other people think."

I dangle my feet in the water and splash.

"So you and Matt are back together?" she asks.

"I think so…but…"

"But?"

"Can I ask a question?"

"Yeah," she says slowly.

"I know you said that your relationship with God is private, but I'm wondering, um, if you're okay with the physical parts of your relationship with Will? Um, that you talked about that day at lunch at the mall?"

She stares across the lake. "It's kind of between me and Will. Like, any decisions we make, we make together."

The conversation with Daddy comes to mind. I can believe in God if I want to believe in God. Parker can do what she wants to do with Will. It's her decision. Just like I have choices to make when it comes to my boyfriend.

"The reason I broke things off with Matt before is because we went too far too fast."

Parker nods.

"I can't figure out how to balance how much I love him with what we do, um, in terms of making out or whatever. And I don't want to upset him by not doing stuff, um—"

"He's not worth it if that's all he's after—"

"No, no—it's that I want to do stuff with him because I love him. But I'm not ready."

Parker pauses. "I slept with Will last week."

I bite my thumb. "You were careful, uh, I hope? Um—"

"Yeah, we were."

"What was it like?"

"It was uncomfortable. But I felt so close to him." She folds her arms across her stomach. "I liked it more the second time."

"Did he like it?" I can't help but ask. "Was it his first time?"

She raises her eyebrows, then nods. "He can't wait for this weekend so we can try it again. Boys." She shakes her head, smiling, and bites her bottom lip.

"Boys," I agree.

"I'm glad you and I are friends," Parker says quietly. "Sometimes I wonder if I got the sign this summer. I really needed a friend." She tucks her chin against her chest.

I splash the water with my feet. Maybe this is where heaven meets the earth. Or maybe because we think we might get a sign, we're more flexible to change and new experiences.

Maybe it's all about a willingness to be open.

"Want to swim?" I ask, and she launches herself into the lake, where we spend the rest of our break splashing, telling stories, and laughing.

That night, I'm walking back from the bathhouse when I hear a guitar crooning in the night. I make my way down the trail past Pinecone to the cookout area, where I find Matt sitting on a picnic table, plucking the strings. He has a lazy smile on his face as he's playing "Rhythm of Love" by the Plain White T's. I sit next to him and play with his hair until he finishes the song and sets his guitar aside.

"Want to take a walk?" he asks, slipping his hand into mine. In silence, we go up to the big field and stand under the stars. It's like we're the only people left on earth.

I wrap my arms around his neck, and the kissing starts slowly. Then he's gently pushing me down to the grass. His mouth is on mine and I fit my body against his.

"I love you so much," he whispers, breathing deeply. I tell him I love him back, and he bends to my stomach. He kisses a trail from my belly button down and even though our clothes are still on, I whisper, "Matt, I can't."

He nods and moves up to lie next to me. I clear my throat. An awkward silence hangs on the air. I love him and want to show him and I can't stop thinking of touching his soft boxer shorts.

My fingers move without permission. I unbutton his shorts and unzip them. He cups my face and runs a hand through my hair.

Then I hear laughter behind me. Matt quickly zips his shorts. We sit up and smooth our clothes.

"Well *that's* appropriate," Andrea says sarcastically, walking by with Carlie. They must've been out at the lake, smoking.

"Now I'm pissed at her," Matt says to me with a laugh.

"Just now?"

He gives me a look and pulls me to his chest. "Ian told me that Brad and Andrea hooked up behind the cafeteria last night."

I shove his shoulder, laughing. "Lies."

"It's true! They were in Ian's spot and he got pissed."

Still laughing, we lie back down in the grass. "You never slept with Sarah, right?"

He curls up beside me and drapes an arm across my stomach, slipping a hand under the hem of my shirt. "No. Why?"

I clear my throat.

He must think I'm asking to have sex because he says, "You don't want to do it out here in the grass…we should wait until we have a bed. And no parental units around asking me to mow the lawn."

Honestly, I can't think of a better place than the big field under endless stars, but it's not the time. "I, um, Matt?"

"Yeah?"

"I might need a long time. To get ready, I mean."

He's silent for a while. He twines his fingers with mine and lifts my hand to his mouth, running his lips along my skin. "How long?" he asks finally.

It could be years. It should be when I get married. What if Matt isn't the one?

"I don't know."

"We can talk about it," he replies, and I'm glad he wants to discuss it, because it seems like the mature relationship-y thing to do, but I'm terrified.

Adult relationships are confusing and scary.

"Bedtime," he says. He disentangles himself from my arms and helps me to my feet. He keeps an eye on my knee, making sure I don't bend it some weird way. It would suck if Matt isn't the one, because I can't imagine anything better than him.

But will he wait for me?

something new

On the last day of camp, we're waving good-bye to the final group of campers. Cars drive down the dirt road leading out of camp, kicking up dust. The sight makes my eyes water.

Then everyone starts cheering and hugging.

Megan blows her whistle. I wince. I want to make it my business to snatch that whistle and throw it in the lake.

"Today's clean-up day," she announces. "Everyone should spend the day cleaning out your closets and packing up your supplies for storage back at regional conference headquarters."

Ian whispers in my ear. "It takes like ten minutes and then we get to spend the rest of the day hanging out at the pool and grilling steaks."

"Medium rare, please," I whisper back.

"You got it." He pats my shoulder, grinning.

We all go home tomorrow. I look around at these people who have become my friends (and enemies!) and feel a pang of sadness that I won't wake up to see Matt and Parker every day.

Sure enough, Ian was right. After we're done packing, we spend the afternoon lounging by the pool. Even Megan and Eric relax, reading. She thumbs through a magazine about motivational leadership or something and his book is called *Build Your Own Swamp*. Will goes to the supermarket and brings back soda and chips and cookies and Ian's steaks.

I lie on a towel next to Matt and hold his hand. We smile at each other, sharing my iPod—each of us using a headphone. At one point I gaze over Matt's shoulder to find Andrea and Brad chatting and laughing together. He tucks her hair behind her ear. What...?

After tanning our brains out—well, Matt tans, and I just get more and more freckles—we stand up and shake the dirt off our towels. Brad waves at me, looking sad.

"Want me to beat him up?" Matt whispers, pressing his forehead to mine. When I told Matt what happened, I nearly yanked his arm out of its socket, trying to keep him from confronting Brad.

"It's okay." I kiss Matt's nose, then walk over to Brad and touch his forearm. Life's too short not to forgive.

"Want to make steak with us?" I ask.

A smile sweeps across his face. "Yeah. Listen, I'm so sorry—"

I interrupt, "You have to keep in touch when you leave. Let me know how you are."

He gives me a hug, propping his chin on top of my head. "I will. I will."

That evening while Ian grills steaks and bakes potatoes over a fire, we have a Bonzo Ball tournament. I get knocked out in the first round. Will and Matt make it to the finals, and we're all screaming and cheering for them. Matt accidentally sneezes and loses concentration, allowing Will to win the tournament as the sun sets.

Before dinner, Ian asks, "Who wants to have one last Critter Crawl?" and Parker shoves him. Right as we sit down to eat, Eric emerges from the trees, carrying three trout he wants to grill.

"I love me some surf n' turf!" Ian says, and Eric beams.

"I made some spices using plants I found in the woods," Eric replies.

"I hope it's weed," I hear Carlie muttering to Ian, and he laughs and kisses her cheek.

When Megan and Eric leave to make sure the camp's gate is locked (Ian asks, "Is that what they're calling it these days?"), the guys decide to play basketball. Andrea and Parker want to watch them, leaving me and Carlie alone.

She looks over and asks, "Can you weave some of your friendship bracelet string into my hair? Like into little braids or something?"

We walk over to the art pavilion, where I dig string out of a packed box and perch on top of a picnic table, motioning for Carlie to sit on the bench between my legs.

"How about pink, black, and blue?" I ask, sorting through the string.

"That's fine."

I braid the colors through her blond hair until the silence is about to kill me. She and I have nothing in common, but she and Ian have been good to me, and I'll never forget how understanding she was during my temporary split with Matt, even though she's better friends with Andrea.

"Listen," I say. "Do you and Ian want to hang out with me and Matt sometime?"

"Like a double date?"

"Yep."

She lets out a little sigh. "I guess that's what you do when you're in a relationship, huh? You go on double dates. You don't get plastered and end up in some random guy's dorm room."

"Nope," I say, laughing. "You go to Chili's. And maybe the Fun Tunnel."

I finish her hair, then we go corral our boyfriends before they end up playing ball all night.

On my first night here, the sky faded to a brilliant purple and orange. Tonight, it's the same colors. Then, I sat in my car and prayed for the sign. God gave me Matt and Parker this summer, but my life still isn't perfect. Emily's not here.

I close my eyes and breathe in the sweet summer air laced with honeysuckle. When the stars are shining vividly, I catch Brad and Andrea sneaking off together, and Matt takes my hand and leads me out to the big field, where six mattresses are set up on top of the giant parachute. My body goes tense.

"Is this for us?"

"Parker, Will, Ian, and Carlie are coming too."

"You didn't ask me about this."

His nose crinkles. "It'll be fun. We're all friends, just hanging out."

I whisper, "Can you and I have separate mattresses?"

He furrows his eyebrows, but then he bobs his head up and down. We push our mattresses close together and lie on top of our sleeping bags, staring at each other.

When Will and Parker arrive, they barely throw us a glance because they are too busy making out. Already.

Then Ian and Carlie appear off the trail. She's riding on his back.

"Hands where I can see 'em!" Ian calls to Matt, cracking up. He and Carlie collapse onto a mattress on the other side of the parachute and start roughhousing, beating the crap out of each other.

"This is totally romantic," I say, deadpan. Matt turns his face toward mine, laughing.

"Don't worry. We can share a bed alone anytime we want now. I have my own room at school this semester. Because I'm a junior."

I circle his wrists with my hands. "I'm, uh, not so sure I'm ready for that."

"To share a bed?" His eyebrow pops up.

"I told you it would be a while."

"But we can't share a bed?" He pulls me closer. "I love lying next to you." He gently kisses my jaw. "We've already spent the night together."

"I love lying in bed with you too…but it's not right for me…yet."

His body stiffens. He pulls away. "Am I not any good?"

"What?" I ask, furrowing my eyebrows.

"In bed," he whispers. "Am I not any good…?" His voice cracks.

"It's not that, Ma—"

"What is it then?"

"I just can't hook up."

His hands tighten around my waist; he studies my eyes. "Is this because of Emily? You think you might get pregnant or something? I would never let that happen."

"It's not about that! It's about me not wanting to do this yet."

His eyes go glossy. "Will you ever want to?"

"I'm not sure…"

"I'm not saying I want to sleep with you tonight, but it is something I want to talk about."

I clasp his wrists. "I need time—"

He drops his chin. "That's what Sarah said. And then she left."

"I'm not her—"

"Why won't you spend the night with me? We don't have to have sex. I just want to be with you."

"I want to be with you too." I rub my cheek.

His expression suddenly changes. "I don't want camp to end," he says. "What if things aren't the same with us?"

I grab his hip. "They will be—I love you."

"I love you too."

We listen to Carlie and Ian screeching and laughing. Then they slip away into the night, probably to fool around behind the cafeteria. Parker and Will are kissing like the world will end in five minutes.

I turn over and fluff my pillow, trying to ignore the disappointment I feel flowing from Matt. It would be so easy to give him all of me, and I know we'd both be thrilled and happy.

Free will comes with sacrifice. And sometimes with heartache.

Jesus sacrificed his entire life for us, but you don't see Him complaining.

* * *

The next morning, I go to the Woodsong Chapel one last time. At the beginning of the summer, I wondered if I could still love this place without Emily. I can't love it like I did when she was around, but I love it in a different way. A new way. I sit there on a log bench, thinking of Matt and enjoying the trees and the sounds of animals and rushing water, before walking back to Great Oak.

I'm signing for my final paycheck when Megan stares me down, as if wanting to ask a question. "Take a seat," she says, gesturing at the chair across from her.

I suck on my bottom lip, waiting for her to speak.

"Are you going to reapply for a job here next summer?" she asks.

I hadn't really thought about it. I mean, I'm still trying to decide on a major. "Maybe," I say. "I'm not sure yet."

She swings her whistle around a finger. "Maybe you should consider not reapplying. I'm not sure you're right for this kind of work."

My mouth drops open. "Really? Why?"

She pulls a piece of paper from her clipboard and examines it. "You had problems starting fires and occasionally did things I asked you not to. You didn't have the best discretion in front of the campers. I heard rumors you sleep with Matt in the big field." She taps her whistle on her desk.

I duck my head. Yeah, some of that's true. But what about all the good I did?

"I worked hard this summer. I can start fires and I'm great at trailblazing and I know about nature and I can pick up craw-daddies now. The campers loved my arts and crafts lessons. I've gotten really good at this job."

"You came to camp on a Sunday morning, when you shouldn't have been here. What if you'd had an accident? The regional conference doesn't have insurance for employees on weekends. You could have ruined my career!" Megan goes all red.

"I apologized for that," I say, wanting to tell her I never broke that rule.

I became a great counselor this summer. Megan can believe whatever she wants. For whatever reason she wants. Parker was right when she said Megan is an OCD perfectionist, and if this is the way she wants to run camp? Fine. There's more than one way to do things and still end up with a great result. It's not one way or the highway.

"I'll apply for the job if I want to apply for the job." I swallow hard, feeling seven weeks of fury leaking out of me. "I'll tell the regional conference that I did a great job this summer. I learned a lot. I hope they'll give me a fair shot."

She twirls her whistle, as if she's bored. "I am recommending that you not be rehired. Good luck."

For a brief moment, I worry that my church will find out. But then I shake those thoughts out of my head. I don't care.

I fold my paycheck and slip it into my back pocket. "Bye."

I turn and march out of the cabin and up the path toward my car.

I don't care what she believes. I know what I know. I lied to save Brad, and I'd do it again to keep him away from a drunk parent. If it costs me a job, so be it. Breaking the rules was worth it to help Brad start his new life.

It's like with art. You can't tell someone how to do it, or it's not her art. You can't tell someone else how to believe.

It's up to God to judge, and for me to help the people I love the best I can.

• • •

At home, I pull on my sneakers and knee brace and fly out my front door, sprinting as fast as I can. It hurts, it hurts, it hurts, but the hurt makes the pain stop. I run around the block fourteen times, then go back home and collapse on my bed.

The moment I hit my pillow, tears burn my eyes.

Once you get hurt the first time, the pain never, ever goes away. Maybe it dulls, but it's always there.

The pain from some things in my life—kids at school calling me a Jesus Freak, Megan being mean, hurting my knee—will never go away. Helping Emily get an abortion will never leave me. But I can work to run with life again.

My cell rings. It's Parker calling to ask if Matt and I want to go out with her and Will tonight. I start tearing up the second she says Matt's name.

I'm glad I told him how I feel, and I guess even if things don't work out with us, I stayed true to myself, and that makes me smile a little.

"What's wrong?" she says.

"Can you come over? Please?" I ask, wiping my nose on my sheet.

"Yeah, I'll be right there."

When she gets here, she plops on my bed and pushes the hair away from my face. She opens her bag. "I brought M&Ms."

She sits next to me against the headboard and I lean on her shoulder, telling her everything that happened with Matt.

"So you told him you won't share a bed with him?" she asks, choosing a green M&M.

"I didn't say that exactly—"

"But you'd already spent the night with him?"

"Yeah."

Her forehead wrinkles. "Did you tell him exactly what the issue is?"

"I just said I can't sleep over with him."

She pours M&Ms into my palm. "And then he asked if he's bad in bed?"

"Yeah." I eat a red one and a blue one.

She leans her head against my shoulder. "You need to tell him you don't want to go that far yet and if he's not okay with that, then you can't date. But you need to explain what the issue is."

"What do you mean?"

"You were willing to let him sleep over and fool around before but you're not now?"

"We got carried away," I say quietly. "I'm afraid if I sleep over with him, it'll happen again."

"He's probably confused and hurt. You need to tell him what you're thinking."

"I sort of tried—"

"If he's not okay with that, he's not worth it. He has to respect what you want."

I wipe my nose again. "What if I want both? What if I want to sleep with him? I know I can't but I can't stop thinking of him."

"Both options are yours."

"Did Will ask to have sex a lot before you started?"

She narrows her eyes and nods, laughing. "Oh, yeah. Will wanted to have sex before we even officially started dating."

I laugh.

She adds, "But we only did it when I was ready."

She pours M&Ms into her mouth and chews. "I have a question," she says through a mouthful, and I nod. "Why the hell do you have all those poor animal heads in your foyer?!"

After she leaves to meet Will for dinner, I turn my cell phone screen on and off. On and off. I won't be able to explain over the phone. I open my laptop and start typing an email.

> Matt—I love you. I need to tell you what
> I believe and what I want...

• • •

Matt doesn't write back. Not that night. Not the next morning. He hasn't called or texted. By lunch, I can't even eat the chicken salad Mom made. I pick the grapes, carrots, and celery out of it and make designs on my plate. Anything to distract me.

Are things over for me and Matt?

Then at like 3:00 p.m., Mom calls from downstairs. "Honey! You have a guest."

Is it Parker? I don't bother putting on a bra or changing out of my short pajama shorts before I trudge down to the foyer, where I find Matt standing with Mom.

"We'd love to have your parents over for dinner," she's telling him.

"They'd like that." He coughs into a fist before saying hi to me. His Adam's apple shifts as he swallows, taking me in. Now I wish I'd put real clothes on.

"Hi," I reply. "Can I get you a lemonade or a sweet tea or anything?"

He kneads his fingers together. "No, I'm good. But thank you."

"I'll be in the other room," Mom says, squeezing my shoulders. She disappears and leaves me standing with the boy I love more than anything.

"What are you painting?" he asks.

"How did you know I was painting?"

He points at my face and hair. I must have orange and yellow everywhere.

"I found this picture of the Australian Outback. The desert. I'm trying to paint the contours of the sand."

"I'd love to see it." He glances at Vincent Moose. I fold my arms over my stomach and try to forget how good his hands felt on my body.

He steps toward me, his blue eyes blazing. "I got your email."

"You could've called," I say playfully.

"I was busy."

"Busy." I lift an eyebrow. "Did you stop at Just Tacos again?"

He grins. "Hm."

"You're in big trouble now."

"Oh yeah?" He grabs my hand and tangles our fingers together, and I remember how this felt on our first date.

Right and perfect, even though we're anything but right and perfect. But being with him smells better than salt on the breeze first thing in the morning at the beach. It tastes better than homemade vanilla ice cream. It feels better than dragging a paintbrush across canvas.

"What did you think of my email?" I ask.

"I understand…let's just keep talking and I'll try not to be an ass, okay?"

My email to Matt said I don't believe in sex before marriage, and that if we share a bed, I'm afraid I'll end up doing everything with him because I can't help it. I told him that I want to do everything with him, but I need time, and I need his support while I figure things out.

I love you, I told him in my email. *Can you trust me? I want us to work.*

"I think God wanted me to find you again," I tell him, stepping close enough to wrap his shirt in my fingers. He stares down at my fists, then up into my eyes, giving me that wicked smirk of his.

"I know God wanted me to be with you," he replies, pressing his forehead to mine. His mouth meets mine and we kiss gently.

"Wait—no way," I mumble, stopping him from kissing me again. "You're totally in the doghouse for not answering my email promptly."

"How do I get out of it?" His lips graze my cheek, leaving me dizzy.

"I'm open for suggestions."

"Ahem." I peek up to find Mom standing there next to Vincent Moose.

Matt and I break apart and smooth our clothes, as Mom goes back into the kitchen. I caught a smile on her face.

"Come onto the porch with me," Matt says, taking my hand.

"Why?"

"I want to get out of the doghouse."

When I step out the front door, I totally wish I had put on a bra and real pants. At least fifty guys are crowded on my street, catcalling and screaming at Matt.

"You pussy!" one guy yells.

"Nooooooooo," Nick, the guy I met at Chili's, cries.

"What's going on?" I ask Matt. I'm bewildered, and maybe a bit scared, but very curious.

He reaches into his shorts pocket—

"You're not proposing, are you?" I gasp.

"What? No!" He throws his head back and laughs.

MIRANDA KENNEALLY

"Good. If you didn't ask my Daddy for permission he'd bring out his shotgun and then you'd be tacked up on the wall with Vincent Moose."

"Asking your dad for permission to marry you would be easier than what I'm about to do."

I raise an eyebrow and look from his frat brothers to him. "Why's your frat here?"

"They're my friends." He looks into my eyes with such a fierce intensity, I know I can never ask him that question again. Regardless of what they made him do with a banana, he cares about them. They are something he believes in.

He loves his frat.

"So when you're not at camp, do you always travel with this entourage?" I say with a laugh.

He smiles. "Not usually…"

Some guy in the street yells, "Brown is an über douche!"

I ignore that lovely sentiment.

"The guys came with me for a reason," Matt says, nodding over his shoulder.

"Are you doing a carwash for the ASPCA? For the puppies and kittens?"

"Is that your way of saying you want me to take my shirt off?'

I pinch his bicep. "You behave."

He grins. Then he reaches into his shorts pocket and pulls out a silver chain. A charm reading ΔTK hangs from it.

"Will you wear my letters?" he asks.

He cares about me more than his frat? My eyes fill with tears. "That means—"

"That I love you more than them," he says, glancing over his shoulder at all the heckling guys. "I want you to know I can wait…whatever you need, we can work it out."

A few months ago, I couldn't even comprehend love or what it meant to be in an adult relationship or how important it is to follow my instincts.

Maybe I can have my beliefs and have the guy I love too.

"I love you more than those guys too," I say with a laugh.

"Thanks, I think." He wipes the tears off my face and we kiss while being heckled.

"What's a girl like that doing with an asshole like you, Brown?!"

We break apart, and he slips the Greek letters over my head. And not even ten seconds later, a roaring mob of guys storm my front porch and carry Matt away. It looks like he's body surfing.

"I love you, Matt!" I yell, then gaze down at the Greek letters. He could've put Megan's godforsaken whistle around my neck and I'd care about him all the same.

Three guys are shoving Matt onto the bed of a truck now. I smile, thinking about how lucky he is to have a bunch of guys who love him enough to come over here and make a big deal out of his love for me.

"Don't you dare tie him to a tree or anything crazy!" I yell at the guys.

I kiss the ΔTK charm and head back inside to call Emily.

I'll never understand why she did what she did.

But if Matt can wait for me—can respect my beliefs—maybe Emily and I can work out our differences too.

• • •

The door to Foothills Diner swings open. The bell dings. Emily appears. She's not wearing makeup and her auburn hair is pulled back into a messy bun.

She slides into the booth across from me and cracks her knuckles.

"Hi," I say, clearing my throat. I close my sketchbook and drum my fingers on it.

"Hi."

A waitress appears, holding a notepad. She pulls a pen from behind her ear. "What can I get you?"

"Rhubarb pie," Emily and I say at the same time. We smile sheepishly at each other.

"I'll take a coffee," I add.

"Me too," Emily says, and the waitress goes to ring in our order.

"Thanks for coming," I tell Emily. I left a voicemail, inviting her to meet me here. It surprises me that she showed.

She pulls two packets of Splenda from the sugar caddy and places them in front of her.

There's an uncomfortable silence until the waitress comes back with our coffees. More silence as we fix them. Half and half with no sugar for me. Two Splendas and skim milk for Emily.

I curl my fingers around my mug. "I, uh, wanted to tell you I'm sorry."

She studies my eyes.

"We don't have to believe the same things to be friends," I go on. "I'm sorry I put pressure on you. You didn't need that, considering everything else."

She sips her coffee and makes a face. She grabs another Splenda and stirs it in. "I'm sorry too," she says slowly. "I'm sorry I wasn't more grateful for how you helped me. I'll never be able to thank you enough."

I sniffle. "Jacob sent me a text, asking how you are."

Her gaze meets mine.

"Have you talked to him?" I ask. "He really wants to talk to you."

"I can't." She chokes on her words. She pulls a napkin from the little rusty dispenser and holds it to her nose.

"I think you should tell him," I say. "He loves you. Maybe he'll understand..."

"How could he?"

"Either he'll forgive you or he won't...Don't you want to risk it?"

She looks down at her lap, dabbing her nose with the napkin.

"You have a boyfriend now?" she asks.

"Yeah, his name is Matt."

"He's cute." She glances up, flashing me a small smile.

"Do you remember him from when we were little? The guy at camp who was always writing songs? He wore glasses?"

"Shut up! That's your boyfriend?"

"Yep."

She bangs her fist on the wobbly table. "The one you made out with behind the art pavilion?"

"It wasn't making out!" I laugh.

"Not then, anyway." The side of her mouth quirks up. "You're serious with him?"

I scrunch my napkin. "We're serious, but not *that* serious."

She nods quickly. "I'm happy for you."

"I'm happy for me too," I say with a laugh.

"Because damn, he is hot."

I laugh again. "He's not just cute?"

She waves a hand, shushing me. "I under-exaggerated before. He's hot."

The waitress drops our rhubarb pie off at the table and we grab our forks.

"So how did you and Matt get together?" Emily slices into her pie and listens as I tell her all about him.

sketch #402

what happened last saturday night, october 20

On Thursday night, I walk into the Belmont dining hall and, after pouring myself a bowl of Rice Krispies, I grab a seat and open my backpack. I push aside my Planned Parenthood volunteer folders and pull out my sketchpad.

The Purdue game is on all of the TVs. It's getting tons of coverage 'cause Jordan Woods is standing on the sidelines in her uniform. I smile up at the screen, knowing there's no way she'll get to play today because she already said so on Facebook. But her standing on the field with her team is huge, and I can't stop grinning.

During a commercial where some SUV is driving through craters on the moon, I start drawing the tent Matt and I shared last Saturday night. I dot the paper with the stars sprinkled above us.

He took me camping at Old Stone Fort, and I grilled burgers for dinner and he fried doughnuts for breakfast. We played this game where we made up new names for the stars in the sky.

My favorite was Shamu. Matt wanted to zip our sleeping bags together to create a queen-size sleeping bag, but I kissed him and told him to stop being such a troublemaker.

"I'm a guy," he said with a laugh. "I'll never stop trying to get into your bed."

We pushed our sleeping bags as close to each other as they would go and I hugged him all night long, trying to ignore how much I want all of him.

Next weekend we're borrowing Matt's mom's van and road-tripping with Ian and Carlie to Chicago, so Matt can run the marathon, barefoot. And I can't wait for the following Saturday, because Matt's taking me to his frat's formal at the Opryland Hotel, where I'll finally get to wear the silk dress Mom bought for me.

I'm shading his dirty blond hair when Emily shows up and grabs the seat next to mine. I shut my sketchbook, slip my pencil behind my ear, and listen to her talk about orchestra practice.

"I think I might have a shot at first chair," she says, wrapping the necklace Jacob gave her around a finger.

I steal a French fry off her plate and smile at my friend.

She touches my wrist. "Tell me what your professor thought of your painting already!"

So I do.

acknowledgments

I've been working on a version of this story since I was eighteen years old. I want to thank my college writing professor, Glenn Moomau, for loving the much darker short story I wrote twelve years ago, and for boosting my confidence when I had very little. Professor Moomau told me I should become a Southern Gothic author. Well, Southern Gothic author I am not, but I do like to think I've explored my roots with this novel. I grew up in a close-knit church community that was always there for me. When I left Middle Tennessee and moved to Washington, D.C., I found that my beliefs began to change. To this day, I don't really know who I am or what I believe, but that's okay. With this story, I want to show you (teenagers) that your beliefs matter—no matter who you are or where you come from. Your opinions matter. You matter.

To me, nothing was scarier than understanding that my truth wasn't everyone else's truth. It took a while, but I discovered that's okay—it's better if I do the things I want to do and believe what I want to believe. I hope you find your truth.

Huge thanks go to Sara Megibow and the awesome people at Nelson Literary Agency. I am most grateful for the support and guidance of Leah Hultenschmidt and everyone at Sourcebooks. Don, I know you would rather be reading Tom Clancy, Lee Child, or Vince Flynn, and, Dad, I know you'd rather be reading Ann Patchett or some dystopian disaster novel, so thanks for reading another one of my teen romance novels. It means a lot to me!

Thank you to Allison Bridgewater, Sarah Cloots, Rekha Radhakrishnan, Trish Doller, Andrea Coulter, Sarah Skilton, Natalie Bahm, Tiffany Smith, Kari Olson, Maria Cari Soto, Jessica Spotswood, Tiffany Schmidt, Robin Talley, Shanyn Day, Jessica Wallace, and Christy Maier for encouraging me as I wrote this book. Without your guidance, it would be a big mess.

Ashley Simmons hosted a contest on her "Books Obsession" blog to name a character in this book. Erica Roberts-Wing won the contest and decided to name a character "Nick" after her friend who passed away following high school. I chose to name one of Matt's fraternity brothers Nick, as he's a very loyal and real friend.

And thanks to my readers! You are all awesome.

about the author

Miranda Kenneally grew up in Manchester, Tennessee, a quaint little town where nothing cool ever happened until after she left. Now Manchester is the home of Bonnaroo. Growing up, Miranda wanted to become an author, a major league baseball player, a country music singer, or an interpreter for the United Nations. Instead, she became an author who also works for the U.S. Department of State in Washington, D.C., planning major events and doing special projects, and once acted as George W. Bush's armrest during a meeting. She enjoys reading and writing young adult literature and loves *Star Trek*, music, sports, Mexican food, Twitter, coffee, and her husband. Visit www.mirandakenneally.com.